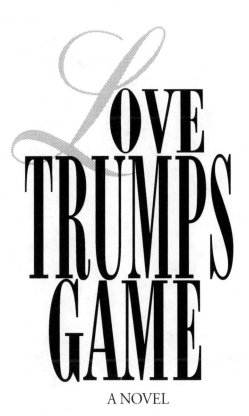

LOVE TRUMPS GAME

A NOVEL

STREBOR ON THE STREETZ

LOVE TRUMPS GAME

A NOVEL

D.Y. PHILLIPS

SBI

STREBOR BOOKS

NEW YORK LONDON TORONTO SYDNEY

ACKNOWLEDGMENTS

Very much like the old adage, "It takes a village to raise a child," getting a book out is pretty similar. It almost takes a village to provide information, advice, feedback, editing and tips on which publishing houses have open submissions and which ones don't. For this, I need to give a few shout-outs.

First of all, giving thanks to God, and yes, even for giving me the audacity and the ability to write an urban tale with a few steamy sex scenes and foul-talking characters. I still say that without Him, nothing worth having can be achieved as a blessing.

Thanks and kisses to my husband, Reggie, who patiently puts up with a wife that, on most days, spends more warm and cozy time with her computer than with him. It takes a special kind of man to put up with this. Reggie, my love, you're that man!

Thanks to a few of my writer friends. I can't remember each and every one of you, but you know who you are: Reon Laudat, Dyanne Davis, Tina Brooks McKinney and many more. Allison Hobbs, a special thanks to you for taking the time out of your own busy schedule to read my project and put in a few words to the powers that be. Good looking out, Ms. Allison.

To my dearest and fondest, Mary Monroe. I can't think of another writer that I admire as much as I admire you. Your friendship is worth its weight in gold.

On the working side, thanks to Charmaine, your down-home

patience is like a life-line to any author who's anxious about what to do next and how to do it. Thanks to my agent, Dr. Maxine Thompson, for talking and explaining "stuff" to me more like a friend than a business associate. If you're on your way to the top, scoot over so I can go with you.

To my all my reading fans taking this journey with me...let's just do the damn...oops, I mean the darn thing!

D.Y. Phillips
dyphil2@aol.com

ONE

Have you ever been in the same room with a monster?

Did you see how he did it? How he used fear as his weapon?

Could you smell, or see, death coming in his eyes?

What Hattie Sims saw when she came out from the bathroom of her home was a tall, muscular man standing in her living room. Her breath caught in her throat. She could have kicked herself for not remembering to lock that metal security door. After all, wasn't that what it was for? To keep devils and monsters out?

"Why are you in my house?"

Topps Jackson was no stranger. Still, she hadn't liked or trusted him from the first time she had laid eyes on him. Something about his eyes; they were dark and threatening. He had nice lips but rarely smiled.

"Chill out, Mama Hattie. I come in peace." A toothpick was restless between his lips. Sneaky-looking eyes panned around her room as if he were casing the place.

"Your type ain't welcome here." Hattie refused to let her nervousness show. "And I'm not yo' mama."

He was dressed entirely in black. Large, muscular arms seemed more like thick, brown tree trunks protruding from the expensive jersey that he wore. "Good thang you not, or you'd be dead by now."

It was probably ridiculous for her to attempt to manually remove him. She was a petite woman with delicate features. Still,

Hattie straightened her back and stood her ground with the father of her grandchildren. His bodacious visit was what she got for not locking her metal security door; thinking that the delivery boy would be there soon with her grocery order.

"What is it you want? Say what you want and get out. You got no business being here."

"Now see, that ain't no way to be treating family." Unfazed by her annoyance, Topps Jackson ambled over to a table and picked up a wood-framed photo of her daughter, Myra. "Pretty," he said, then grunted. He placed the frame back and ran a finger along the top of the table. "A little dusty in here. You might wanna take care of that when I leave."

"Look, if you're looking for Neema, she ain't here."

"Not looking for Neema. Looking for you; the mama that keeps putting nonsense in Neema's head. You know, that shit about taking my kids and moving away." Topps sniffed, looked around her old, cozy living room. It was clean, but worn-looking. He frowned like it was a shame to have an average existence with no frills.

Hattie couldn't imagine what Neema saw in him. True, he was tall, handsome, cunning and, from what she'd heard, drug-dealing rich. He had materialistic wealth, yet, he represented everything a mother should warn her daughter about. *Stay away from men that degrade women. Men that hurt women. Stay away from men on the opposite side of the law. Stay away.*

"Like I said, you have no business being here."

"I disagree. I feel like this. If my kids spend a lot of time over here, I need to know what's up. How you hanging. You know what I'm saying, don't you?" All six feet of man turned and slowly walked down her hallway, padding along her carpet in his expensive-looking black sneakers. "How many bedrooms you got here, ole lady?"

"You listen here, young man…" Hattie was right behind him, clutching the collar of her floral housedress. "You need to leave."

"You gotta man up in this mutha?" Topps inquired as he opened doors and surveyed one room after another. "What? No nigger laying that pipe down? That explains a lot."

"That's not your business," Hattie snapped. *The nerve of this fool; talking this way to me.*

"That's how I feel when you stay all up in my business with Neema. See…" He grunted, looking down at her. "If you had a man tapping that ass, you wouldn't have that problem."

"Neema's my daughter. I gave birth to her; not you."

Topps turned to get up in her face. "I don't care if you shot Neema out your wrinkled, gray-covered ass twice. She's my boo-bitch now. Mine; so get over it."

"I'm calling the police," she said.

And she would have, but he was blocking the narrow hallway with his bulky frame. She could smell the toothpaste and cologne he'd used earlier; that's how close he stood. The monster grinned; eyes red and nostrils flared. He snatched up her hand like she was some bratty child trying to slip away.

"Ouch, you're hurting me!"

"This the deal here. You need to stop putting crazy ideas in Neema's head. She ain't no child no more. She ain't going no muthafuckin' place. You understand what I'm saying?"

"Let me go!"

His dark-eyed stare was so intense, it could have made a baby cry. Hattie felt like howling herself. The scowl on his face promised worse.

"I'm warning you, ole lady. If I hear my boo-bitch say she wanna take my kids and move away from me one more time, I'll have to come back. We'll be doing some real talking next time. Know what I'm saying, ole lady?"

When she didn't answer, he squeezed her hand harder, causing a hot sting to zip through her hand and up her elbow. The pain nearly brought Hattie to her knees.

"You hear me or not?" he prompted again.

"I…I hear you…" She wanted to scream. Not being able to do anything about his presence grated on her nerves. At five feet three, one hundred and eighty, she was no match.

"That's better," Topps said, smirking. Hate was in his eyes. He patted the top of her head, much the same he would have a pet dog. "See, mama-bitch. I'm not so bad, am I?" It could have almost been misconstrued as a term of endearment. Clearly, it wasn't. All women were bitches to Topps Jackson. "You alright." He released her hand.

"I want you out of my house." Hattie massaged her hand while Topps removed a moist cloth from a packet in his pocket and wiped germs from his hands.

"Not so fast." Topps made a show of checking out the ceiling, knocking on a couple of walls. "Not a bad house, but if my kids gonna be coming and going up in this muther, you need to be living better. Check this out. If you ever want to sell this dump, I'll give you a hefty price. Enough to get you a new house that smells better." Frowning, he sniffed a few times. "Smells like loneliness and mothballs in here. What you think?"

Hattie didn't answer.

"Yeah. Just what I thought. You need some time to think that shit over, huh?"

Her front doorbell rang. It had to be the delivery boy with her grocery order.

Topps acted like he owned the place, the way he headed for the metal security door and greeted the delivery boy. "What's up, my man? It's all good. How much I owe you? You can sit those bags down by the door."

He took a wad of cash from the pocket of his black sweatpants and peeled off two crisp hundred-dollar bills. "Keep the change, bro."

Once the pimple-faced delivery boy was gone, Topps turned back to Hattie. "One last thing, ole woman. You mention this little visit to Neema and I'll have to come back to see you. Maybe I can stay longer next time. Better yet, I might have to take my frustration out on Neema's sweet little ass for even bringing yo' name up."

Hattie waited until her security door banged shut, rushed over to it, and locked it. Frowning, she watched the monster walk to his big black vehicle, get in, and drive off.

TWO

"I said, c'mon now. I don't have all day, Brandon. You get yourself up those steps now! You, too, Raynita."

Neema Jean wiped beads of sweat from her honey-brown forehead as she stomped up the dusty, concrete steps to her mother's house with her two kids in tow. It had to be over ninety-nine degrees in the shade; add a summer breeze and it felt like she was inside somebody's new convection oven. She used the ball of her fist to bang hard on the metal security screen door.

"Who is it?"

"Who you think it is?" Neema was surprised to find the door locked. In no time her mother was at the door unlocking it, then ambling back to her seat. Neema marched inside after her children. The heavy door banged shut behind her.

"Lock my door," Hattie ordered.

Neema made a face. "Why? You ain't been locking it."

"Neema, I said, lock my door behind you."

"Whatever." Neema stood and blew out a weary breath. "Mama, can you watch my kids for a few hours?"

The Compton house was almost as suffocating as the August heat outside, only adding to her irritation. She fanned her face and looked around, like she was expecting her sister Myra to be lingering in the house someplace. Myra was always around, brown-nosing.

"Mama! I said, I need someone to watch my kids. I can't find a job if I don't have no babysitter." Remembering to pout, Neema rolled her big brown eyes and folded her arms over her ample chest.

Hattie rocked a few times in her new La-Z-Boy chair. A recent gift for her forty-ninth birthday, it was the nicest piece of furniture gracing her living room. She was still a little upset about that fool, Topps, popping up at her house, but didn't dare bring it up. Topps could make a believer out of Satan. If she mentioned his threatening visit, there was zero doubt that he would take it out on Neema. Even worse, possibly even take it out on the kids.

"Hi, Nanny." Raynita waved her little hand.

"Hey, baby. How y'all doing?" Hattie barely blinked in Neema's direction as she reached over to click on her tabletop fan. Cool air, mixed with heat, ruffled the hem of her thin housedress. "Come give Nanny a hug."

The heat was enough to fight the devil, but Hattie remained unfazed. Surely she hadn't been foolish enough to think a Saturday would slip by without Neema contacting her in need of something.

"Mama!" Neema stomped her foot. "I know you hear me talkin' to you."

"Not really," Hattie said calmly, picking up a magazine to fan her face. "Child, I feel too blessed to be stressed today."

Thank God, she had a high tolerance for drama; especially when it came to her youngest child, Neema Jean. "Drama" should have been Neema's middle name. Hattie kept her eyes trained on her television set where *Soul Train* was on. The volume was lowered to a comfortable level. The sight of smiling faces and young bodies gyrating to music made her wish for younger days when no one used to barge into her home with demands.

wisdom to Neema had become futile. "Take 'em to their father. Let him watch 'em."

"He can't. He's off on business."

"I bet he is." *The business of harassing good Christian folks.* She resisted bringing up Topps' earlier visit.

Neema sighed. "Mama, don't start that mess about Topps. He's a fantastic father and you know it."

Hattie bit her tongue lightly. "Try asking your sister to watch the kids."

"You know it's over an hour drive to Myra's house."

"And it's a nice day for a long drive. Nee, stop making excuses."

"Fine, Mama! I guess I can't go to the damn interview then!" Like a spoiled child, Neema huffed and hopped up. She blew out a hard breath before stomping off in the direction of the small bathroom and then slammed the door.

"Well, you wanted to be a mother, so be one," Hattie mumbled, then shouted in the direction of the closed bathroom door. "And don't be slamming no doors in my house or using that kind of language with me! You not that damn grown!"

Smiling, Hattie went back to her program. Happy people with smiling faces were dancing to "Blow the Whistle" by Too Short. "I'm the one that shoulda never had kids," she mumbled as she picked up her chilled lemonade and took a sip. She glanced over at her grandchildren, who hadn't said another peep the entire time. They were standing like stiff, brown trees next to her loveseat.

As much as she hated to admit it, Brandon carried that same handsome hardness of his father. A head full of curly, black hair; piercing dark eyes; the same strong jaw line. Raynita, on the other hand, was the spitting image of Neema Jean with her honey-hued complexion, thin lips, and large brown eyes. A smile could bring the deepest dimples to her plump cheeks. *Poor things.*

"Nita, why you over there looking so sad?" It was cute, the way Neema kept the child's hair in neat cornrows with colorful beads dangling from the ends. Their shoes and outfits looked expensive, making them well-dressed kids for a mother that didn't have a job to speak of. "You two look hot and hungry. How 'bout some cold milk and some of Nanny's homemade cookies?"

Raynita's eyes lit up. "Nanny, you have chocolate chip? They're my favorite."

"I don't want no damn chocolate chips," Brandon said with a scrunched-up face. "Peanut butter cookies taste better."

"Boy, you watch your mouth before you get a bar of soap in it. You start that cussing in my house and the next thing you'll be getting is a leather strap on your behind!"

"Hell, I didn't want no stupid cookies anyway." Brandon stuck his small chest out. "I hate chocolate chips."

"Hey! I said, watch your mouth." *Good grief.* Hattie got up and headed to her refrigerator for some cold milk. Raynita and Brandon followed behind her like puppies. She fetched her cookie jar down from the shelf. "I don't have chocolate chip cookies, but I have oatmeal raisin with walnuts."

Both kids took a seat at her table. The day before she'd baked two dozen cookies, knowing her grandkids would be back over soon enough. "You've tried the rest, now try Nanny's best."

She ignored Brandon's tight lip at the mention of a leather strap. The child didn't know it, but her words were mostly idle threats. The only time she had felt justified to take a belt to one of them was the day she had found Brandon hiding in one of her closets playing with matches. The little fool had almost set her house on fire.

"What about you, Brandon? You sure you don't want some cookies?" Hattie took pride in her baking and often contributed her baked goods to various church functions.

The boy put his head down.

"Suit yourself then."

No matter how much she tried to instill good morals into her grandchildren, the more it seemed like a losing battle. For a seven-year-old, Brandon knew more curse words than she did, and didn't mind using them. Raynita, on the other hand, was plagued with sticky fingers. More times than she could recount, the girl had been reprimanded for stealing small trinkets from some local store. Hattie had to hide her purse when Raynita was in her house.

"Brandon, you sure you don't want some cookies?"

Brandon glared at her with tight lips.

"Nanny, can I have some more?" Raynita asked, after wolfing down two cookies and half a glass of cold milk.

"I said, I don't want no stupid cookies. Stop punking me!"

"Punking? What? Boy, please. Honestly, you starting to act more like your father every time I see you. And don't take that as a compliment."

Brandon frowned up at her. "Don't be talking about my daddy either." He stood up with balled fists.

"Boy, I'm forty-nine years old and this is my house. I can talk about what I want." Hattie fought the urge to laugh. In her heart, she knew that they were good kids, but she also knew their tendency for waywardness stemmed from a poor environment. The Crenshaw District, the area where Neema lived, was infested with people who had long given up on the idea of doing better. As a result, many lived in poverty, their normal lives filled with baby-making for a payday, prostitution, drugs and violence. "Is that how your mama teaches you to behave?" Her tone softened. "Nita, of course you can have more cookies." Then to Brandon, "And you, young man, you need to work on your attitude. You hear me?"

Hattie was waiting for the boy to say something smart back when she heard her screen door being closed gently. Just one more sassy word from that boy's mouth and she'd whack him one good time to show that she meant business. Next came the sound of a car engine starting up, and the peel of tires spitting dirt as they sped away.

THREE

"What?! I know that trifling Neema didn't tip out my…" Hattie put her cookie jar down, hurried to her security door, and stepped outside in time to see Neema's 2006 black Range Rover burning rubber away from the house.

"Neema! You get yourself back here right now! Neema!" Furious, Hattie tried running a few seconds behind the car, but it was hopeless; not to mention dangerous with all the heat. Besides, she didn't see the sense of giving her nosey neighbors something to talk about. Her legs ached, and smoke and dust stung her eyes.

"Damn her!"

After a cloud of dust cleared, she pursed her lips and headed back to her house to discover Raynita and Brandon arguing over a cookie.

"Cut it out, you two." Hattie went straight to her phone to call Neema's cell phone. *How dare she pull a kid-dumping stunt?*

"It's mine, give it back!" Raynita screamed, about to clobber her brother.

"Make me, ho." Brandon was daring her with a clenched fist. A cookie was clutched in his other hand. "Don't make me hurt you!"

Hattie hung the phone up and stared in disbelief. "Brandon! What's wrong with you?" This wasn't the first time she'd seen the two argue over something so trivial, but it was the first time she'd heard the boy call his sister a derogatory name. "Young man, I don't know what your problem is, but we don't talk like that in this house."

The two were at her house a mere three days ago and Brandon had seemed fine. She couldn't imagine what had transpired enough to change his attitude in such a short time frame.

"Nanny, he snatched my last cookie!" Raynita yelled loud enough for her neighbors to hear. "He's always doing stuff. That's why I hate him."

"Alright, you two. Nita, you don't hate your brother, and Brandon, if that's her cookie, give it back."

Brandon tossed the bitten-off cookie to the table. "Crybaby. That's why I can't stand you either. You nothing but a snitch. That's why Daddy likes me better than you."

"Brandon, stoppit! Nita is your baby sister and you're supposed to look out for her." Lord have mercy. This was exactly what she wasn't in the mood for—kids bickering back and forth, and acting like baby hoodlums. "I don't know what's wrong with you, but I'm tired and it's too hot for all this." She loved her grandkids to the core, but sometimes, after spending a day or two with them, she was ready to yank out her own hair.

"I can't stand her; that's why." Brandon looked ready to throw some blows.

"This is what happens when mothers spare the rod." Neema was forever claiming that she was doing her best to provide structure and discipline for her offspring, but Hattie was having a hard time seeing the evidence.

Brandon yelled, "It's too hot in here! I wanna go back to Daddy's house. I didn't wanna come to your stupid house no way."

"Boy, what in the world has gotten into you?"

"I hate snitches; that's what."

"Brandon, you do not hate your sister."

"I do so, and when I go live with my daddy, I won't even miss her telling butt."

"Umph." Hattie shook her head as she sauntered back over to the cookie jar and removed a few. "I know your mama ain't foolish enough to let you live with that man." It was wrong to bad mouth Topps to their faces, but she couldn't help how she felt. Topps was notorious for his gang affiliations and drug dealing. Maybe even a few murders. People talked and she'd heard enough. It was difficult to feel warmth about a man who had allowed his own mother to starve to death. "If you wanted some cookies, all you had to do was ask. Whatever has gotten into you, you need to control it while you're at my house. You hear me, Brandon?"

His only reply was a stubborn pout.

Raynita talked with a mouth full of cookie. "Mama said he acting mannish 'cause he spent the night at Daddy's house. She said Daddy musta let him do weeds or somethin'."

It felt like Hattie's heart thumped and skipped two beats. She patted her chest. "Is that true, Brandon? Your father let you try drugs?"

"I ain't no snitch like Nita."

"Little boy, please. Snitching is when you talk to the police. I asked you a question. Did your father let you do drugs?" Hattie waited with a hand on her hip. It was hard to keep her face from frowning. *So help me to God, if Neema is allowing that man to abuse this child, I will go crazy on her behind!* "You can tell Nanny the truth, Brandon."

Every now and then, the boy spent time with his father, but each time he returned, there was a remarkable change in his behavior for days. He acted funny, looked funny, and walked funny. Heck, sometimes Hattie thought Brandon even smelled funny after such visits.

"Dang, Nanny, why you all up in my bizness?" Brandon wiped crumbs from his mouth with a paper towel before tossing it to the table. The tone of his young voice suggested irritation.

Hattie raised a brow. "Boy, at seven, you don't have no business." She couldn't control her kids' lives, but if she could convince Neema to move to a better environment, meet a nice young man and settle down, maybe Brandon and Raynita might have a chance. True, Topps Jackson was the children's biological father, but it didn't give him a right to exploit them. It also didn't give him the right to contribute to their budding delinquency.

"I'll just say this. Your father might be crazy, but I know he ain't that crazy, to be letting you try drugs. I better not hear something like this again, I know that."

"I said, it's my bizness, Nanny. Know what I'm saying?"

Brandon looked upset enough to fight, but it didn't stop Hattie. If there was something she needed to know, she planned to find out one way or another.

"That's it. Maybe you need to take time out to work on your attitude. Get yourself on in that bedroom."

For a few seconds, there was a stand-off, two contorted faces glaring. Hattie couldn't believe how defiantly the child was behaving. She must have been getting soft because when her own kids were coming up, it wouldn't take much for her to go get a leather belt or a switch from her peach tree out back and get busy. "Did you hear me, Brandon?"

He still didn't move.

Hattie stepped closer. "Boy, I am not playing with you. I said, get yourself into that bedroom. Now!"

Without another word, Brandon got up and stomped from the room.

"Lord, give me strength. I'm getting too old for this mess."

Hattie forced herself to calm down. "Nita, what's your mama's cell phone number? I have it around here somewhere, but don't feel like searching for it."

"Uh…I don't know. She didn't tell me her new number."

"What new number?" Grandmother or not, she needed to find out when Neema would be picking the kids up. The sooner she came back, the sooner she could get back to her peaceful existence. "When did she get a new number?"

Raynita stuffed the last of her cookie into her mouth. "Daddy bought her a new phone yesterday. He took her old phone and threw it away. He bought me and Brandon a phone, too, but I think I lost mine. I don't know Mama's new number."

"Oh, that's just great." Hattie blew out a weary breath. "No way to reach your mother in case of an emergency." Hattie shook her head. She didn't understand it. A lot of the young mothers of today were certainly a different breed from when she was coming up. "Oh, well…" She sighed. "Maybe she'll call later tonight to check on you two."

As much as she hated the idea of it, she would have to wait it out. Knowing Neema, it could be days before she even called to see what was going on. And then again, she might not call at all. Hattie knew one thing—when she did hear from that girl, she planned to have a serious talk with her about Brandon and his visits to his father's house. Topps Jackson shouldn't have been allowed to have unsupervised visitation with stray puppies. Neema would probably say it was none of her business how she raised her kids, but Hattie didn't care. When it came to her grandkids, she planned to make it her business.

♦ ♣ ♥ ♠

FOUR

"Yo, boo, you working that dress." Topps Jackson smiled in appreciation the second Neema opened his front door and stepped inside his house. He clutched his cell phone tighter while his free hand did a slow massage of his shirtless chest, before finding its way down to his groin area. "Yeah, man. I'm still here."

"You like?" Neema threw her head back seductively and deliberately ran her tongue along her red lips. She catwalked over to the white leather sofa where he sat and placed her oversized Gucci bag down. Slow-motion-like, she spun her body around, only to stop to give him an ample view of her high and perfectly rounded "asset."

"Hell yeah, boo. I like it a lot."

Good, she had his attention. Nothing turned Topps on more than watching what he often referred to as her "bubblelicious" behind. Neema made her lips look pouty as her hungry eyes caught the stirring in his sweatpants. "And no panties to get in the way," she whispered to keep from being heard by the person he was talking to on the phone.

"Is that right?" Topps was licking his lips with mounting excitement. "Check it out. My little freak of the week is here. Yeah, I'm feeling you big time."

Neema sat down next to him and began rubbing his wide chest, marveling at the results of what four days per week of pumping iron could do. Washboard abs felt like hard rubber beneath her manicured fingers. "Did you miss me?"

"Slick…man, hold up a fucking minute." Topps took the cell phone away from his ear. "Hell yeah, I did. What took you so damn long to get here? You know I hate to wait."

"Baby, I know you do, but I had to wait for him to get the money from his safe, and then he started counting it and talking about nothing. I got here as fast as I could." Neema rubbed one of her hardened nipples to keep his mind focused on the pleasure they would be having later.

"The hell you did, but that's alright. Check this; let me finish handling my business and I'll deal with you as soon as I'm done. Know what I'm saying? Matter of fact, make yourself useful and go make me a sandwich real quick. Don't forget to wash yo' hands first."

"Excuse me? Make you a what?" She knew better. One look at his twisted sneer confirmed that her response jumped off incorrectly.

"Bitch, did I stutter? You heard me. I said, I'm hungry and for you to go make me a damn sandwich!"

A few seconds of defiance flashed in Neema's big eyes before she came to her senses. *Oh, damn. What the hell am I thinking?* Disobedience was a no-no. Topps Jackson was a man who hated to be told no. At thirty-five, he was twelve years her senior but looked younger. A young face that belonged to an old spirit. If Topps told you to do something, regardless of what the task was, you sucked it up and you did it. End of story.

"Sure, Daddy." She sniffed and stood up. "What kind of sandwich would you like?"

"Try using your brain for a change and surprise me." His words had come out more like an insult. Too bad. He watched her walk away, knowing that he had to hurry up and wrap up his business so he could deal with her. "Lucky bitch."

He smiled to himself. He could name a slew of freaks waiting to take her place. Neema happened to be the flavor of the week. When he got through with her luscious behind, she wouldn't be able to walk straight for weeks. The thought made him grin. He put his cell back to his ear. "Yeah, man, like I was saying, that area is ours and we don't back down. Hell, send some soldiers out to pop their asses. Every last one."

In the large room, Neema could barely contain herself. "What an asshole," she mumbled, looking around the state-of-the-art kitchen. Topps had owned the three-thousand-square-foot home for all of two years and she still wasn't used to it. Each time she paid him a visit, her top-of-the-line, expensive surroundings in the split-level dwelling nearly took her breath away. *Ooh wee, and just think, this could all be mine one day. Mrs. Topps Jackson.* Hell yeah. That shit had a good ring to it.

She popped her fingers and danced herself over to the sink with the intention of washing her hands. "Forget him. Germ-crazy bastard." She reached under her dress and rubbed her hands back and forth over her pussy. "There. Eat some good-coochie germs, nigga." She then walked over to the wide Sub-Zero refrigerator. Imported tile and marble were everywhere she looked. Everything was tastefully done with a mere hint of a woman's touch; thanks to the services of a professional interior decorator.

Quiet as it was kept, Neema felt that she could have done a better job, but Topps had acted funny every time she had broached the subject; even going so far as to joke, "Yeah, and then you'll be moving yo' shit in." More than once he'd made it clear that he wasn't ready for cohabitation; at least not with her.

"Whatever," she mumbled. She didn't need to be underneath him twenty-four-seven anyway.

She pulled out plastic containers filled with assorted deli meats and cheese and got busy.

Fix me a sandwich. Count this money for me. Pick my package up. Neema, do this, and Neema, do that. She didn't like it. The way he talked to her sometimes, his quick temper, nor the way he treated her when his so-called cronies were around. Just because he was the father of her two kids didn't mean he owned her. Topps Jackson was arrogant and demanding. She couldn't say that she loved the man, but the love of his money, and the lifestyle he provided, remained solid.

"Must think I'm his damn maid or something." Neema had known from the beginning that their relationship would be a difficult one. They had met over seven years ago at The Pink KittyKat over on Slauson and Overhill Drive where flashing fake IDs had gotten her and her running crew in. Flashing big bank practically all night, Topps had ended up buying them a truckload of drinks. Chillin' like a big-baller, Topps had even shared news about an off-the-hook party. He had singled her out with his sexy smile and suggestive eye contact, and she had enjoyed every minute of his attention; sucking it up like a sponge absorbs water.

They met, they clicked, and less than a week later, he was dicking her down good. Good friends with benefits. On the real, Topps treated her better in the beginning. Still, she stayed because she loved that new Range Rover he'd bought her and spending his money. Having access to drugs and being his baby's momma, his first lady, was the icing on the cake.

"Nigga, yo' azz need to learn how to treat a woman. That's what you need to do." Neema was putting the finishing touch on a monster sandwich. She turned around to find a plate for her culinary masterpiece and there he was. "Oh!" She jumped, startled. "Dang, Topps. Don't be sneaking up behind me like that. You scared me." Damn. She hadn't even heard him come into the room. He was like that sometimes; quiet and sneaky like a cat. "Baby, you ready to eat?"

Her query was about food but the look in Topps' eyes suggested something else.

"Hell, yeah, I'm ready. I'm starving." He grabbed the sandwich and bit into it, but after a few bites tossed it aside. "Guess that takes care of one appetite."

"Hey. Thought you said you were so hungry. I took my time with that sandwich."

"For real? Guess that means I have to take my time with you. But first, did you take care of that business for me? Took yo'ass long enough. You know I hate waiting."

Like he had to ask. "Don't I always?"

"You have my money, right?"

"Don't be silly. Of course, I have your cash." Topps was standing so close that she could smell the soapy scent from his recent shower. Thick hair from his chest brushed against her arms. "Baby, you know I'm always on target." She moved her body closer into his for a long, hard kiss. Tongues battled for position before someone had to come up for air.

"Damn, girl, you always excite the hell outta me. You know that, right?"

She moaned. "Umm, and that's a good thing. What say we take this to the bedroom?"

He hefted her body up to straddle his like she was as light as a feather. Her clingy, red dress rode up and over her hips to expose her "bare asset."

"Hell, yeah. But you know how I am? Cleanliness first."

Too caught up with kisses to her neck and nibbles to her sensitive earlobe, Neema knew exactly what he was hinting about. Topps was a man who enjoyed a good tongue-probing between her honey-brown thighs, but such a treat always followed a bath or steamy shower. Always!

"Ahh, baby, let's just do it. Live on the edge."

Still straddling his body, Neema allowed him to carry her into the spacious master bathroom where he eased her meaty rear end onto the marble countertop. His tongue was practically down her throat as his hand fondled the sweet and delicate pink between her womanly folds. Neema was about to explode with her first release before he abruptly stopped.

"I'll turn the shower on for us."

Damn, Neema thought. *Here he goes again with that mess.* "Baby, I'm already squeaky clean. I took a long bath before I dropped the kids off at my mom's." She planted a few gentle kisses on his neck. "And you smell good already; like you just showered." She grabbed the rim of his sweatpants and playfully tugged. "Let's get naked and get busy."

He smiled at her, but something about his eyes took away from it. "I showered a couple of hours ago, waiting for you. Now take that shit off."

"Topps, I told you. I don't need another shower. I'm good." Her tone was firm.

"Bitch, how many times I have to tell your ass about giving me a hard time?"

He walked over, grabbed a clutch of her hair, and pulled her, screaming and all, over to the marble shower stall where he cut on the water, adjusted the temperature, and pulled her into the stream. They were wedged between two large potted palms that graced the large shower area.

"Topps, stop it! I don't want my hair wet. Stop it now! I'm not playing."

"Shit, neither am I!" He pulled the ruined wet garment up over her head and flung it to the floor.

Before she could protest more, he had his body pressed hard into hers. All six feet of man, complete with a six-pack and a half. Neema squirmed and wiggled but he was a brick wall that couldn't be moved. Warm water pounded flesh as he nuzzled his lips against her neck with her still trying to assert rejection.

Topps reached for the bottle of liquid soap. "Here," he said, passing it to her. "You wash my back, and I wash yours."

Stubborn at first, she took it and began the process. His back, his buttocks, tight like a drum, the back of his legs. He turned around to face her, his dick pressed against her wet thighs.

"Damn you, Topps. You be tripping." One minute she had been ready to claw out his eyes, but such aggression rolled away when his mouth locked onto hers. "Look at my hair," she swooned, coming up for air. "It's all jacked up now."

"Yeah, but don't I make it worth your while?" He took the mango-scented soap from her hands. "Don't be mad, girl. Spread them pretty damn legs."

"Nigga, you didn't have to ruin my dress." She turned her back to him, but that had never stopped him before. It was always Topps' way or no way. His hands lathered soap onto her perfect rear like a professional waxing an expensive vehicle.

"You still feeling mad at me?"

"Ooh, Daddy, no. That feels so good." She moaned as his hands soaped between her legs, slowly lathering her delicate spots, fingers slipping in and out of wet warmth. She could feel him using the handheld showerhead to rinse the places he wanted to get to.

He kissed her before placing the showerhead back on its cradle, then pulled her down onto the thick, rubber-matted shower stall that was large enough for four bodies to lay side by side. He was a comfortable fit, and felt her shiver as he kissed the inside of her thighs, his tongue tasting sweet nectar.

"Love how you taste, boo."

"And I love how you taste me."

The thrill of his warm tongue between her legs, the lukewarm water cascading down on them, made her back arch and welcome every sensual second of it.

"What's up now? Still mad about yo' hair?" he asked, rising up on his knees to slide ten inches into her.

The sounds of pleasure filled the room, mixing with the patter of water hitting their tangled bodies.

FIVE

"Mama, call the police. Call Children's Services. Call somebody. That's what I would do." Myra Bradshaw was extra careful, smoothing back the gloss along her dark-auburn French roll. From her Coach bag she pulled out a gold-crusted compact to check her reflection. Perfect. Not one strand was out of place. Too bad she couldn't say the same for her mother's hair. Dry and lifeless, it looked like a neat bird's nest. Several times in the past she'd offered to hook Hattie up with her stylist, but her mother seemingly preferred the old and frumpy look. Maybe it was stress.

"Nah…" Hattie shook her head to the offending suggestion. "I'll give her more time. You know how Neema does. Eventually she'll show up."

"Mama, please. That could be days, maybe even weeks. Think about it. Why should Neema rush back to see about some kids when she knows they're in good hands with you?" Annoyed, Myra tossed her compact into her purse.

"You're right…but—" Hattie reflected on her words. Myra was her oldest. Maybe even her favorite. As much as she hated to admit, the woman was right—Neema was taking advantage of the situation. Still, she didn't see how turning Nita and Brandon over to Child Protective Services would teach Neema much of a lesson. If anything, it might further traumatize the kids. "It's bad enough their mama left 'em. Then some police officer or social worker coming and taking 'em away from here? I couldn't do that."

"Humph. You a better woman than me. I wouldn't put up with that mess." Myra walked her thin, regal frame over to open the sliding door's screen so she could holler at one of her twins for throwing rocks. If it wasn't so darn hot out she'd go out and shake some sense into that child. She knew better. "Val, don't make me tell you again. Leave them rocks alone!" Besides, she couldn't risk getting dirt on her white linen, two-piece outfit.

Every other Sunday Myra gathered up her three children and took the hour-and-a-half drive down from the high desert of Victorville to her mother's house. Valena and Kalena, her six-year-old twins, still looked forward to seeing their grandmother, but not eight-year-old Trayvon, who preferred staying at home with his video games. On this visit, it was only her and the twins.

"Where's Tray?" Hattie didn't look up from stirring a pitcher of grape Kool-Aid.

Myra took a deep breath, thinking about that boy. "At home with his father in front of the PlayStation 3. You know how those two love playing video games." There had been times in the past when her husband, Glen, had made the trip with her, but lately, the burden of being a top oncologist with a large hospital in Rancho Cucamonga had taken care of that. Glen refused to do long drives on his days off. "It's called abandonment. I still say call the police and let them deal with her kids. That should teach Neema a lesson."

Myra fanned herself. Though she lived in a hot climate herself, she had access to central air, which she utilized. However, Hattie's house was old and wasn't blessed with such. How the kids could stand being outside in all that heat was a mystery.

"Myra, you know I wouldn't do that."

"Mama, why not? Stop letting Neema take advantage of you like this. How long have you had the kids this time?"

"Since yesterday." At her stove, Hattie removed the top from her pot of beef stew. She stirred the heavenly smelling brew with a large wooden spoon before tasting it. Perfect. Another twenty minutes should do it. Laughter from her four grandchildren playing in her backyard gave her a warm cozy feeling but that was short-lived. "I tried calling her apartment but either she's not there or won't answer."

She slid on an oven mitt, opened her oven, and pulled out her skillet of jalapeño cornbread and set it on top of the stove.

"You try her cell phone?" Myra asked, checking the makeup on her honey complexion for the umpteenth time. Her need to feel and look glamorous never stopped.

"Tried that, too. Nita said her mama has a new cell phone, but I guess she forgot to tell the kids her new number. Guess she forgot to tell me also."

"Like hell she did. She should be ashamed of herself; dumping hers kids off on you like this. You know it won't stop 'til you put your foot down."

Hattie snorted. "My foot was down when she dumped them off yesterday." Sometimes Hattie felt weak; like she had to endure nonsense to make it to forgiveness. Maybe God hadn't forgiven her for what had happened to her baby over almost thirty years ago.

"I feel sorry for you, Mama. I really do." Myra shook her head.

"How come Glen didn't drive down with you?" Hattie's attempt to change the subject was thin. Sunday dinner was almost done. Normally she looked forward to Sunday dinners with her immediate family. But, this thing with Neema was weighing heavily on her mind. Neema loved her two children. At least that's what Hattie wanted to believe. How was it that she could run off and leave them for days at a time and not even call to check on them? The thought nagged at Hattie, making her feel exhausted. The sooner she could get everybody fed, packed off, and headed back to their own space, the sooner she could get off her feet and relax. "I miss when Glen used to come with you."

"Yeah, well, you know how it is being married to a doctor, Mama." Myra was talking, but her mind was really on her dog, Princess. She was worried about whether Glen would remember to feed her. "Their first love is their job. Glen doesn't like to do much on his off-days. Golf and playing videos; that's about it."

"Even doctors need to spend quality time with their wife and family." Hattie took up a spoon to stir her mushroom risotto. She was sure that she'd made enough. Thank goodness, she'd made the salad earlier. Of her two daughters, Myra loved to bake. The lemon coconut cake she'd brought down with her would go well with some ice cream. "Can you set the table for me?"

"Tell me about it." Myra fetched plates and arranged them along the table. Silverware came next. "I really can't complain about Glen. I realized what I was getting myself into before I got married."

One of the twins opened the sliding door and ran into the kitchen. "Nanny, Brandon called me a bad word!"

"He what?" Hattie feigned anger. That child could be a cussing fool and she knew it. "You tell Brandon I said one more bad word and I'll be using a bar of soap to wash out his mouth."

Hattie refused to get her feathers ruffled up about it, but Myra didn't think the same. In a split second she was at the sliding door again with strong words for her nephew.

"Brandon, if I hear one more complaint about you, I will come out there with a belt and wear your little tail out. Don't believe me? Try it!"

Brandon didn't back down. "Go to hell. I ain't afraid of you either!"

Myra's eyes bugged as she gasped. "Oh, no, he didn't just talk to me like that. Oh, hell no. Let me find a belt for his behind."

"Myra, please." Hattie stopped her. "He's showing out for his cousins." Granted, the boy had no business talking to his aunt that way, but the last thing Hattie needed was Myra beating on him. "Don't worry 'bout it. I'll deal with 'im later." She didn't want to have to hear Neema's mouth about Myra disciplining her son.

"Mama, I don't let my own kids talk to me like that."

"I know, I know." Hattie gave her a pleading look. "The boy is going through something right now. That's why he's acting out. Don't worry; let me get to the bottom of it."

"Oh, he's gonna be going through somethin' when I get finished with his behind. Talking to me like that. Humph."

Hoping to quell Myra's anger, Hattie stopped what she was doing and moved to the door. "Brandon! You come here. Now."

The boy stood stubbornly rooted. "For what?"

Hattie gave him the look she used to use on her own kids when they were younger. Myra and Neema Jean were her only two, but not her first child. God was still punishing her for what had happened to her first child. Neema Jean was that punishment. Maybe even Brandon, too.

Raised in a rural part of Alabama, overly strict parents had prompted Hattie to run away from home at the age of fifteen, right into the arms of twenty-year-old Macon Winston. Things were lovey-dovey perfect until the baby was coming and Macon skipped out. Hattie still remembered how hard it was to crawl back home to her parents, all the while hiding her pregnancy. Sometimes babies come with or without doctors, and when her time came, Hattie found herself outside, in the barn at the rear of her parents' house, alone and scared, giving birth to a baby boy that she quickly left on a nest of warm hay. Terrified of her parents finding out, she had hurried to the house to clean herself up and dispose of any evidence.

Once her parents were asleep for the night, Hattie tiptoed back down the stairs and out the back door to go check on the baby. Her son. But the child was no longer breathing. Panic filled her heart as she tried taking the infant up and gently shaking him to prompt breathing that wouldn't start back. After hiding the stiff infant under the hay, Hattie had waited a day later to place the lifeless little body in a shoe box and dig a grave for him at the rear of the barn. She had the good sense to pile on heavy rocks to keep the dogs from digging her misfortune up.

It was her secret. Hers and God's. A secret that dropped so deep into her soul that it made a sound as hard as a drop hitting water for the first time. She couldn't tell one soul about her dead son, but God hadn't forgotten. Surely He hadn't. That's why God was putting so many trials in front of her. Like that hardheaded Brandon.

"Brandon, I said bring yo' behind here now! Boy, don't make me come get you."

The two women watched Brandon stomp toward the house. Hattie snatched the screen back and ordered him inside. "You apologize to your aunt."

The boy was as stubborn as two mules on meds.

"Forget getting to the bottom; let's paddle his bottom."

"Myra, no. Brandon didn't mean what he said. He'll apologize. Right, Brandon?"

The twins and Raynita ran inside to watch the festivities.

"He need a whuppin'." Raynita's eyes lit up with the anticipation of her brother getting his behind tore up. "Mama don't whup him enough. That's why he be acting like he do."

They all waited for Brandon's apology.

"Apologize, Brandon."

Brandon's face was one big frown. "I ain't saying shit!"

Myra wailed. "Oh, hell no! I need a belt, or a switch! Somebody go get me a belt!"

"I'll get it." Raynita sprinted to the bedroom, obviously happy to oblige.

Hattie had to stop the girl. "Nita, no! There will be no ass beating today. Not now."

"Nanny," one of the twins squealed and giggled. "You said a bad word, too."

SIX

*T*he first time he had seen a man popped, he had recently turned ten. Topps Jackson still remembered that night as if it had happened last week. The pop had been over money, and his father, Mack Jackson, had carried out the task like he had been shooting a BB gun at empty cans; cold, easy and heartless.

"Pay attention, TJ," his father's gruff voice had demanded. "This is what you have to do when niggas stomp on your loyalty. And when niggas try to take advantage of your generosity. Are you paying attention?"

"Yeah, Daddy."

Topps' ten-year-old legs had trembled so bad, he thought that he would collapse as he stood in the Long Beach warehouse where his father had run one of his business out of. The massive building was for automotive parts storage, but behind the scenes, it served double-duty as a lucrative marijuana and cocaine operation. The four "soldiers" who had brought the man to Mack had been sent away.

"A private lesson for my son," Mack had told them. "Take a walk."

"One thing you have to learn about this business, TJ, you have to check behind your soldiers. No matter how much you think you can trust them, you still have to check. You see, son, greed is like a cancer that can get to anyone."

"Is he gonna scream like a bitch?" Topps had asked; mostly because he had felt like doing so himself. Screaming and running. But he knew better. His father couldn't stand weakness in his only son.

Mack had chuckled at that. Like father, like son. "Probably so. But remember this tho', real men die brave."

"For real." Topps didn't see anything brave about the dark, thin man down on his knees, crying and begging for his life.

His father had the gun in his hand, trained on its target. "Take this nigga here. He's what you call a skimmer. You pay him well. Treat 'im like he's family and still he skims off the top of your money. Stealing like he deserves it. You give his ass a break. Give 'im time to return what he's taken, but he don't listen. Punks you in front of your soldiers. That ain't good. See what I'm saying?"

Topps had bobbed his head. "Yes, Daddy."

"Mack, please," the man had tried to plead. His hands had taken a praying position. "Man, don't do this, please. I'ma get your money. I promise."

Mack had snorted back, "Man, that's what you said last month, so shut the hell up!"

"C'mon, man. You know me. We like brothers. You know my woman just had a baby. It was borrowing; that's all. You know, for milk and diapers."

Mack had hauled his hand back but didn't slap him. "Man, didn't I tell you to shut the hell up? Ain't nobody trying to hear that sorry shit. The game is over for you."

Topps had felt sorry for the poor fool. He wanted to close his eyes until it was all over, but he couldn't. His father would think that he was weak.

"Here, lil' man. You wanna pull the trigger?"

His father had passed the heavy gun to him. The feel of cold power had been in his small hands, right at his face. He felt like he was in control. Like he held the power of life and death. But he couldn't pull the trigger.

"Daddy, I can't." Topps had tried passing the gun back.

"Pull the trigger, TJ. Don't think about it. Pull the damn trigger!"

Tears had sprung to his eyes. "Daddy, I don't want to."

"Nigga, what the hell!" Mack had angrily yanked the .38 from his young hands. The gun popped off twice and the begging man fell over with bright red seeping from the center of his head. A few splatters of blood and brain went everywhere, even some on Topps' hands.

"Now you listen to me." His father got in his face. "One day this whole damn operation will be yours. You understand me? Yours! And you can't be giving chances and slipping when it comes to your damn money. Ain't no forgive and forget in this game. Niggas get popped every damn day. You get they ass before they get you. That's the goal. You understand me?"

"Yes, sir." Tears had rolled down Topps' ten-year-old face.

"Next time I tell yo' weepy ass to pull the fucking trigger, you pull it. You understand me?!"

"Yes, sir."

"Standing here crying like some sissy. Go wash yo' damn face!" Mack walked away to get his soldiers to come clean up his mess.

Topps had hurried into his father's private bathroom to wash his hands and face. He had never felt so dirty in his life. Blood felt like it was burning on his skin. He had scrubbed with a frenzy, but the more soap he had used, the dirtier he had felt. Never the less, his father's words had remained with him. "Get their ass before they get you. Pull the damn trigger!"

The next time came two weeks later. Another soldier was caught stealing. Mack gave the order. Fearful that it was either his life or the perpetrator's, Topps popped him. He became a ten-year-old murderer, ruthless and cunning. He never dwelled on it. Shit happened. People did what they had to do in life.

That was twenty-five years ago. Eight years later Mack was dead. Set up and murdered by a jealous woman. Money had to be watched and women couldn't be trusted. That's what it taught Topps Jackson in his thirty-five years of life.

Now, not a month went by when he didn't have to pop a nigga behind his money, his drugs, or his privately owned pussy. Popping niggas left and right was no big deal. It was almost like popping popcorn. Quick. Easy. Dirty business, but very lucrative. Still, he'd been trying to wash the germs of sin and murder off ever since.

"Here's to money and pussy," Topps said, holding up a flute filled with Cristal. "The two best things in life."

"Got that right." Slick grinned.

"The two things that will get you killed quick." Topps toasted Slick, who sat across from him in his private office. "If only we could bottle those two things and sell it together, we'd make a killing. Money and pussy. Give it a catchy name like 'Monussy.'"

"Monussy? Man, you whacking out. Pussy already on the market. Nothing new there."

"Nigga, I'm talking bout the essence of money and pussy combined, like an energy drink or somethin'. You feeling me?"

"Hell, nah!" Slick laughed. "You been smoking too much bud."

"Yo, see if you be saying that when my new energy drink hits the market legit."

Slick had been running one of Topps' two distribution operations for over seven years. The two had met in grade school. Their first meeting had been a fight over a cute girl who had gotten them both suspended from school. The girl had hooked up with another fifth-grade boy less than a week later, leaving Slick and Topps feeling so stupid that they both had to laugh about it later. They had apologized for their knuckle-dancing and became good friends.

Slick wasn't much in the looks department, not with his dark face being pockmarked from old acne. Some even called him ugly behind his back. Still, Slick had a good head for business. His bugged-out eyes gave him a froggish look that Topps felt would keep most gold-digging women away. That way, the man could concentrate more on running a business and making that paper instead of chasing tail.

Of all his soldiers, Topps thought of Slick more like a brother that would do anything for him. At least that's how it was in the beginning. Just like Topps, Slick ran a tight ship. Any problems with a sergeant working under him was dutifully reported and handled.

On the desk in front of them sat a small pile of coke. "Man, this shit is the best we've copped." Slick took up a razor to chop and scraped out some lines. "Check this out, bro." He used a rolled hundred-dollar bill to fly some coke up each nostril before passing it to Topps, who refused.

"Nah, man, I'm straight." Another thing his father had taught him about the business was not to use or abuse his own product. Occasionally he flew a few lines up his nose. But that was only if he was tired and needed a quick pick-me-up. Flying lines for recreation was rare, and he made it a point not to rock, smoke, or drink too much alcohol. Even smoking a blunt was on rare occasions. Smoking crack was a no-no. He'd seen too many niggas lose their footing with smoking crack. Not him. He wasn't going out that way. Not when there was money to be made.

"Wonder what's taking Neema so damn long. She should be back by now." Topps stood and gazed out of his office window at his operation, in full swing. The place was as tight as Fort Knox. Soldiers paraded up and down the assembly lines watching every move of the scantily dressed female workers. The job was easy and fast-paced. Measuring and bagging rocks and white powder for street sale. Larger packages were handled by well-trusted runners. Not only did it pay well, but it was a lifetime job. Once a person was recruited to work the business, there was no such thing as quitting or retirement. Workers who tried to quit came up missing. End of story.

"Yo', man, speaking of Neema, you still thinking about playing wifey with her?"

"She the mother of my children, ain't she?"

"Yeah, true that but what of it? You gotta kid by that skank, Tia, too."

Topps gave him a side look that should have been enough to say 'stay the hell out of my business.' "Thought I told you not to bring her name up again?"

"Oh yeah," said Slick, turning on the flat-screen computer on the desk. "I keep forgetting."

The subject of Topps' ex-girl, Tia, had turned sour after Topps discovered the woman had stolen a quarter of a million dollars from him. Tia had been his number one woman before Neema came on the scene. Tia had been more sophisticated, but Neema was more fly in dress and looks. Neither women knew about each other, and Topps planned to keep it that way. Besides, he couldn't even see his daughter by Tia because her scandalous mama was still hiding out from him. Topps knew it was only a matter of time before he found out where the woman was and dealt with her. Daughter or no daughter, he took stealing personally. No one got away with stealing from him. No one.

"What, you got something against Neema?" Topps kept his

back to him. His eyes zoomed in on soldiers, watching for workers who might try to sneak a small rock into their mouth or the rim of their panties. Skanks were sneaky like that. It was in their blood.

"She alright," said Slick half-heartedly. "Better than some I've seen you kick it with. But once she becomes wifey, she'll be knowing more about yo' business. That's all I'm saying. You think she can be trusted like that?" Slick had his back, but he didn't know how to tell him that his woman was a b-hopper. Meaning that the girl would hop in any man's bed. Half of Topps' army knew that girl was a bona fide freak because they had sampled her juice. *Hell*, he thought with a smile on his face, *I was all up in that pussy two nights ago myself.*

"Slick, you bugging, man. Of course I trust her ass. I wouldn't have her transporting my big-money packages all over the place if I didn't trust her. Know what I'm saying? Why? What's up? You have something to drop on Neema?"

"Nah, man. I was just saying, I mean, you know how it is with skanks sometimes. They be trippin' like they all into you, and they love you deep, but they be skimming big time." Slick watched him go to the sink to wash his hands. The sixth time so far. At least a brother was getting better. Times in the past, Topps washed his hands ten to twelve times in the span of an hour. The cleanest nigga he knew. "I'm just saying we have to be sure. A woman as fine as Neema brings a lot of competition. Niggas be sniffing behind her, and that's a lot of temptation for any woman. Any nigga try'n to get to you would step quick to her. That's all I'm try'n to say."

He couldn't mention the fact that he'd caught some feelings for Neema. Throwing out negative thoughts about the woman was his ploy to keep Topps from catching on. Actually, Neema deserved better. She deserved a man like him, but only if she stopped b-hopping.

Topps snatched a paper towel off to dry his hands. "Yo, bro, like I said, if you know something you need to tell me, drop it now." He turned around, adjusting his blue-and-black Sean John sweatshirt, waiting for Slick to say something else, but the man was quiet. "Other than that, I'm handling mine."

"Yeah, you right." Slick went back to looking at the computer screen.

The four solid gold chains around Topps' neck were enough to finance a small car. A smirk found its way onto his handsome face. It irked him when niggas made sly comments about his woman, but weren't man enough to drop the truth. On the real, Slick was probably jealous because he didn't have the skills or looks to pull a classy-looking number like his Neema. He could dig that. What normal man wouldn't be jealous? Still, Slick was his closest confidant. Damn near like a brother. Any other nigga talking like that about his woman and he would have taken his pistol out and went upside his head. But Slick was his boy from back in the day. He was the only one he'd take that mess from.

"Matter of fact," Topps tossed the paper towel in the trash, "get Neema's ass on radar now. See where the hell she is with my money."

Slick was happy to oblige. "I'm on it." He punched in the code for the computer's software that linked GPS tracking to the cell phone that Neema carried. Topps had convinced Neema that the reason he was supplying three new cell phones was for their top-of-the-line features: camera and MP3 player. In truth the three units he'd given Neema and their two kids were sophisticated tracking devices.

It took a couple of minutes for her location to flash on the screen's digital map. "She's nowhere near Hollywood; that's for damn sure."

"No shit?" Topps came around him to check out the screen for himself. Equipping all their soldiers with GPS cell phones had been Slick's idea. Expensive, but the best idea so far. This way, he always knew where his soldiers were with his money or his merchandise. Niggas trying to slip away couldn't get far. "Where the hell she at? Her ass should be back by now."

"Looks like the Crenshaw District."

"Crenshaw and Martin Luther King. That dizzy-ass woman. Looks like she's at her crib to me." Topps pulled out his cell phone and speed-dialed her digits. Neema answered on the third ring.

"Hey shawty. What's up?" He listened to what he knew would be lies.

"Where you at now? Hollywood? No shit? On your way back, huh? Hey, it's all good." Just like he thought, she was straight up lying to him. "Alright then. Check you when I see you at the house. Later." He punched off. "Damn, my boo bitch is lying like a rug."

Slick gave him an I-told-you-so look but held his tongue.

"Damn. She's been my best one yet." For a second, it looked like his eyes tried to fill with water. He was hurt. They had been kicking it for over seven years and had their ups and down like any other couple, but Neema kept convincing him that she had changed her sneaky ways. And yeah, there had been a few discrepancies over the years, but nothing major. Caught in her web of lies more than once, Neema always promised to do better. Topps had believed her and was getting to the point of thinking that he could take her as his wife. Maybe have a couple more kids. Live happily ever after. Yeah, right, like that shit really happens to people like him. "No sweat. My boo loves that bling-bling living. She's wicked as hell on a nigga, but I caught feelings for her ass and she got my kids. I'll get her straight, fo' sho.'"

Slick thought he heard commotion out on the line. "What the hell?" Always alert, he shot up to go investigate but it was nothing serious. A soldier thought he spotted a worker tucking a rock beneath her hanging breast. A quick check had revealed nothing. Everyone was back to work.

"Man, women are like small children; you have to keep an eye on they asses at all times."

Topps wasn't listening. He was back at the sink washing his hands again. Shaking his head, Slick watched him.

"Topps, man, you know they have medication for yo' condition."

"My condition?" Topps turned around to regard him. His look was vexed.

"Hell yeah, man. Had an uncle had the same affliction. Couldn't touch a damn thing without washing his hands all fucking day. Not even pussy. Hell, he almost washed the black off his ass, he washed so much. You need to check on some meds."

"Medication?"

"For real, my nigga. Medication works."

"And what would my affliction be, Slick?" Insulted, Topps' expression turned serious. "What, you saying I'm weak now?"

"Hell no. Hey, man, I'm just try'n to help. Damn, stop being so sensitive and twisting my shit up."

"Fuck it!" Topps was clearly irritated. He couldn't stop thinking about Neema and how she kept trying to play him. Always lying to him. Always begging for more money. Probably still stealing from him, too. He had to do something about her. Make her an example so others could see that he didn't play. "I'ma slide outta here. Got some business to take care of. You know what to do, if you need me."

"No problem. I'ma hold things down 'til close-up. It's drop day, you know. We got major paper coming in. But I'll swing by your place first thing in the morning with profits."

"Sounds tight. I'm out."

The two knocked knuckles before Topps headed for the door. Disappointment with Neema had his shoulders slumped. Seemed like the more he tried to trust her, the more she proved that she couldn't be trusted. At least he had Slick. Slick was his man, his ace, his dawg. It felt good to have at least one person that he could expose his back to.

"Yo', dawg," Slick called behind him. "Whatever you do, don't be too hard on her. Neema is just being Neema."

"Nah. I wouldn't do my son's mama like that. Still, I'ma deal with her. That's word. Later."

It wouldn't be right to pop his own son's mother over some money. When his son was old enough, he would be next in line to fill his shoes. Thoughts of Brandon made him smile. Already the boy was showing signs of being hardcore and fearless. He dug that shit big time. Maybe he'd slide by Hattie's place again to see his kids before heading to the crib to wait on Neema. Nah. Neema first.

SEVEN

Ten seconds after her doorbell rang, Neema Jean ran to it and looked out the peephole. The neighborhood where she lived wasn't the best. Plus, she had to make sure that it wasn't her mother or that pesky sister of hers, trying to bring her brats back home. Good. It was her home girl, Kaykay.

Neema unlocked and swung the door open for her. "What's up, my homie?"

"Did you get it?" Kaykay asked, waiting with hungry eyes.

"Hell yeah, I got it, and damn it's good." Once Kaykay stepped inside, Neema closed the door behind her. "Didn't think you were coming, so I started without you. It's some of his best."

"That's what I'm talking about. Let's get this party going then."

"Ooh, I forgot. Shit, lock my damn door behind you. Can't have Topps sneaking up on a sistah before we can get our head right."

"I know that's right," Kaykay agreed, turning the deadbolt. Truth be told, if she never saw Topps Jackson again in life it would be too soon. She'd been around the man on several occasions and from what she'd observed, he had a temper like a firecracker that sizzled before going *bang*. She'd seen it with her own eyes, how he could beat a man down until he begged for his life. If he knew how Neema was topping off with his drugs, no telling what his crazy ass would do.

"C'mon in. We can fly a few lines before I have to leave to square some business. That fool Topps got me on his damn clock. I should be on my way back already from my drop in Hollywood. I don't feel like hearing his mouth today."

"Hollywood? Dang, girl, I feel sorry for you. That's too far for this time of day." Kaykay was about to step on Neema's imported white Persian rug but checked herself. She took her shoes off and felt good for it. The new heels she had on were killing her. "Damn, girl. You got it fly up in this 'mutha." It had been weeks since she'd been to Neema's place. Their meet-and-chill spots were clubs, the mall, and sometimes at Kaykay's place. "When all this jump off?"

"A week or so." Neema beamed. "You like it?"

"Hell yeah!" Kaykay panned her view, admiring all the new touches: paint, furniture. A creamy vanilla leather sectional with matching coffee and end tables. A fancy looking painting adorned the walls. Everything was too fly, in glass and leather. Any fool would be shocked, stepping up in the place, since the outside of Neema's Crenshaw district apartment was old and rundown. But the inside was the difference between Compton and Palos Verdes. She walked over to the smoky glass dining room table where Neema had some coke piled on a mirror. "Looks like you're doing good, for somebody unemployed. Hell, girl, I work six days a week and still live in a shack."

"That's because you not hooking up with the right niggas." Kaykay was a true get-money chick who mainly dated big-ballers, but occasionally she went through a dry spell. Neema wasn't sure who her main man was now, but the last she'd heard, her girl was involved and stalking a married man who had to uproot and leave town with his wife and family to end their relationship. "Hell, I was tired of my place looking like a dump while that nigga Topps kicked it in luxury. Shoot, I like nice things, too."

"You ain't never lied."

Attired in a short, yellow sundress, Neema sashayed over to the table where she had Topps' package wide open for her dipping pleasure. "Make yourself at home."

"Hell, yeah," said Kaykay, pulling out a chair. Her hungry eyes locked on the white blow like a kid lusting behind chocolate cake. "Good looking out for inviting a sistah over for a lift party. I sho' appreciate it."

"Kay, you know how we do? You my homie. We share." Neema took a seat across from her. She took up an index card and sectioned off four generous lines. "Here you go." She passed Kaykay a cut-off straw, then watched that greedy girl fly two lines up so fast that it made her shudder. "Girl, look at you. You a dope fiend crackhead." The two shared a brief laugh.

"Yeah, right, Miss Pot-Calling-the-Kettle-Black. I do a few lines every now and then, but I ain't no crackhead. I can't stand smoking no crack."

"I know that's right." Neema flew the last two lines and stood up feeling as light as air itself. "Want something to eat?"

"Nah. Maybe somethin' to drink. Nothing with too much sugar in it. You got any diet Coke?"

"Diet? Girl, please."

Kaykay was one of her closest friends. The two had met during jury duty a couple of years back. The girl was constantly crying broke but always dressed like she was running with a big-baller with heavy pockets. She wore diamond rings on all fingers, and gold dangled from her neck and wrists. Kaykay's long, reddish-brown hair, as usual, was fly to perfection; even if it was a lace-front wig. Neema admired the slamming black miniskirt with a matching top over a red Baby Phat tank she wore. She resisted the urge to ask where she'd bought those jamming Jimmy Choos she'd kicked off. The look was way hot for a chick with a hot body—something Neema appreciated from her friends because she couldn't be seen in public with skanks who didn't know how to dress to impress. Truth be told, Kaykay could pass for Ciara's twin. At least from a distance. Up close she had a mad scar on her left side from a car accident three years back.

"You know you still look good. Yo' man wouldn't let you get fat and you know it."

"Word. That fool keeps my gym membership paid up."

"Are you serious?" Neema laughed but knew she wasn't lying. "Well, who is he? What's his name?" With two kids and running product for Topps, Neema stayed pretty busy herself. The two friends rarely got together anymore, so Neema wasn't quite sure who Kaykay was talking about. "Is he a true baller or what?"

"Let's just say he treats me good."

"Whatever. Anyway, if you ain't doing nothin', come make this run with me."

"You mean, ride dirty for Topps?" Kaykay snorted with a mock frown. She took out her compact mirror to check herself. Pink-manicured nails primped at her expensive lace-front wig. "You know I can't stand that nigga. No offense. I don't want shit to do with his mess."

"You wasn't saying that when you was flying his shit up your nose."

"Humph. That's different. And I ain't trying to tell you how to handle yo' business or nothing, but you need to cut that fool loose before you find yourself in a world of trouble. Take me, for example. I likes my freedom. Got me an old gangsta on the side. Keeps me happy. Hear what I'm saying?"

"Kay, I'm not asking you to suck his dick. Come ride with me. You can keep me company. Once I handle business, we can sprint over to that fancy eating place called Crustacean in B-Hills, have lunch, and a few apple martinis. My treat."

"Girl, you trying to tempt me, but no. Maybe next time." Perplexed, Kaykay sniffed and looked around. "Dang. Them kids of yours are too quiet. They napping or what?"

"They not here."

Hell. That reminded her that she needed to call her mother to check on her kids. Neema dreaded the task like going to the dentist. After three days, her mother had to be pretty pissed off about the kids being dumped on her. She took up her cell phone from the table, flipped it open, and looked at it.

"Nah. Maybe later. I don't feel like hearing Mama's mouth right now. She a Christian and all, but my mama keeps it real. You piss her off, she libel to swear and curse and tell you how she really feel."

She tossed her phone back, went into her kitchen and returned with a can of cola and a box of baking soda. "Here you go." She passed the soda to Kaykay. "I better wrap it up and get going then." Opening the plastic bag containing the cocaine she was supposed to deliver, Neema replaced equal amounts of the white powder. "That should do it," she said after using a scale to check the weight. "Perfect."

Kaykay eyed her suspiciously. "What the hell are you doing?"

"Covering my ass. What else?" Neema zipped the plastic bag up, then carefully placed it in her oversized tote bag on the table. "You know that nigga Topps keep his shit down to the nit, and his clients all know it, too. I gets mine from the top, but I know to be careful."

Kaykay found her antics comical. "What, those niggas can't tell the difference between pure blow and baking soda?"

"Girl, please, sometimes I run outta baking soda and substitute with foot dust."

Kaykay cracked up laughing. "No you didn't say foot dust."

"Girl, I'm for real. If you sand your feet and catch the dust, it almost looks like cocaine. Especially if you mix it with pure blow. You can't tell the difference."

"That's some crazy shit. You one crazy and bold bitch."

"Screw them fools. They shouldn't be dope fiends if they can't take the risk."

The two laughed even harder. "Shit, my foot dust probably the best shit they asses ever flew up they nose." All that laughing made her bladder wake up. "Damn, now I gotta go pee. Still, you need to come ride with a sistah. I'll make it worth your while. Think about it while I go pee."

Neema hurried toward her bathroom, already hiking up the floral hem of her sundress. She made a mad rush of doing her business and washing her hands. Her perfect lips were just forming the words, "Let's raise up outta here," when she heard the distinct click of a key turning in the lock of her front door. "Who the hell..." She froze in place; eyes wide and trained on the door.

"Girl, what is it?" Kaykay whispered loudly, noticing her face. She jumped; scared.

Neema felt her heart speed to a drum beat as her front door slowly opened and in stepped Topps like he owned the place. He had that cocky look on his face that she couldn't stand. Those cold, dark eyes of his were staring straight through her.

"What's up, ladies? Looks like Mister Topps got here right on time for the party."

EIGHT

"Topps! How the hell you get a key to my place?" Neema tried to play it off like it was no big deal, even though she had posed the question. After all, he did pay her rent from time to time. The times when he didn't, the money she had stolen from him did.

"I been had a key."

Neema rethought things and decided not to play a damn thing off. She was mad that he had barged in to her crib. "Well, a nigga coulda told me that shit. You stepping in here unannounced ain't right."

She sniffed to keep her nose from losing some of the blow she'd flown earlier. Honest to God, she was getting tired of this man constantly checking her like she was some lowlife criminal. "I mean, I know you sometimes pay the rent on this mutha, but damn, boo."

"I'll keep that in mind."

Screw you, she thought. Neema headed to the kitchen, came back with three bottles. "Here bitch, have some water." She tossed one bottle to Kaykay before placing one on the table and shooting Topps an irritated look. "You have a key to my crib; I should have one to yours. That's how I feel about it."

"Yeah, right." Topps closed and locked the deadbolt behind him, then put the chain on for extra assurance. "I was in the neighborhood and spotted your ride parked outside. Thought I'd stop by. Hope I'm not disturbing you ladies."

"Nah, boo. You not disturbing nothing. I ran to the crib to use the restroom. You know how I am about using public facilities. I was on my way back out." She had to admit, he looked good in those super-creased jeans and dark knit shirt. Gulping water, she watched him.

"On your way to deliver? No shit?" He walked slowly over to the table where he spotted her tote bag with his product in it. He snatched it up.

"Boo, I said I was on my way out. I had to pee real bad."

"When I talked to you earlier, you were on your way back from dropping off. Ain't that what you said?"

"Yeah, but, that was because I had to pee, baby. You know how you feel about public restrooms. They full of germs."

"True dat. But still, you lied to me, Nee." He took his bag of product out for a good examination. The weight felt about the same, but that didn't mean shit. "I know you not standing there saying that you drove to Hollywood but had to come all the way back to this mutha just to take a piss."

Kaykay stood up, fumbling for her purse and keys. "Uh, look, girlfriend, I see you have some business to deal with, so I'll give you two some privacy."

"Sit yo' bitch ass down!" Topps' eyes dared defiance.

"Nigga, who you calling a bitch? I ain't yo' bitch. You must have me confused with…"

"And shut the fuck up!" He pulled out a twenty-two, one of his favorites because it didn't make a lot of noise, in case he had to pop a bitch in her own community. "Now say something else."

Oh shit. This is getting outta hand! Neema jumped in with, "Baby, what's wrong? Why you tripping like this?"

He aimed the gun at her. "I'm not playing, boo. You need to shut the hell up, too."

"Now I know you done lost your ever-loving mind, coming up in here pulling a gun. What's wrong with you, Topps?" Neema walked up on him, but froze in her tracks when he aimed the gun higher at her head. The bottle of water dropped from her hand.

"You my boo and all, but don't get it twisted when it comes to my money, Nee. I'ma find out what the hell is going on up in this mutha."

"So what you gonna do, Topps? You gonna shoot me now?" Neema made a wide gesture with her arms. "You gonna shoot the mother of your kids?!" Her hands began to tremble, but her face remained straight. It was hard to put on a brave front with a man so unpredictable. Instinct told her to chill.

"I might have to. You know how this shit goes, baby. You play the game wrong, you lose. Damn, don't take it so personally. Now…let's see what's going on here. You and your little bitch friend here go stand next to the wall and chill while Topps check things out. Know what I'm saying?"

"Hell no, I don't know!" Neema rolled her eyes at him.

The two women did what they were told, with Neema huffing and puffing and shaking her head about the injustice of it all. She glanced sideways at Kaykay's hands trembling so badly that she could barely get the cap off of her bottled water.

"Girl, don't sweat him, he's going through one of his male PMS moods; that's all. It'll be okay. Ain't that right, Topps?"

"I'm not playing with you, Nee! You need to shut the fuck up!"

Neema took a deep breath, trying to calm her nerves. She never should have invited Kaykay over for a noontime pick-me-up, knowing how crazy and sneaky Topps could be. He was forever popping up unexpectedly. This was the third or fourth time that fool had hemmed her up about his product not arriving on time, or money missing. If it wasn't one thing with him, it was something else. She didn't see why he was always sweating her when he had plenty of money and product to deal with. *Should have been a damn detective or a lawyer.* Obviously, the fool had some trust issues. Maybe it was time for a new man.

It took some time, weighing the package. Tasting the product and eyeing the open box of baking soda, the deal wasn't hard for Topps to figure out. "Skimming bitches."

"Look, I need to get going, if you want that package delivered. You know how that traffic can be. We can argue over this shit when I get back."

"Nee, don't worry about it. I'll call my client and explain that we had a little delay. I'm sure he'll understand."

"So what now?" Neema challenged, her face frowned up. "You gonna keep us as hostages, like I did something so wrong? Hell, Topps, I gotta pick the kids up from Mama's house."

Topps chuckled at that. In fact, he seemed to relax some. "No. In fact, you know what? I'm not even mad at y'all little party with my shit. It's cool. Plenty more where that came from. But check this out. Maybe we all need to chill and party together. That would make Topps really happy right about now." He looked from one face to the other. A wicked smiled tugged at his lips.

"What the hell that's supposed to mean? And why you keep talking like that?" Neema wished she could go get a wine cooler from her refrigerator to mellow out her nerves. She had known all along that Topps was crazy, and not one to be messing with, but damn, she had no idea he'd pull a gun on her.

"Like I said, don't worry about it. Y'all want some blow, let's do some blow." He placed the gun down on the table before taking a seat. "C'mon, let's get this party started. Y'all want some blow?"

"Nah." Kaykay shook her head. "I'm trying to stop. That shit ain't good for you. I…I need to split back to my crib. My man is waiting on me."

"Bullshit, Topps says we gonna do some blow. Y'all gonna love this shit 'cause I carry only the best for my friends, so let that nigga wait like everybody else. Get yourself over here."

"Topps, stop it. The girl told you that she needs to get home."

"Yeah. I heard, and she will after we party a little bit. No party, nobody leaving this mutha, and that's word. Now, do as I say and bring yo' asses over here." From his pocket, Topps took out a small brown vial and removed the black top. "Like I said, I keep the good stuff for good friends." A tiny pile of the white powder was spread on the same mirror Neema and Kaykay had utilized earlier. "Come try this," he said, after sectioning off five lines with the same index card. "Yo, who's going first?"

"This stupid-ass, childish nigga," Neema mumbled under her breath. She took a quick glance at her Cartier watch before stomping over to the table. As much as she liked flying lines up her nose, his offer really wasn't a problem. She kept it quick. "Here, Kaykay," she said, offering the cut straw. "Might as well get it over with."

"Bitch, you crazy. How you know it ain't poison he try'n give us?"

Topps took the straw and flew one short line. "Like I said, only the best for good friends. You wanna leave here, we party first. Your choice, shortie." Topps didn't look up at her. "We could be here all night. Days even."

"Hell, Kaykay, just do what he says so we can get on with our lives. I gotta get up out of here to pick up my kids."

Kaykay walked over. Hesitantly, she snatched up the straw and flew two lines. "There," she hissed, throwing the straw down. "Freaking satisfied?"

"Yeah, bitch. You could say that. But I'ma be more satisfied when we get this party in full swing." Topps stood up. "Now, it's time to get clean."

"Topps, baby, please...please don't start that shit. You got a problem with me, deal with me."

He took the gun up. "You know how I do it, Nee. Let's take this party to the shower."

Neema screamed, "I'm not fucking playing with you!"

Topps was in her grill in a flash. He grabbed her. "Do I look like I'm playing, Nee?" His harsh words were followed up with a back-handed slap. "This ain't no game; this real."

Neema grabbed her face before making a lunge, but Topps was quick-aiming. Would he actually shoot her in the face? "Crazy fool! You didn't have to hit me like that."

"You bitches are too much, you know that? Stealing my shit and acting like I'm wrong when you get caught. Fucking crazy. Now get your asses in there."

"Ain't nobody stole shit from you! Why you bugging?"

"Oh, it's 'bout to be crackin' in a minute." He aimed the gun in their direction. "Like I said, we taking this party to the shower area. You play, you pay. So you got two choices. Party and go home alive, or refuse and get popped. I can have a few of my soldiers here to clean up my mess in no time, and be on my way."

Seconds passed with a stare-down.

"What's he saying, Neema? What the hell he planning to do? I ain't into no freaky-deaky shit with no female!"

"Hell, Kaykay, I don't know, but c'mon. Just do what he says."

The women walked ahead of him to the restroom. The gun was still in Topps' hand. In a matter of minutes he had the two women undressed in the shower and soaping up each other like it was a video being made for profit, but not before applying a few licks upside Kaykay's stubborn head to help her cooperate.

"Oh yeah. This shit pleases Topps very much." He swooned as he watched the two brown bodies lather up one another in soap. Once the powdered "E" he'd given them earlier had kicked in, the two seemed more natural at trying to please him. At least they weren't fighting it. Hell, it seemed like they were enjoying it.

"Kaykay's ass needs more soap on it, baby. Lather that mutha up good." Topps licked his lips. He put the gun on the bathroom counter so he could shed his own clothes, and then sat on the chair he'd dragged into the bathroom. "Don't forget those pussies, ladies. They need some soaping, too. Yeah, just like that. That's what I'm talkin' 'bout. Soap that juicy shit up good. Get up in it."

"Boo, how long we have to do this?" Neema asked, her words slurred.

"Until I say stop. Oh yeah, that's sweet. Rub those nipples good. And let Kaykay wash your snatch good, too. That's right, open that shit up and make it clean like a mutha. Hell, y'all good at this shit. I need my camcorder right about now."

"How much longer, boo? We tired."

"Hell, we barely getting started." Topps got up and walked to the shower to join them. "Nothing like a little 'E' to get a party rolling."

Neema's shower wasn't as commodious as his, but there was enough room for three bodies to get close. "Yo, turn y'all fine asses around. Face the wall. You know how I like cleanliness," he said lustfully, lathering soap from one tight round ass to the other. There was no need to worry about either woman trying anything because all three were feeling pretty good from the "E." In fact, the women seemed to be enjoying the shower as much as he was.

Topps wasted no time running soapy hands up through their thighs to their hot privates. He inserted slippery fingers into double moistness as his body rubbed up against both backsides. Damn, he was in second heaven with not one but two pussies. All for him.

"Damn. This the lick here. We can take this party to the bedroom."

Taking both by the hand, he pulled them to the bedroom where he wasted no time putting on a condom and pumping one, then the other. His manhood was still in full bloom when he lay back along the bed.

"Brain time. And this the deal. The one that gets me off first gets to leave first." He looked from Neema to Kaykay. "Hell, the way I'm feeling, I might let you bitches leave without the bonus beat down I was planning."

"Here, I'll go first." Kaykay grabbed his rod like she owned it. She got straight busy with it, like there was no tomorrow.

Jealousy flashed in Neema's eyes but she couldn't say one word; watching her good friend mouth-clamp her man's dick. If it hadn't been for her greed, they wouldn't be in the predicament to begin with. It made her mad to watch, and yet, in a way, it also turned her on. *Yeah, girl, suck that big dick like your life depends on it*, she thought. And in a way, maybe it did.

NINE

A promise was a promise. Sunday after church service, Hattie headed to the nearest Walmart where she planned to let Brandon and Raynita pick out one toy each for behaving so well during Reverend King's sermon. The weather was perfect, not too much sun, not too little. Just right.

"Who wants to climb in the basket?" Hattie asked, steering the metal cart toward the store entrance. Reverend King's sermon still had her feeling good inside; despite the fact that it had been eight days since Neema had dropped the kids off without so much as a phone call.

"I do, Nanny! I do!" Raynita wasted no time climbing in, leaving little room for Brandon. She placed her little purse in her lap and adjusted her dress like a proper, little lady.

"What about you, Brandon?"

Brandon gave a weary look. "Nanny, that's for babies."

"I ain't no baby!" Raynita protested.

"Yes, you are. Daddy says you are. A big crybaby."

"I'm not."

"You are. Big crybaby, and a snitch, too."

"Okay, okay," Hattie interrupted. All of her good church feelings started slipping away. "You two need to stop all that bickering over nothing. Didn't you two hear a word that Reverend King preached earlier? Families need to stay close and love one another; not fight all the time."

Raynita rolled her eyes. "He started it. He always talking 'bout somebody."

"Big baby! Big baby!" Brandon teased, making a face at his sister.

"You make me sick! I hate you!" Her purse in the air, Raynita threatened to hit hard.

"I said stop it!" Hattie snapped. She dared either one to say another word. "If you two don't behave, we can forget about getting toys and go home. Maybe some time out in bed will help you two think about your behavior." Hattie stopped and gave them "the look" again. Heck, the "stern face" used to work good for her kids when they were little, but her grandchildren were different. "The look" didn't mean a darn thing.

"Nanny, why you look crazy like that?"

"Hush up, Brandon, before I pinch a plug outta your arm."

"And I'll tell my mama."

"Boy, what good would that do? Y'all mama been gone for eight days now. I hardly think she'd worry about you getting pinched. Shoot, when I see her, I might have to pinch her behind a few times."

Raynita giggled. "Nanny, you can't pinch Mama."

"Humph. Wait and see." Hattie had to bite her tongue to prevent herself from saying more. She was upset. No, she was beyond upset. How dare Neema presume it was okay to dump her kids off for more than a week and not leave an emergency number? What if one of the kids got sick? Or some kind of emergency came up? She had no power-of-attorney, no health insurance card, no medical records, no nothing. If it hadn't been for her scrupulous saving over the years, she wouldn't have the extra money to feed extra mouths or take the kids on a shopping trip. *Oh well!* She sighed. All she could do was make the best of it until Neema came to her senses and showed back up.

"Excuse me." Hattie maneuvered her shopping cart around a fat woman with four kids. The woman looked too tired and too old to be the mother. *Probably another poor grandmother being taken advantage of.* "Do you know where the toys are kept?"

The plump-faced woman frowned back at her. "Do I look like I work here?"

"You don't have to be rude about it. Geez."

It took going up and down a few aisles, but Hattie located the toy area. "Remember now. One toy only and nothing over twenty dollars 'cause I'm not rich." Both children picked two and three items and whined for them.

"Please, Nanny, please."

"Nita, what part of *just one toy* didn't you understand? You and Brandon also need other items." As usual, the store was crowded and Hattie wanted to get in and out so she could get back to her place to relax and soak her feet. The plan was to pick up a few clothes for the children as well, seeing how Neema hadn't packed enough. Both Brandon and Raynita needed more underwear and some house slippers. "I'm tired of washing y'all clothes every other day."

"Are we going to school tomorrow?"

"I don't know, Brandon. I might have to take you if Neema don't show up." The kids had already missed a week of school. Hattie couldn't see them missing another one. The school they attended was quite a distance away, but if she had to, she'd take them.

"I like school," Raynita announced, playing with the new doll she picked. "I wanna see my friends."

"I hate school." Brandon tossed his toy into the shopping cart. "It takes too long and it's stupid. Gangstas don't haft to go to school."

"Boy, stop talking crazy before I pop you upside the head."

"Nanny, that's child abuse. I'll call nine-one-one."

"Brandon, hush up."

Shopping done, Hattie got in line to pay for her items before proceeding to the store's main exit. "Let's go home and have some lunch. Y'all hungry?"

Raynita asked, "Can we stop at McDonald's? Please, Nanny, please."

"Please nothing, and no, we can't. We have food at the house." Hattie smiled down at the two, who seemed happy with their selections. Brandon had chosen some kind of plastic gun that worked with rubber darts, after promising that he wouldn't aim it at his sister's face. Raynita was still going on about the fancy-dressed Barbie she picked. *Look at 'em*, Hattie thought with pride swelling. *They really are good kids. They just need more love, guidance and attention.*

"I have five Barbie dolls now, Nanny."

"That's nice, sweetie," said Hattie, waiting for the door clerk to check her receipt. This Lakewood location was the only Walmart she knew that checked the receipts of the blacks and Latinos as they exited the building.

"Thank you, Nanny."

"You welcome, sweetie." Hattie handed the receipt over and waited for the clerk to mark it with a yellow highlighter. "Have a nice day." Finally they were on their way home. She couldn't wait to get out of her hot go-to-church dress and relax. The second she stepped through the door scanner it sounded off. The clerk was right behind her, asking her to please step to the side.

"What? What's wrong?" Hattie asked, perplexed. Instant embarrassment flooded her senses. She shopped at Walmart all the time, but had never been stopped after having her receipt checked.

"It's probably nothing, ma'am." The clerk asked to see her

receipt again, then looked through her bags to re-check her purchases. "Sometimes the cashier forgets to deactivate the anti-theft tag. You don't mind if I take a look in your purse, do you?"

"Why would you need to do that?" Hattie asked, making a face. This was the first time that she'd ever experienced something like this. "Sure," she said, opening her purse up for inspection.

The fat, brown clerk was still looking for something when a pink-faced man walked up and identified himself as store security, then instructed Hattie to follow him to the back. Feeling like some convicted criminal from *America's Most Wanted*, Hattie wanted to hide her face from the shoppers that stopped to watch them. She had never felt so embarrassed in her life. If they didn't find something to justify being treated this way, she'd get a lawyer and sue. They had a lot of nerve, treating decent church folks this way.

"Why? What's going on? I paid for my items." Regardless, Hattie did what she was told and followed the casually dressed man to a back room where she and the children were asked to remove everything from their pockets and purse. "I don't understand what all this is about. I hope you don't treat all your customers like this." Now that she thought about it, she'd seen that same man several times in the same aisles with them, pretending to be a shopper.

"There? Satisfied?" All their belongings were laid out on a big wooden table where two store security personnel stood waiting for Raynita to empty her purse. The girl was clutching the thing like her very life depended on protecting its contents.

"Nita, give the man your purse so we can hurry up and get out of here. I might have to go home and call Jacoby and Myers about this. It makes no sense. I shop at Walmart all the time and never had this kind of problem."

"No, Nanny, it's my purse!"

"He's not asking to borrow the thing, Nita. He just wants to look inside. Give it to him."

"No. Nanny!'

"Here, I'll do it, Nanny." Brandon got up from his chair and snatched the purse hard away from her. He ignored her wail of protest as he turned it upside down and out tumbled a few items that Hattie hadn't paid for, along with the new cell phone her father had given her.

"Nita, what in the world…" Hattie felt her heart sink. She looked up at the pink faces that looked down at her.

A first-time offense, that's what they called it. Hattie couldn't have been more grateful that the store security let them go with a strict warning and of course, Nita was banned from that Walmart. Heck, Hattie didn't know if she was welcome again in Walmart, thanks to Raynita.

"I really appreciate this. You can believe that it won't happen again. I had no idea the child would steal. I'm so sorry." Hattie couldn't thank the people enough for not calling the police and having them taken down and booked like common career criminals.

"I can't believe this little nappy-headed child," Hattie mumbled to herself as they made their way out the store and to her car. A good belt whipping? No dessert and no television? What would be the best punishment? She felt like taking Raynita and shaking the black off her right there in the parking lot, but fear of catching a child abuse case stopped her. "Lord, please give me the patience…" She blew out a hard breath. Stealing was bad enough, but that girl stealing while she was out with her took the cake. And another thing that disturbed her, that darn cell phone. Raynita had that cell phone all along and never mentioned it. She felt like slapping her.

"Nita, I hope it was worth it." She seatbelted the girl in and slammed the car door.

"I'm sorry, Nanny." The child had big crocodile tears streaming down her face. "I wanted some new clothes for my Barbie and you said no."

"A crybaby and a thief. Wait 'til I tell Mama."

"Brandon, hush up, and I mean it. And how long you had that darn cell phone, Nita?" Hattie started the engine and waited a few seconds before backing out the parking space.

"I been had it. Daddy bought it for me."

"Girl, I specifically asked you if you had your mother's new cell number and you told me no. Didn't you?"

"Yes, ma'am." Nita sniffed, crying silent. "I forgot I had it."

"What about you, Brandon. Where's your cell phone?"

"In my backpack."

"Is your mother's new phone number in it?"

Brandon shrugged. "I don't know. I haven't used it yet."

Well, I'll be darn. "Little nappy-headed kids probably had a number to reach their mama all along. I'm very upset with you, Nita. Very upset. And you can forget about that Barbie doll I bought today. Right now I don't think you deserve it."

Raynita cried harder, but Hattie wasn't falling for that "instant pity" act.

"Humph. I can't stand no stealing! You better hope I'm feeling better about all this by the time we get back to the house. And stop all that crying before I pull this car over and give you something to cry about!" All her good Christian feelings flew straight out the open car window.

TEN

He'd never been a deep sleeper. The slightest movement on the bed made Topps go for the small-caliber gun he had placed under the pillow his head was laying on. His eyes flew open in time to see Kaykay standing in the corner of the room easing back into her clothes. The vision both excited and irritated him.

"Yo', where the hell you think you going?" Topps raised his head up, looking around. Neema was still passed out on the bed from drinking too much wine. The party had turned wild with frenzy and all three had fallen asleep from all the drugs, alcohol and sexual fatigue. It was close to seven and already dark outside. Looked like Miss Kaykay was trying to sneak out on them.

Alarmed, Kaykay swirled around. "Look, I have to leave. I'm already late."

Topps sniffed. "Is that right? And who said this party is over?"

"Topps, please…I…I…"

"Don't go there, shorty." Topps hopped up with one fluid movement. With no clothes on he was quite a towering specimen of ripped muscle and hard body. The heady scent of sweat and sex was still on him. "We got more partying."

"You two have fun. I'm out." After all the licking, sucking and screwing they'd done, Kaykay was too ashamed to look at his nakedness.

"And what if I'm not ready for you to leave, Miss Kaykay? Did yo' sweet ass forget that I'm calling the shots here?" He put the gun down on the dresser. The idea of repeating a threesome was a turn-on. Normally, Neema wouldn't have gone for it. Hell no. But that's how it goes when her hand is caught in the cookie jar. "This party ain't over yet. You'll leave when I say you can leave." His growing erection became more evident.

"Look, I did what you wanted. You gave your word. I need to get home." Fully dressed, Kaykay had her purse and tried to walk away.

"Like I said, I'm calling the shots here." Topps grabbed her purse. A tug-of-war ensued.

Kaykay screamed, "Get yo' punk-ass hands offa' me!"

The two were in full struggle when Neema sat up, asking what was going on. She got out of bed with the intention of stopping the mayhem before things got out of control. "Topps, let her go! What the hell's wrong with you? Let her go!"

"Nah. Not until I teach you bitches a real lesson for stealing! Nobody steals from Topps and gets away with it. Nobody!"

"She didn't steal shit, it was me. You need to deal with me!" Neema tried to pry his fingers from Kaykay's clothing, but a hard back-hand slap sent her falling to the bed. She watched Kaykay put up a good fight, but she was no match for Topps' male strength. Kaykay clawed into his face, making him madder and more aggressive. He spun her around for a good back-hand slap that sent her thin body flying over to the wooden dresser where the temple of her head caught the dresser's edge with a large thud. Kaykay gave a yelp before she went down hard. Blood oozed from her mouth. "Topps, stoppit! Leave her alone!"

"Bitch, get up!" Topps walked and stood over her. His face felt hot from where she had tried to dig her fingernails deep. He could kill her ass for trying to mess up his face, but she wasn't moving. He knelt down and felt against her neck for a pulse, held her arm and pressed two fingers at her wrist. "Damn. This bitch ain't breathing."

"Ohmygawd!" Neema jumped up, ran and knelt down and shook her. "Kay? Ohmygawd, Topps, what have you done?!" She sprinted up for her robe and then the cordless phone at her bedside. She ignored the flashing light indicating that she had messages waiting to be retrieved. Probably her mother called about the kids. "She's hurt bad. We hafta' call somebody."

Topps snorted. "Yeah, we gonna call somebody alright."

Neema's shaky fingers dialed 911 but before a voice could pick up, Topps was at her side, snatching the instrument from her hand.

"Are you crazy?" He slammed the receiver back down. "This ain't no damn Hollywood movie."

"She's unconscious, but if we call somebody, they might be able to save her."

Topps shook her head for no. His cold, piercing eyes bored into hers. "The paramedics will bring the cops, Neema. We can't have no damn cops stepping up in here."

"And why not?"

He stood looking like *'are you crazy?'* "What you gonna say, Nee, that she stumbled and hit her head? How you gonna explain drugs in her system? Hell, you got product like a muther in yo' living room. You think I'ma sit up here and wait for the pigs to slide up?"

"But…but she might die." Tears slid down her face.

Topps found his underwear and stepped into them. "It was an accident, Neema. Accidents happen."

His cold eyes said that there would be no negotiations on the subject. No compromise. No help coming. "Don't worry 'bout it. I suggest we get in the shower and get this smell off of us. Get some food in us, then I'll have my clean-up crew take care of this. Did she drive herself over here, or did somebody drop her ass off?"

Neema felt too numb to answer. Her hands shook as tears streamed down her face. It was like being in a bad movie and she was one of the main characters, only she didn't know what the script wanted her to do next.

"I said, did she drive her own damn car over here?" When Neema didn't answer fast enough, Topps grabbed her by her hair. "Bitch, I'm 'bout two minutes from whipping yo' ass 'cause this is all yo' damn fault! If you had done what you were supposed to do, we wouldn't be in this mess, now would we?!"

"Ouch, you're hurting me!"

"I asked you a damn question about her car!"

"Yes! She drove her car. A green Jeep. I…I guess it's in front of the building." She tugged away from him.

"See what happens when you don't take care of business, Nee? You see?" He hissed at her. "Now go get that damn shower water going. I'll make a few calls."

It was pointless to protest. Shaken, Neema went into the bathroom and turned the water on. She could hear Topps' cell phone ring, could hear him talking. Sounded like he was talking to her mother, who was probably calling again to see when she would be showing up to pick up the kids. *Oh gawd, my poor kids.* She had been doing her own thing and partying so hard the last few days that she'd completely forgotten about picking them up. It probably was for the best. She knew that they were in good hands at her mother's house.

She heard Topps say: "Yeah, Neema. She's been feeling a little sick with a cold. I been looking after her at my place. Yeah. She's better now, in fact, she went to the store, but I can have her call you when she gets back. How the kids doing? For real? Damn. No problem. She'll definitely be there tonight. You can count on it. Yeah, sure thing."

Neema came back in the bedroom and stood watching him tell lies to her mother. She made it up in her mind right then, when this was all over things were going to change. She'd go get her children, take the money she'd saved out the bank and move far away where Topps couldn't find her. She had skimmed enough of his money to do it, too. On the real side, it was time to make some serious changes in her life before she didn't have a life left to change. Topps hung up. "Who was that?"

"Yo' moms. She says that Nita got caught stealing in Walmart today, and you need to come pick our kids up."

"Why didn't she call my cell?"

Topps shrugged. "Beats the hell outta me. Did you give her yo' new number?"

"Not yet."

"That's why she used one of the kids' phones."

That was something to muse over. Maybe she had overlooked giving the new number to her mother. "And Brandon?" Hell, who was she fooling? Her mother would have been blowing her cell up after day two if she'd given her the number.

"She said Brandon's been giving her grief. But why wouldn't he. He's just like his old man." He patted his wide chest. "Strong and fearless. He got a good head on him, too. Always thinking and calculating shit."

Neema looked down at her friend crumpled along her beige carpet. A few seconds of dizziness tried to claim her, but she fought it off. The truth was out and it wasn't pretty. Her baby daddy was a bona fide, hellified monster and her life could very well be in danger. All she knew was that she wanted out: Out of the game, out of Topps' life, out of California. "Let me put a sheet over her." She snatched a sheet from the rumpled bed and laid it over Kaykay's still body.

"Yeah, you do that," Topps sneered. "Is that water ready for us? I know I'm hungry as a muthafucker. Hope you have some bacon, eggs and grits up in this mutha 'cause I could eat a whole pig myself." Topps walked to the shower area and stopped and looked at her. "You coming?"

Two hours later, Topps' main man Slick and two other thuggies were in her apartment with drinks, food, an oversized trunk, and some cleaning paraphernalia. The men smoked a blunt, talked trash, laughed, and joked around as they got busy. Blood was cleaned from her carpet. To Neema the scenario was akin to party. All fingerprints were wiped down, and Neema watched, in horror, as they lifted Kaykay's body up and stuffed it down into the large trunk like it was an old brown quilt. For a minute it looked like her legs wouldn't fit.

"No problem," said the biggest thug on the crew, who took one of Kaykay's legs and folded it over with a bone-breaking crunch, then folded in the other leg like it was no big deal.

"Ohmygawd." Neema felt lightheaded and had to hold on to the door frame to keep from passing out. She felt so bad for her friend that she didn't know what to do. Thank goodness Kaykay wouldn't be leaving behind some poor orphaned kids, but still, her man would no doubt come looking for her. She wasn't sure if he knew where she lived or not, but Kaykay had been friends with Cheeka who did know where she lived. Cheeka would no doubt lead Kaykay's man to her apartment, and then what? Damn. How could she let herself get mixed up in this madness?

Topps reclined along the bed, watching her. "Yo', Nee, what's up? You don't look so good. Maybe you should lay down and take a nap or somethin'."

"I don't need a damn nap." Her stomach was queasy, like the breakfast food she'd eaten an hour earlier was trying to come back up. She moved into her bathroom to splash cold water on her face.

"Stop trippin' over that shit. It's all taken care of. One of my boys will drive her Jeep away and dispose of it. The body is on its way to the furnace. It's all over. Chill out."

"They gonna burn her up? Ohmygawd." She felt like throwing up. She turned off the water and took up a towel to pat-dry her face. "It's not over. Kaykay was well liked. I hardly think her friends and family will say, 'oh well,' and not try to find out what happened to her."

Topps smirked. "You let me worry 'bout that, Nee."

The cleaning crew finished up and left. Slick came into the bedroom to announce he was out.

"Man, the guys will call and let me know when the deed is done. So far, everything is flowing. I'll check y'all later." Slick looked over at Neema with a knowing look. "You gonna be okay, Miss Neema?"

"Hell, yeah," Topps almost yelled at him. "She's fucking fine. She gonna be even better once we tie the knot, jump the damn broom, whatever you wanna call it. Ain't that right, boo?" Reclined on the bed, Topps was smiling big time.

"Later, man. Gotta go check on a few things." Slick turned and left.

Topps waved him off. "Damn. Thought they'd never leave." He got up and walked to where Neema was still standing at the bathroom sink, looking at her troubled reflection. "Looka here, shorty. You still my boo, right?"

She allowed him to turn her around to face him. "Yeah, I'm cool, I…I, mean no, of course not. Nothing's changed. It's just that she was a good friend of mine. Just like you said, this is all my fault. She'd still be alive if I hadn't called her over here to get high…it's all my…"

"Stop it. We can't fold up behind no…" He paused. He wanted to say "bitch," but seeing how sensitive she was. "…friend of yours. It was an accident, baby. You know it was, but we have to get beyond this." He kissed her forehead. "And I meant what I said about us getting hitched. I wanna wife you, if you still want me." He lifted her face. "Put you in a nice house. A better car, something like a Bentley. You know what I'm saying. You deserve the best. You still want it, right?"

Damn. This fool is like night and day. Hot and cold. She had to be careful of what she said. This was no ordinary man that she was dealing with. An ordinary man could never let his own mother starve to death while she lay sick in bed. Yeah, she knew about that shit, after hearing Slick spill the truth. A man that could kill his own mother could kill her without a second thought. Playing it safe meant going along with the program. "Baby, you know I still wanna be with you." She kissed him hard, feeling his manhood swell against her thigh.

"For real, Nee?"

"Hell yeah, for real-real. Let's do this shit."

Topps looked at her hard and serious. "Okay. This is the plan. You go and pick the kids up from yo' moms, then come back here to start packing up yo' stuff. Tomorrow I'll hire a moving company to haul all your shit to storage."

"Why my stuff gotta be shit?"

"Yeah, whatever, Nee. You going to a furnished house. Ain't no room for all this stuff you have here, so don't give me a hard time. We can look into a marriage license and all that shit once you and the kids get settled. You still feeling me?" He kissed her forehead as gentle as a mother kissing a baby.

"Hell, don't be so romantic about it." Neema looked away. Hell, her face was still sore from where he'd slapped her earlier. It was a good thing that fool couldn't read her mind or he'd see the words *I hate your punk ass* scrolling across.

It took a while before Neema could gather her composure. After she'd showered and donned a maroon, velvet warm-up suit and sneakers, she was hoping that Topps would take off and go home, but it was almost like he was hanging around her place to watch her. Like she might pick up the phone and call the police and drop a dime on him. The minute she announced that she was finally going to get the kids, Topps' cell phone rang.

"What kind of damn trouble?" Topps was asking somebody. His tone was serious.

Thinking that it might be her mother calling again, Neema froze in her step at the front door, listening.

"What the hell you mean the old man won't do it? He what? Alright, alright. We on our way there."

ELEVEN

e? Oh hell no! Neema stepped out her apartment and headed to her vehicle. It was getting later and later.

Driving to her mother's house was the only thing on her immediate agenda, and she wanted to get there before they were put to bed.

"Yo', hold up, boo." Topps stepped out right behind her. He checked her door to make sure that it was locked.

Neema cringed before turning around.

"We need to make this run real quick. It seems that the old man running the crematorium is giving my crew a hard time. Gotta go straighten his ass out. Ride with me."

"That's between you and yo' boys. Why should I have to go?"

"Because we wouldn't be having this conversation if you and that Kaykay hadn't been stealing my shit. That's why."

"I don't wanna go."

"I didn't ask you. We'll take your ride. Yo', Nee, stop tripping. This shouldn't take long," Topps told Neema as he steered her Rover down Crenshaw Boulevard to Stocker and took a right. The windows were down, allowing cool air to splash their faces. Bose speakers blared Pretty Ricky singing something about talking dirty to somebody. Topps bobbed his head to the music. "You gonna be upset all night or what?"

Neema acted like she didn't hear him.

"Fuck it, be that way then. Shit happens in this business, Nee. You should know this by now."

"Look, just get there. Do what you need to do and get it over with. We don't have to talk about it, too."

"Yeah, aw'ight." Topps grinned at her. The selling of drugs had been lucrative, but not enough to be his only financial venture. Once he had accumulated enough money to draw more greed, it seemed only natural to want to invest money in preparation of retirement. As a result, he owned a few apartment buildings, two food franchises, and a stripper nightclub on Imperial Highway. All businesses were good for laundering money, but his prized investment was Harmond's Funeral Home in the Crenshaw District. "It's probably some trivia bullshit. You know how it is with old people. They get stubborn every now and then. Know what I mean?"

"If you say so," Neema deadpanned, keeping her eyes on the straight ahead. Her lips were poked out and all she could think about was her friend, and how they would never be able to hook up again. No more shopping. No more lunches. No more scamming high-rollers. No more nothing. She knew one thing; she wasn't getting out the car to go see them do more awful things to Kaykay. No way. It wasn't happening. "I'll wait for you here," she told Topps after he parked and shut the engine off in the parking lot.

"Nee, you coming in, and I don't want no damn grief about it."

"Why I need to go inside? Hell, I said I'll wait in the car."

"Nee, I ain't playing with yo' ass. You can either walk your sweet ass in, or be dragged in, so what's up?"

His expression told her it was best to get out of the car. "Damn you, TJ. I'm sick of this shit." She rolled her eyes and smacked her lips. She hated him.

The gray brick building known as Harmond's Funeral Home looked small from the outside, but for those who passed through the thick, double doors, they soon learned that the place was sprawling. Inside, they moved past the viewing room where several caskets sat with the recently deceased, prepared and waiting for the loving family that would come before their final resting.

"I hate this place," Neema hissed, recalling the two times she'd accompanied Topps to the facility to take care of business. Each time she'd waited patiently in the front, refusing to see what took place behind the scenes.

"Too bad, my shorty. Business is business."

A two-bedroom house was built at the back of the building. Harmond had lived there alone for years after his wife passed three years ago. The self-containment of the business included everything needed by a grieving family: an office to negotiate burial plans, a facility to prepare the body for final resting, a modern-designed chapel, a flower shop, and facilities for cremation. Topps favored the latter. In fact, it was the facilities for cremation that had signed the deal. He saw the business as the perfect channel for getting rid of the myriad of bodies that came with his line of business. Old workers trying to leave his employ ended up here, as well as enemies who thought they were clever. The establishment also did its share of legal business.

"It stinks in here." Topps walked up into the pastel-blue main office where his crew had old man Harmond waiting at his large desk. Clutter was everywhere. Topps rarely visited the place because there was always a scent in the air that made him feel nauseous; death and despair. His last visit had been over two months ago to check out some damages done by some burglars. No doubt druggies who sought the embalming fluid they loved for dipping cigarettes and blunts in. Since then security bars had been installed on all the windows.

"Here you go, partna." Zoot, one of his henchmen, got up from his seat so Topps could sit down.

"I'm aw'ight. What seems to be the damn problem here?" Topps asked, taking a pack of Wet N' Wipes to cleanse germs from his hands. He chose to stand.

Rolling her eyes, Neema walked over, pulled the chair back from the desk and plopped down hard enough to break a hip.

"I don't burn on Sundays," Harmond half stuttered.

"And why the hell not?"

"It's the Sabbath." Harmond looked to be in his late sixties with thick gray hair and cloudy-looking eyes that set back in an old, wrinkled brown face. Topps paid him good. More money than he'd ever made when he was the sole owner of the place. The only reason he was still working in the business that he no longer owned was due to fear. The fear of trying to retire. A man that knew too much of Topps' business couldn't retire. He, of all people, knew this.

"Is that right?" Topps smirked at him. "Last time I checked, I was paying your salary. I don't care what muthafucking day of the week we bring trash here, you fire up the damn pit."

"She wasn't trash!" Neema yelled. She started crying quietly, resenting Topps for implying such about Kaykay.

"Shut up, Nee! Trash is trash."

Harmond frowned up at him. "Uh-huh…well, that's another thing. I've seen what y'all call trash and it don't look like what you usually drag up in here. Burning up those street thugs is one thing, but that there in that room look like a young, innocent woman to me. I don't want no part of it."

Topps almost laughed at the man. He panned his view of his four-person crew that had delivered Kaykay's body for disposal. "I can't believe y'all niggas couldn't handle this shit without calling me. Harmond here says he ain't firing up the pit; then one of you niggas fire that shit up. And throw his old ass in the flames when you through."

Harmond's rheumy eyes widened. "Now…now just a minute, young man. I've been a loyal worker for you."

"True that, but that was in the past, old man. When you get to thinking you running my shit, it's time to go." Topps looked around. "Who else here know how to fire the burners up so we can be done and get the hell on?"

Harmond was quick to throw in, "What's wrong with tomorrow? It's a normal working day. I don't want to, but I…I guess I can do it then."

"Don't wanna wait, old man." It had to be Topps' way or no way.

Zoot spoke up. "I've been here and watched his ass a few times. I believe I can do it." Tall and lanky, Zoot gave the appearance of a man that loved drugs and would do anything to obtain money to feed his habit. His dark eyes always had that hungry look.

"Get his ass up and out to the pit," Topps snapped.

The crew members followed orders, wrestling Harmond up. They traveled to the back of the building where bodies were cremated.

"Last chance, old man. Fire the burners up and handle business, or you'll get to see what it feels like."

Zoot grinned. "Shit, burn his old ass anyway. We don't need 'im."

"Very well then." Harmond pulled himself away from their grasp and walked over to the controls that started the incinerator. "Better hope no one notices the smoke and calls the authorities. Might look suspicious to be cremating this late on a Sunday. There's been a few complaints about the smoke and smell."

"Screw that. Get the shit over with 'fore I pass the hell out in here." Topps sniffed.

"I'll go wait in the front." Neema made an attempt to leave, but Topps grabbed her arm and pulled her back.

"Yo, Nee, you stay. You need to see what happens to people that steal from me. People that don't handle my business right."

"TJ, I don't wanna see shit."

"Too bad."

It took two men to carry the large trunk containing Kaykay's body to the incinerator room. Neema watched them remove her friend's jewelry and hand it to Topps who tried to pass it to Neema. "Here, a few souvenirs for you."

Rolling her eyes, she refused to take it. "Screw you. I don't want that shit." Once the proper temperature was reached, Harmond pressed a button that opened the heavy doors. Flames released radiant heat into the room as the body was shoved inside the incinerator. Neema was looking into the mouth of hell. That's exactly what it would be like if she didn't get her life right. "I don't need to see this." Neema started to cry.

Topps warned, "Better not close yo' eyes, Nee."

The coldness in his eyes, the crude, sadistic smiles on all the faces except for hers and Harmond's, made Neema want to puke.

"Yo, can you smell yo' homie cooking, Nee? Huh, can you?"

"Smells like crackling to me." Somebody had the nerve to joke and laugh.

"My boo like crackling, don't'chu, Nee?"

"Fuck you! A bunch of sick pricks." Neema pulled away from him, stormed toward the door and turned. "I'm going for my kids."

"Yeah, you do that," Topps sneered, tossing her keys in the air for her to catch. "I'll get a ride back to the crib."

It took some driving around trying to calm herself before using her personal cell phone to reach out for help. "Meet me at the place," was all she had to say.

TWELVE

"That's right. Let Slick make it all feel better. Yeah. You like that?"

"Ooh, baby, yes. Do it harder. Oh yeah. It's so good."

"And whose pussy is this?"

"Ooh, baby, it's yours. It's all yours for now." Neema pressed her head back into the pillow and closed her eyes. She had been under so much stress earlier that the only way to relieve it was to bust her a nut a few times. Since bad vibes still flowed toward Topps, she had to utilize the next best thing. Slick. To her, Slick was ugly as hell, but he had the longest and the fastest dick she'd ever seen on a man, and she'd seen a lot of dicks to know.

They had decided to meet at a faraway motel on the opposite side of town. It wasn't the first time, and it probably wouldn't be the last. It was their secret den of lust. To Neema, love didn't have a damn thing to do with it. Plus, she couldn't take any chances with that sneaky, always-suspecting-and-checking-her-ass Topps.

After leaving Topps and his goons at the funeral home, she had all but burned rubber away from the place. First she stopped at Fat Burger to get something to eat hoping food in her stomach would calm her nerves. It didn't. She had thought about stopping for a wine cooler but didn't care for drinking while driving. The more she had driven around, the worse she felt. She had no choice but to pull out her other cell phone, the one that Topps knew nothing about, and call Slick to plan their rendezvous. It wasn't top-of-the-line amenities, but the room was clean and spacious with a vibrating bed and cable television that boasted free porn.

"Oh yeah, work that shit good, baby." Neema lay back with her legs wide open like Slick was her brand-new gynecologist doing a full examination. His thick, black rod was his examination tool and he knew how to work it in and out at the right pace.

Nigga got my kitty kat purring like a 'mutha. Every now and then he gave her a power-thrust that sent both a jab of pain and pleasure through her love tunnel. "Ooh, hell yes!" Neema was like a junkie going through total withdrawal.

"You like it?"

"Hell yeah, I love it."

"Tell me how much now." Slick pumped it to her harder. "You better say it."

"Your shit is the bomb. It feels so good. Don't stop. Do it, Daddy, do it."

Neema opened her eyes and watched his powerful-looking ass from the ceiling mirrors over the queen-sized bed. *Damn, brotha.* She could see every tight muscle working in that ass pumping like new pistons in a high-performance engine. He pumped straight before going sideways, then back to straight, causing a volcano of ecstasy to push its way up through her core. For him to stop now would kill her, or she'd probably snap and have to kill his ass. She needed the sweet release that his sex would give her.

"You want this dick?"

"I want it."

"I said do you want this big dick or not?"

"Nigga, please, stop talking so much and just do it!" She loved a good orgasm like the next person, but too much dirty talk was distracting.

A few more power thrusts and she could feel Slick's body quivering on top of her. He was about to come. She could always tell because his dick seemed to swell up more once his quivering started. Neema wiggled her hips and clenched the walls of her vagina to milk him tight. A good open-and-clutch motion was all it took to bring it all home. Her own climax came at the same time as his. The two sweaty bodies rested for a few seconds before disengaging.

"Damn, girl," Slick panted, falling to her side of the bed. His breathing was so labored he could barely catch a good breath. "You almost killed a nigga."

"Sounds like your ass getting too old for all the snow you be flying up your nose."

"Shit, that's the icing on the cake." Slick wiped sweat from his forehead.

"Yeah, right." Neema grinned. She got up and pranced her perfect body to the adjacent bathroom for a face towel to sop up the juices between her legs. Then she hopped in the shower.

Slick was kicked back on the bed smoking a blunt when she came out with a large towel wrapped around her. "I can't kick it too long. Gotta get to my mom's house and pick up my kids. I know she's fit to be tied by now."

"I'm sure you know how to sweeten her back up."

"Hell yeah. A few hundred dollars should do it."

"That's for real, but what you gonna do?" Slick flicked ashes onto the carpet.

"I just told you, I'ma slide by my mom's place." She almost caught an attitude, thinking that Slick might be checking her. Hell, Topps' constant checking was one thing, but two niggas drilling in her business was more than she could tolerate. "Dang, Slick. Somethin' wrong with your ears, too?" She picked up the pillow and playfully hit him with it.

"I'll ask you again, Miss Neema, 'cause you ain't listening to me. Whatchu gonna do?"

Irritated, she smacked her lips. "About what, Slick?"

"About this mess you in." He offered the blunt to her.

Neema made sure that her towel was secure before she took the blunt from his hand. She took two big draws on it before blowing a cloud of smoke in his direction. Between flying lines up her nose and smoking herb, doing lines was her favorite. But the way she was feeling she needed something to maintain calmness—something to take her mind off everything that represented Topps Jackson. She looked over at Slick's spent love bone. That had helped some, but two more treatments might be warranted.

"Hey, how come you don't have a wife?'

"Haven't found the right one yet."

"Are you looking?" Neema put it out there, hoping to change the subject.

What they were doing was dangerous. Screwing around behind Topps' back. But Slick was always nice to her. Kinder. He never talked down to her the way that Topps did. Slick was someone who didn't mind cuddling later if she needed it. He was an ear that would listen. These were her justifications. True, he wasn't handsome like Topps, but Neema saw him as a prince trapped in a frog's body. The only reason he wasn't her main man was fate had her meeting Topps first. Switching horses in the middle of the scene could get one or both of them popped and pushing up daisies.

"Not really, but you changed the subject. What'chu plan to do about yo' situation?"

"I'ma get my kids and do what my man wants me to do." She flounced down on the bed beside him, then rested her back against the wooden headboard. Taking up her tote, she fished in and found a small bottle of vanilla-scented lotion.

"You thinking about splitting, aren't you? Don't lie, Neema. I can see it in yo' eyes."

"Nigga, please," she countered, working the silky fluid into her arms and legs. "I'm about to be Mrs. Topps Jackson. His big ballerette. Watch and see that we don't be picking out some rings by next week."

"Nee?"

"Topps loves me. He'll do anything for me. Why would I wanna sky up and leave all that?" Even to her the lie didn't sound right.

"Nee?"

"What, nigga?! You got somethin' to say, just say it." She slammed the lotion back into her bag and took up the blunt for a few puffs.

Slick turned to face her. His stare was hard and serious. "Topps is my boy and all, and yeah, we go way back from the 'hood, but I know how that nigga be thinking sometimes. Topps got a problem, I got a problem. The way I see this shit right now, you've become a problem for him."

"Slick, you paranoid. You need to slow yo' roll on that coke. Hell, you bringing my high down. I gotta split." Neema went to move off the bed, but not before Slick grabbed her arm.

"We talkin' about a man that let his own mother die. A man that didn't shed one tear when his own father got popped. Need I say more?"

"And?" Neema challenged. "I mean, if he so bad, why you still working for him?"

"'Cause I got bills to pay like the next nigga. But what I'm try'n to say is that my boy got you on radar. You think he was watching you before? Please." He snorted, removing the burned-out blunt from her hands. "He'll be watching yo' every move now. You won't be able to fart without him knowing when and how much gas was passed. You got the power, Nee."

"What damn power?" Slick always had some kind of advice to give her, usually about what transport jobs to take and which ones to stay away from. Most of the time she didn't mind, but this was not one of them. Getting out the game was heavy on her mind, but it was something she didn't even trust telling Slick about.

"The power to get 'im caged behind yo' girlfriend dropping. It's one thing to get caught with yo' hand in the cookie jar, Nee. Topps is sharp. He knows you been skimming from him for years now."

"That's bullshit…I don't steal from my own…"

"Nee, please. It's me, Slick. You can cut all that false jaw-jacking. Yo' hand in his cookie jar is one thing, but now we talkin' about murder."

She squirmed along the bed. Neema tried to play it off, but he had her full attention because she was scared. Scared to leave and scared to stay. "Hell, Slick, you act like it's the first time my man dropped somebody. Thought y'all been bragging about popping punks since kindergarten."

Slick sniffed. "Check this tho'. You ever seen 'im pop a nigga with yo' own eyes?"

Neema thought about it. She'd seen a few brutal beatings, fingers cut off, and a tongue sliced in half. Once even, she witnessed a fallen soldier take a bullet to the spine. Topps had pulled the trigger. The soldier didn't die, but she was sure he'd never walk again. But now the writing was on the wall. She'd witnessed a murder. Accident or no accident. Kaykay wasn't coming back. Tears threatened her eyes. "I hadn't thought of it that way."

"Now you listen to me, Nee. That little friend of yours was getting around. She was kicking it with Rocco, better known as 'Bulldog Roc.' I'm sure you've heard of 'im."

"One of Topps' old rivals?" Her heart raced. That explained why Topps was riding the girl so hard behind some coke. "So it wasn't about the stupid coke after all."

"You hear me now? Bulldog Roc is an old gangsta that went into retirement some years back. That's the same nigga that popped his father for sleeping with his bitch over twenty years ago. I didn't wanna say nothin' when I was at yo' place, but I recognized her then."

"I am so tired of all of this." Again, thoughts of Kaykay dying almost brought tears to her eyes, but the blunt she'd smoked earlier was helping her to cope. A couple of glasses of wine would make it even better. "Swear to God, I can't do this no more. I can't."

"This is on the real, Nee. That nigga Rocco is known for being crazy. He'll have some of his old cronies out sniffing around to find out what happened to his girl. That's a fact."

"It was an accident though."

"Yeah, try telling that shit to an enemy. But yeah, accidents do happen. They happen all the time."

Neema looked away, thoughts clicking a mile a minute. "Maybe I need to cut my losses and move the hell away."

Slick shook his head. "Good idea and bad idea."

"I gotta do something, Slick. I just want out."

"Look, fo' sho you need to get yo' kids and run like crazy, but you need to move yo' moms away, too. Maybe even that sister of yours."

"My sister?" She shot him a look of disbelief. "What about my sister?"

"My boy Topps is an obsessed man, Nee. He's been keeping tabs on you like a mutha. He knows where your moms lives, and that prissy little sister of yours. What's her name? Mia? Myra? Living in Victorville, right? Married to a guy named Glen, a doctor. Three kids. He thinks her twins are too cute."

"Ohmygawd." Neema felt sick to her stomach. It was worse than she thought. Topps wasn't just checking and keeping tabs on her because she sometimes transported his product; he was stalking her family.

"Running could be a dangerous thing right now. Go along with the program for a while. And if you gotta do the wifey thing, do it. Once Rocco gets word that Topps had somethin' to do with his girl's drop, he'll be gunning for 'im. And you don't wanna be around when that happens."

"Nobody knows about it but me, him, and you."

"And the cleaning crew. Enough money can make anybody talk. And that fool they call Zoot, hell, I wouldn't trust him around his own mama. That nigga's mind is whacked."

She rubbed her hands along her tired face. "I gotta go."

Slick grabbed her hand again. "Look here, shortie. I like you. I like you a lot. All I'm saying is, I don't wanna see you get hurt behind all this, but I see it coming." He wanted to warn her about the cell phone that Topps had given her, but Neema could be a hot-head at times. He could see her storming over and confronting Topps about the tracking device. That would blow his position. "Stay put for now, go along with his plan, but don't be car riding with 'im too much. I'll keep my ears open for you."

"Why you spilling to me like this, Slick? Thought you and Topps were like white on rice."

Slick let her arm go and got up from the bed. "We are." He grinned as he headed for a shower. "But that don't mean I have to agree with everything he does. Now do it?"

Neema admired his muscular body as he headed to the bathroom. He was a chocolate, walking, dick-thick, Wesley Snipes-looking man except for his bulging eyes and bad skin. A nice smile though. Shorter than Topps by an inch, Slick had more muscles in the right places. His high behind looked powerful, like a good time promised. She smiled at the thought. *How right they would be.* "Thanks for the advice."

"No problem."

Neema was dressed by the time Slick walked back into the room. "Can I ask you something?"

"Shoot," said Slick, sliding back into his silver-and-dark gray Sean John walking suit.

"If Topps is tracking my every move like you say, how the hell can you be sure he don't know that we're here now?"

"You thinking smart. I like that. But check this, when you hit me up on my cell, my boy and I was kicking it at his place after I dropped off his money."

"You sure?"

"Nee, you think I'd be here with you if I wasn't sure?"

She found some comfort in his words. "Well, I'm out." Neema grabbed up her gear, walked over and gave Slick a quick peck on the lips. "You a good friend, Slick."

"I know." He kissed her forehead. "Oh yeah, shortie, before I forget." He picked up his jacket, reached into a side pocket and pulled out a banded wad of one hundred-dollar bills. "A little somethin' to sweeten yo' day."

"Good looking out. Thanks."

"You welcome," he said, patting that ass as she turned and headed out.

Neema stuck the money in her tote without another thought and headed to her SUV. She got in, started her engine and waited a minute before pulling off to finally get her kids from her mother's house. Too engrossed in her thoughts of how her mother would act once she arrived, she didn't notice the black panel van parked across the street from the motel.

Inside the van, the blue-eyed private detective had taken three pictures of Neema: exiting the motel, opening her car door and getting in.

"Looks like a done deal," he mumbled lowly to himself, then

sat back and waited for her male companion to exit the same motel room. He didn't have to wait long for Slick.

His client had paid him good for his service. More than any other client he'd dealt with. *Click. Click. Click.* "Look this way and smile for the camera." Two more clicks. "That's a good boy." He smiled.

THIRTEEN

"Topps did what?!"

"He picked the kids up."

"Mama, why would you do that?!"

Hattie Mae felt flustered. Plus, she didn't like the way Neema was talking to her. Hell, she was practically yelling at her. To keep from saying something to hurt the girl's feelings, she got up from her La-Z-Boy and went into her kitchen to turn on the oven. No doubt it was too late to be baking, but she'd promised to bake three cakes for her church's fundraiser on Tuesday. Now was a good time to get started. It was bad enough that she'd almost been carted off to jail earlier with Raynita trying to steal from Walmart. Then Topps had shown up asking for the kids, and now this.

"First of all, you need to lower your voice. I don't like no yelling in my house, Neema Jean."

"Mama, I'm not yelling, I'm just trying to figure out why you gave my kids to Topps."

Hattie shook her head. "Could it be because he's their father?"

"But Mama, you knew I was coming to get the kids. Didn't he tell you that earlier?"

"I told you, Neema, he popped up at my door, said you had a migraine and that you sent him to pick up the kids. And they wanted to go with their father." Hattie poured sugar into softened butter and turned her stand mixer on low. "Them kids missed a whole week of school fooling with you. Don't make no sense. It was time for 'em to get back home."

"Well, in case you don't know, my kids make good grades. Missing one week won't hurt 'em. B'sides, school will be out next week. End-of-the-year testing is done with."

"Not the point, Neema." Hattie shook her head. Neema always had an answer for everything. "Dumping those kids off the way you did, you didn't even consider if I had doctor appointments or anything. You can't be selfish all your life, Neema. You're a parent now. You have responsibilities."

Neema turned her back so she could roll her eyes. "I said I'm sorry, Mama. Dang. I wouldn't have left Nita and Brandon like that if you had said yes to watch 'em for a few hours. I get tired, too. Sometimes I need a break."

"Humph," Hattie snorted back, unconvinced. She needed to vent and Neema wasn't getting off that easy. "Didn't even call to check up on 'em the whole time. What kind of caring mother does that, Neema? You tell me that." She turned her mixer off and picked up one of four eggs and cracked it. "Not enough clothes or underwear. No extra food for 'em. Nothing."

"It won't happen again, Mama. I'm sorry you don't enjoy spending quality time with your own grandchildren. Most grandmothers do." Neema knew she had it coming. Though her mother wasn't the high-energy woman she used to be, she still enjoyed her church functions, Monday night bingo and shopping trips to the mall. Dragging two kids along had to be hard on her. "Maybe you don't love my kids like you love Myra's."

"Oh hell no, you didn't!" Hattie shot a hot glare at her. "Don't you dare use that psychobabble with me, Miss Thang! I love all five of my grandkids the same, but when I spend quality time, it should be when I choose to do so—not because they mama ran off from 'em." She snatched up a second egg and felt like throwing it at Neema. "Got some nerve saying that mess to me."

"Okay. Okay. You're upset about it. I get it, but I didn't run off, Mama. I took a break." Neema had been standing at the kitchen door with her arms folded over her chest for the last five minutes while her mother fussed up a storm, but she'd had her fill. "I had an important appointment. Three hours of your time; that's all I wanted from you."

"Then how does a few hours turn into eight days, Neema? Explain that! Then you have the nerve to come up in here questioning me on why I let Topps take 'em? Like I want that man coming to my house. I can't stand his behind and you need to get the hell outta here with that mess!" Hattie could feel her heart rate speed up. Of her two daughters, why was it that Neema could always bring out the worst in her?

"Well, I'm back now, Mama, so get over it." Boldly, Neema trudged over to a chair and plopped down. She looked around and blew out a deep breath. She had more important things to worry about, like how to save her own life, and how to get her mother to move away from Compton. *Here goes*, she thought. "This house is paid for, right?" She placed her tote bag on the table.

Hattie looked over at her like she was crazy. "Thank God. Don't owe one cent." Maybe a change of topic was for the best.

"You know you could probably get a good grip for this house. Maybe enough to move and pay cash for a brand-new house."

Hattie didn't look up from adding flour into her mixer. "If I was thinking about selling, I guess I could."

"Maybe you need to think about it, Mama. I mean, couldn't you stand a change of scenery? We both could leave California together."

"Why would I want to move away now, Neema?" Hattie gave her a curious look. One thing about her youngest daughter, the girl was full of surprises and there was never a dull moment. Something was always going on with Neema. The soft purr of the mixer filled the room. "Why, what's wrong?"

"Nothing, Mama. Dang. You so suspicious. I'm just thinking out the box. You know, thinking about the future and what's best for the kids."

Batter done, Hattie clicked the mixer off. "What's best for the kids, huh?"

"Never mind, Mama. I gotta go." Neema stood, fumbled through her bag and pulled out the wad of money Slick had given her. One hundred, two hundred, three, four, five hundred. She laid the crisp bills on the table. "This should be enough to cover the kids' expense. I'll be talking with Nita about that little stunt she pulled at Walmart. You won't have to worry about seeing the kids for a while."

"If that's drug money from Topps, I don't want it." Hattie found her little performance amusing at times. Neema had been a drama queen since she learned to talk. She simply didn't get it. Doing what she wanted, when she wanted. Always thinking about herself and treating others with little respect or with no regard for good morals. Neema being Neema.

"I swear, it's not Topps' money." Well, it wasn't, it was Slick's money.

"You don't work, so where did the money come from?" She resisted the urge to ask about the new furniture the kids had informed her about.

"Mama, I earned it. Okay? Dang. You always drilling in my business."

Hattie turned her attention back to her cake batter. "Somebody need to be in it."

Neema shoulder-strapped her bag. "So how long ago did Topps come for the kids?"

"About an hour ago."

She had been getting her nut busted about then. The delicious thought tingled between her legs. "Did he seem upset?"

"No, Neema. He didn't. Should he be?"

"No. I mean, not really. I'm just asking, Mama. Jeepers." She watched her mother pour batter into a Bundt pan. "Next time, Mama, please check with me before you hand my kids over to someone else."

"And next time, you need to leave a damn contact number so someone can check with you about your kids. Hell, if you don't trust Topps to pick up his own kids, you should have said so before you abandoned them."

"Mama, I didn't abandon...never mind. I have to go." Neema tossed the bills on the table and headed out.

"Let me say this before you leave." Hattie closed her oven door and dried her hand on a towel. "I'm praying for you, Neema. Praying that you come to your senses, find a good man, get married and get back in school. You have a smart head on you, so use it."

"Topps is a good man, Mama, and college wasn't for me." She wished her mother would stop throwing college up in her face. Right out of high school, Neema had thought she wanted to be a registered nurse. But wanting to be one and sticking out two to three years to make it happen was easier said than done. She gave the nursing program a good five months before realizing that running product for Topps paid a hell of a lot more than sticking needles in the asses of sick people. "He wants to marry me."

"He's a 'good man?' Is that why you here interrogating me about why I let him take his own kids, cause he's a 'good man?' Neema, all I'm saying is that this fast living is going to catch up with you. That's why I keep praying."

"You praying?" A sneer found her face, and Neema folded her arms across her chest. "Well, while you at it, Mama, maybe you can ask God why He never answered none of my prayers when I was younger. I used to pray, too. Prayed for Daddy to stop being so mean and stop hitting you. Prayed for Daddy to stop drinking so much. Where was God then?"

"And you say that to say what, Neema?"

"That God don't give a shit about me, Mama. And you either. That's what I'm saying."

"Neema, you be careful what you say."

"I'm talking truth. As far as I'm concerned, there ain't no God!"

"Neema!"

"That's how I feel, Mama. You need to hear the truth. All prayer don't work."

"That's not what His word says."

"The Bible? Get real. It's a book written by some stupid white men to keep stupid black people in control. That's what the Bible is, Mama. And that's the truth."

Hattie's mouth sagged open. For a second or two, the room felt like it was spinning and she would surely pass out.

"See? I knew you couldn't handle the truth." Neema waited for Hattie's rebuttal but none came. "Got it? Good! I'm out. Thanks for watching my kids for me."

FOURTEEN

orty-five minutes later, Neema pulled her vehicle into Topps' driveway. She cut the engine and sat for a while, dreading to go inside. More mess was coming and she knew it. It was always that way with Topps. Questions of her whereabouts. Who did she see? What did she do? More drilling. Intimidation. Shouting. Drama. And she might have to take a wash-up, two showers and a bath before she could get some peace and quiet. She was exhausted already. How did she let her life get so out of control? All she wanted was to collect her kids and get back to her own place for a little peace of mind.

"This nigga bet not give me a hard time. I swear to God I'll drop a dime…" She got out, and made her way to the door with her keys in hand. Before she could knock, the big, wooden door swung open, swishing air around her. Topps stood in the doorway with a glass of wine in his hand.

"Yo', where you been, Nee?"

"I stopped to get something to eat." Neema stepped in, closing the door behind her.

"You and who?"

"Me, myself, and I. Then I stopped over a girlfriend's house for a minute."

"What girlfriend?"

"Dena. You don't know her."

"Yeah, I bet."

"Look, you could have called and told me that you would slide by Mama's to get the kids. I told you that's where I was headed."

"Maybe I thought it was taking you too long." He undid the belt to his satin smoking jacket but didn't take his eyes off her. His hard scrutiny suggested that he didn't believe her.

"Where my kids at?" Neema put her bag down.

"Your kids?"

"Our kids. Whatever. I don't feel like playing games. Give me the kids so I can go home. I'm supposed to be packing up my stuff, remember?"

"Yeah. You should be packing alright." Topps half smirked. "That's why I got to thinking that maybe I should keep the kids here with me. You know, so they won't be in yo' way while you packing up. I called the moving company like I said. They should be there day after tomorrow." He went back to the great room where a basketball game was playing on a fifty-inch plasma.

"Stop playing around and tell me where my kids are. And I don't appreciate you going to my mom's house and getting 'em without my permission."

"Didn't know I needed yo' permission to get my own damn kids."

"You've never picked them up before without letting me know what's going on. Why you doing that shit now?"

"Maybe this is the new me." He patted his chest like some Mighty Joe Young making a point. "You better get used to it."

"Forget you, Topps." She pushed past him and marched down the marble hallway to one of two guest bedrooms. Inside she found Raynita down on the floor playing with some Barbie dolls while Brandon didn't bother to look up from the X-Box he was mesmerized with. "Hey guys. I'm back."

"Mama, Mama!" Raynita squealed, jumping up for a hug.

"You miss me?"

"I sure did. What took you so long? Where have you been?"

Neema kissed her cheeks and forehead. "I'm sorry. I had some business to take care of. But it won't happen again. Did you have fun at your nanny's house?"

"Nita got caught stealing," Brandon casually announced. His attention stayed on the game.

Neema's shoulders slumped. "Yeah. I heard. But that's not going to happen again. Right, Nita?"

"Brandon stole somethin', too," Nita said, frowning over at her brother. "...but he didn't get caught."

"Alright now, what I tell y'all 'bout that telling just to be telling?"

"Snitches can't stop telling." Brandon made a face at his sister.

"Yeah, well, like I said, it's not going to happen again. You two know how I feel about stealing." Neema felt like a hypocrite. Her vice of stealing from Topps was one thing. It was part of survival. Still, she constantly tried to instill in her kids about right and wrong. Despite her own shortcomings, she had higher expectations for Raynita and Brandon. Her kids would grow into college-educated adults with good moral judgment, even if it killed her. "Can't have that going on with you two, but we'll talk about it again later."

"We going home now?" Raynita wanted to know. "I wanna go home."

"Maybe. And what about you, Brandon? No hug for your mama?"

Brandon managed to pull himself away from his video game, jumped up and hugged her. "Take Nita home and I can stay here with Daddy."

"I don't think...what's that on the side of your ear?" In disbelief Neema pulled a thin-wrapped reefer joint out from its tuck. "Who the hell gave this to you?" She knew the culprit already.

"Daddy."

Brandon had shrugged and said it so casually, like he was talking about a stick of chewing gum. Topps had been introduced to drugs at an early age, but Neema didn't play that mess. "Fucking moron," she hissed to herself. "Y'all get your stuff. We going home." Neema went back to Topps to throw the weed stick at him. "Don't be giving shit like this to my son!"

"What? A blunt? Big damn deal, Nee. Shoulda have seen 'im earlier shooting my gun in the backyard. My boy has a good aim. Gets it naturally."

Neema looked at him like he was insane. "What's wrong with you? Are you freaking crazy?"

"Nah. Not really. He gotta learn to shoot eventually."

"Topps, if you want to do something good for your son, try acting like his freaking father and not his buddy! What asshole gives weed and a gun to a seven-year-old?"

"Hell, I was smoking herb when I was six. It's relaxing to over-active kids. Better than that shit the doctors pass out to 'em. Look at me; I turned out okay." He aimed the remote and changed the channel.

"Guns and weed this time; what next, Topps, coke, and a bomb-making kit? Maybe some Ectasy? What's next?"

"Yo' Nee, whatever it takes to get 'em ready. You have to know a product to be good at operating a business selling it, and the boy gotta learn how to handle a gun."

"I don't care if your daddy stuck a joint in your mouth the minute you came out your mama's twat. You don't even give a damn aspirin to my son without asking me!"

"Bitch, you need to watch yo' mouth." He was up on his feet in a flash. "What? You think I'm some little punk ass you can talk to any kind of way? You better think again."

"Look, I don't wanna fight. I'm taking my kids home with me. They have school tomorrow."

"Why the hell you so damn concerned about the kids all of a sudden?"

"Forget you, TJ. I'm taking my kids!"

"You can go," Topps said firmly. "The kids are staying here tonight."

"Raynita! Brandon! Let's go!"

Topps took her by the arm and walked her back to the front door. "In case you didn't understand what I just said, let me lay it out again. You go back to your place and do some damn packing while you still have a chance."

Both Raynita and Brandon showed up with their backpacks.

"Get your hands offa me!" Neema tried to snatch away but not before Topps twirled her around for a backhand slap.

Seeing her mother being abused, Raynita screamed and ran back into the room crying.

"Brandon, get in the room with yo' sister. Y'all get ready to take a bath and get ready for bed. Yo' mama was just leaving. Say good night." He waited for Brandon to leave the room. "As for you, Neema, take yo' lying, conniving-ass home and pack. I'll take the kids to school in the morning and pick 'em up."

"What about their clothes?" Neema asked, rubbing her face.

"They have clean clothes with 'em." Topps twirled her around and pinned her arm behind her, pushing her hard against the door. "And the next time you disrespect me in front of my son, I won't be so nice."

"Ouch! Stop it, fool! You're hurting me. Why you doing this?"

"Because I'm not blind, Neema. I know what's up."

"Oouch. And what the hell that's supposed to mean?"

"You'll figure it out. Now go on home and do what you have to do. I'll expect you at the warehouse tomorrow. Ten sharp. Don't be late. Slick will have a package for you to transport. We can talk when you get back."

"Maybe I don't wanna deliver shit for you no more."

"Like I said, Nee. Ten sharp. You know how you love money. It's not like you to turn down twenty-five grand."

"Why can't one of your other hoes do it?"

"Because, Nee, this is big money we talkin', and I trust you'll do the right thing. That's why. I can't have some new skank handling my big packages. Know what I'm saying?" He released her, and turned her around.

Their eyes locked in hatred for a few seconds. Neema felt like spitting in his face, but she wasn't that crazy. Was it really possible to love and hate a man with the same degree? Hell yeah, it was. She hated him, but at the same time the tingle between her thighs was heating up.

Topps kissed her lips, softening his tone. "Look, Nee. We just going through a rough spot right now. The kids will be fine here with me. Stop sweating it. Things will work back out to smooth soon." He stroked the side of her face with a gentle backhand. "Plus, you don't need 'em in the way while you packing up your place. Now do you?"

Deep breath. Neema exhaled slowly. His words made sense. "I... guess not." A little hope was somewhere inside her, that he would kiss her again, put his tongue down her throat, throw her on the couch, snatch off her clothes, pull her hair and make hard-thug love to her. *Do it, nigga. Do it now!*

"Once we get married and you my wifey, you can stop transporting for 'sho. Count on it." He kissed the tip of her nose. "Now, go on home. We'll talk about it tomorrow when we both feel better."

FIFTEEN

*I*t was early Monday morning. Neema sat in the Ford Escape at the intersection of Del Amo and Avalon waiting for the traffic light to change. The specially equipped vehicle was one of several owned by Topps. It was used often because of the hidden gas tank where product could be stashed and transported.

Her mind was still clicking. While she was packing items the night before, she'd done a lot of thinking on how she needed a change once this was all over. The heck with what Slick had said about waiting and playing it out. She'd be a fool to stay and marry Topps after what had gone down with her friend, Kaykay. Moving drugs was one thing, but murder was another. It was time to go. Neema felt ready for it. This would be her last delivery. It had to be a special client for Topps to go out of his way and let her use one of his private vehicles. He also had promised her twenty-five thousand in cash once the job was done.

"Piece of cake," she mumbled. An actress is what she should have been. She could play a part to the hilt. She was always crying broke, but the truth of the matter was that years of putting money aside had accumulated over two hundred and twenty-five thousand dollars in her savings account under another name. Her checking account was nice, but to keep from drawing suspicion she never kept more than a grand in it.

A delicious smile tugged at her lips. It was all money well earned from transporting, stealing from those that had it, and sleeping with big-money rollers that didn't mind giving it up for that precious commodity all females have. If she needed more money for her escape, she could probably hit Slick up good before she left. Heck, the more she thought about it, Topps kept a safe at his house. A safe full of cash. She didn't have the combination, but from time to time he opened it to either put more cash in or take cash out. She could wait for the right opportunity and then...

"Oh my God, listen to me. I'm just as bad as him."

Nah. Slick was the best answer if she needed more cash for her escape. With the kind of money he was pulling, a hundred grand was nothing. For a good cause, he would give it to her, too. Getting her kids to a safe place and away from Topps was definitely a good cause. A depressing thought flowed through her. Her mother.

What was she going to do about Hattie? What Slick had told her last night at the motel was probably true. Topps was a madman who didn't care who he hurt to get what he wanted. She had to try one more time to convince her mother to pull up roots and move away. If not out of California, at least to a new location where Topps couldn't find her.

Once the light changed to green, Neema pulled the vehicle over, and undid her seatbelt to reach over to get her cell phone from her tote bag. For a minute, she was alarmed at not seeing her wallet with her driver's license in it. Soon she recalled that she hadn't brought any identification with her. It was Topps' bright idea in case she was pulled over by the police. Just like it had been his brainy idea to burn her natural fingerprints off a few years back. "Yo' Nee, they can't find out who you are if you don't have prints. Can they?"

"His stupid ass." As far as she was concerned, Topps had a rude awakening coming. Once this was over, she could pick her kids up from her mother's house, leave all her material possessions behind and hit the highway. See ya! Where they would live, where they would go, and how they would manage, were all minor details.

First she dialed Bianca's number. Bianca was a close friend to Kaykay. The thought of Kaykay saddened her. If she had never invited her friend over for their little coke party, Kaykay would still be alive. Twice a month, Kaykay, Bianca and Bianca's sister, Kimmie, dressed up as sexy as hell and did girl's night out to see who could hook the most big-ballers with money. Any news about Kaykay, Bianca would know.

Act normal, Neema told herself before Bianca picked her up. "Hey, girl. What's crackin' up yo' way?"

"Going through it right now."

"What's wrong?" Neema asked, making her voice sound concerned. Bianca's didn't sound right. Her voice sounded thick and nasal—like she'd been crying.

"Our girl is missing," Bianca relayed over the line.

"Who?" Neema felt bad. She knew damn well who. Still, she had to play if off.

"Kaykay didn't come home last night. Her man Roscoe said when he slid by her crib and waited, she didn't show. We been blazing her cell phone like crazy, but no answer."

"What? Ohmygawd. Anyone know where she went last?" Neema was fishing for information. If her girl Kaykay had told anyone that she was driving over to her place, it was something that she needed to know.

"Not really," said Bianca, sniffing. "You know how Kay was sometimes; always doing her thang but secretive about it."

"Wow. I just talked to her yesterday, too. We talked about hooking up this weekend and hitting a few clubs."

"Did she mention anything about where she was going, anything like that?"

"Nah," Neema lied with ease. She was going to hell for sure, but she couldn't tell the truth. "She said something about some nigga she had met a few days ago. She sounded a little excited about hooking up with 'im. But you know that girl; she probably somewhere getting her new freak on but didn't want nobody to know."

"Yeah. I hope so. Her moms tried calling in a missing persons report, but they talking shit about waiting for so many hours before you can file. Probably 'cause she's a black woman. You know how they do."

"Dang." It was time to cut it short. The more she talked about Kaykay, the worse she felt. "I'm sure she'll show back up when she's ready. I was calling to see if y'all wanted to hook up this weekend and party, but I can check back."

"Maybe another time, Miss Nee. Once our girl is home safe, we can do the town and stir it up old time."

"For sure." Neema had to keep it as real as possible. "Don't worry, she'll show up."

"Yeah. Hope you're right, Ma. But I'll holler at you later when I hear something."

"For sure, Bee. Anyway, I'm out."

She dialed her mother's number. Hattie picked up on the third ring. "Mama, I need a big favor, and please don't give me a hard time. I need you to go pick the kids up from school early." She had known there would be some protest. "I have an emergency and I need you to go get them now. Before dismissal time." Topps would be parked outside the school waiting at dismissal.

Hattie gave her some words of concern about her request.

"Mama, I promise I'll be over to pick them up tonight. Whatever you do, don't wait until two-forty-five dismissal time. Plus,

I need to talk to you again about…well, about you moving from that spot. I hate to tell you this, but you might be in danger staying there. I know, I know, Mama. We'll talk about it when I get the kids tonight."

Before she hung up, Hattie had insisted on confirming her new cell phone number, Topps' cell phone number, and his house phone number. It would have been comical if Hattie hadn't been so adamant about it.

"You know where their school is, and I always put your name down as an emergency contact, so it shouldn't be a problem to sign them out early. Oh, and one more thing, Mama. Don't give my kids to Topps. We fell out big time, but I'll explain it all when I get there tonight. Thanks, Mama."

Topps ain't as smart as he thinks. Neema smiled, putting the Ford in gear and pulling away from the curb. She turned the air conditioner on. It was getting hot in the light-brown velour warm-up suit she had worn. In no time she was waiting at the intersection of Del Amo and Alameda for the Metro train to clear before proceeding. While she waited, she thought about all she needed to get done before she could pack up her kids and leave. Two hundred and twenty-five thousand dollars wasn't exactly rich. But she'd heard that she could actually pay cash for a decent-looking house in Hutto, Texas or another small town for about seventy or eighty thousand. Maybe even buy her mother a house, too. She could get a job, maybe take some classes to better herself. Heck, she might even get back in college. Everything was going to work out just fine once she put some distance between herself and that fool Topps Jackson.

"Let's go, let's go." The Metro was taking forever. Neema looked around surprised that there wasn't a lot of traffic yet. Compton was not one of her favorite cities, so the sooner she could deliver her load and get back to her own vehicle, the better. Not one car was to her right or her left. Her glance caught the rearview mirror, a sight that made her stiffen in her seat. From the rear view, she could see a large black truck speeding up to her rear. It didn't look like it was going to stop, but instead, accelerated. The Metro train was in front of her, which left no means for her to get out of the path of the speeding truck. It was obvious that the truck would plow into the back of her vehicle.

"What the hell is he doing?" Neema couldn't take her eyes away from the rear view. The Metro train finally cleared, and the guard rail went up. She made an attempt to floor the accelerator hoping to move her vehicle to the side, but not fast enough. The huge, black Chevrolet Suburban plowed into her at a speed meant for freeway driving. The slam and crunch of metal against metal echoed loud through the early morning air. The compact Ford Escape lurched forward fifty feet into a utility pole, crushing the front of the vehicle. Without her seatbelt on her body was airborne out the shattered windshield. Her head hit the pavement hard on landing.

Neema groaned in pain. "Help me...please."

Everything on her hurt. Blood was on her face, in her eyes. It felt like she couldn't breathe. As she lay there, she heard voices—Spanish-speaking. Footsteps came over to her, and someone said something in Spanish, then there was the sound of feet running away from her. She didn't have the strength to lift her head, but could hear a vehicle moving past her.

Thoughts in her head felt like they were in water, sloshing around. Nothing made sense. Not even the sound of a voice saying, "Can you still walk? Don't be afraid. I'll get you some help." Someone was handling her, picking her up. Carrying her. She was light as air. Like a feather moving through the cool morning air. It was the last thing Neema recalled.

SIXTEEN

*O*ne monkey don't stop the show. It was Topps Jackson's personal mantra, and he lived by it. He had an hour before he had to drive to Kinsley Elementary and pick up Brandon and Raynita. That was all the time he needed to give Gina, his second main squeeze, a good joy ride.

Thanks to him, Gina had a bomb place to kick it. Her Baldwin Hills condo was small, but nicely furnished with the best of everything: large plasma televisions; oriental rugs and top-of-the-line Italian furniture. Imported. Not to be confused with cheap imitations. Not one soul knew about the place except for he and Gina, and he planned to keep that way. Plus, it was a hop and skip away from Neema's crib, and ten minutes from his kids' school. He had everything he needed: good sex, a safe place to rest his head, a freezer full of food, and access to any alcohol or drug that he could possibly want. Of course he didn't need anything to cloud his head or get in the way of what he had in mind for Gina.

He'd been knowing Gina for a good six months after scoping her out at a nightclub. Hell, the same one where he'd met Neema. Gina had tried to play that hard-to-get shit in the beginning, but that didn't last. Topps smiled thinking about how money attracted pussy and pussy attracted money. It was all about the "Monussy." Money was how he had hooked up with Neema, too.

He shook his head thinking about Neema. A spell of disappointment tried to invade him. His girl was playing out and Gina was next in line as her replacement. Neema didn't know it, but the delivery he'd sent her on was more than her last; it was a set-up. Sent her straight into the hands of one of his enemies with poison powder. Instant death. The receiver would take one test snort of the white powder and collapse, then kill Neema for bringing it. The plan was brilliant. Even his righthand man Slick hadn't been told what the plan was. And why should he when he and Neema were screwing behind his back. *Yeah. Niggas thought I didn't know about that, huh?*

Payback is a mutha, ain't it? First Neema, then that nigga Slick later on. They must have thought he was some dumb ass they could fool. The two fucking behind his back was one thing, but even if he had married Neema, it wouldn't have dismissed what she knew about him and that bitch friend of hers, Kaykay. Neema was like most women—the minute she felt scorned, she would no doubt turn on him like a pit bull. Probably even drop a dime. A scorned female was dangerous in his line of business. His father's death had taught him that much. Topps had to think about his safety and his freedom. Only a fool would leave loose ends hanging. Neema was a loose end.

"Stop daydreaming and come and get this good pussy, baby."

"What?" Topps' mind had been going a mile a minute. He looked up and admired her thickness. Something about a big-legged, big-eyed woman made him feel weak. Gina was his own personal Beyoncé but with shorter hair done in twists. Gina was blessed with a nice ass, too, but not as nice as Neema's. Her breasts were higher and firmer. Plus, she'd had no babies to stretch her pussy out like Neema's.

"You heard me," Gina half purred in her sexy way. Shower water was still dripping from her high, rounded rear end as she strolled from the shower into the room to slather some lotion on her honey-brown body.

"Maybe a little dance might help." Topps only had on a black-and-red smoking jacket. His manhood peeked through the satin as his body reclined on the chaise lounge in the spacious bedroom.

"Anything for my daddy." Gina moved to her open closet and slid on a pair of red stilettos and threw a red, feather boa around her delicate neck. The feather boa covered both nipples of her "D" cups. "Let me get some music going."

Topps stroked his swelling manhood as he lay back and watched her glide over to the Bose system to turn it on. "Paradise" by Sade filled the room. "Do yo' thang, girl," he cheered as Gina's onion ass began to catch the music's rhythm with gyrations. She was the bomb like that. She could move her body in ways that could make a blind man see naughty things. "Yeah, girl, you working that ass." Topps felt like he was in paradise.

"You craving it?"

"Big time, for real."

Gina was two years older than Neema, but more limber and agile. Hell, the way Gina could bend and mold herself into shapes and positions was an act that should be in Circus Ole. Topps couldn't take his eyes off the way her head appeared between her own legs.

"Damn, you like rubber, girl." His mouth watered as he admired the light and dark of Gina's fuzzy feminine mound from behind. She straightened her body and turned to face him as she sat at the bed's edge.

"Yeah, like that. Now do slow motion for me."

"Like this?" Gina moved slowly along the bed's edge, gyrating her hips. She gave him a wide leg flash of her wet, pink sweetness before putting her shapely legs up in the air.

"That's it, girl. Damn, you so nasty. You got me harder than a damn coliseum full of jawbreakers." He could barely control himself, watching Gina lay back on the bed and run that red boa over her swollen clit like she didn't have a shame in the world.

"Looks like you been a bad girl," Topps said, moving to where she lay, flipping her over. A few open hand slaps to her behind jiggled some flesh. "You one sexy bitch and you know it." He knelt in front while she rolled onto her back. Her pink pearl was swollen in waiting and calling to him. He flicked his tongue lightly over it, causing Gina to throw her head back with a loud moan. A few more flicks and deep sucking had her begging for more. Topps wasted no time positioning himself over her, giving her every inch of himself. Just like him, Gina liked it hard and rough. Fifteen minutes later, the two collapsed side by side, but not for long. Topps hopped up and headed to the shower.

"I know you ain't leaving me now. We got seconds coming."

"Maybe later," he said over his shoulder. "School is almost out. Gotta pick my kids up."

"Thought they mama did that shit." Gina reached for a cigarette.

One thing he hated was a woman smoking cigarettes. A blunt was one thing, but nicotine turned him off. Now she was trying to get in his business. "They staying with me for a few days."

"Who? Yo' baby mama?"

"Yo', my kids, Gina. Stop sweating me."

Gina knew about Neema, but Neema knew nothing of Gina. Hell, he was a single man who could see who the hell he wanted. Neema wouldn't be around much longer anyway. No need for her to find out either. If his plan went right, Neema was out of the picture. If he didn't care for his kids so much, he would have terminated Neema.

Gina rolled her eyes at him. "Does that mean they mama gonna be at your house, too? 'Cause if it's gonna be like that, maybe I should see other men, too."

A large bath towel around his waist, Topps left the shower water running and casually walked back over to Gina. Why was it that the beautiful women always tended to be mouthy? It was one of his pet peeves. He walked right up to her and slapped the taste from her mouth, then stood and waited for Gina to say something else he didn't like. She didn't.

"You got somethin' else to say?" He stood there glaring down at her like a crazed mental patient, his eyes cold as death. "Fucking bitch, I didn't think so. You knew the deal when we first hooked up. Maybe you forgot whose money is paying the damn bills around this mutha."

Stunned, Gina sat there holding her face while he walked back to the bathroom for his shower.

Twenty minutes later, his shiny, black Denali with the tinted windows and twenty-one-inch, kill-me-quick rims was parked across the street from Kinsley Elementary. Topps had five minutes before the school bell sounded, and kids would be all over the place on the lookout for parents and babysitters. Most adults were stupid and too lazy to walk their big fat asses to pick up their kids. People like that made him sick.

A toothpick dangled in his mouth. Topps gave a good look around making sure no friend or foe was trying to slide up on him. Catch him off guard. Everything looked calm. Once the bell rang, he'd get out and cross over to keep Raynita and Brandon from crossing the street to get to his vehicle. But for now he sat listening to Akon's upbeat tune "Trouble Nobody."

The school bell rang. Kids running around. Kids playing. Kids yelling back and forth. Kids were everywhere. Topps got out and crossed to the front of the school where he waited like the rest of the group for teachers to walk their classes out in an orderly manner. No sign of Raynita or Brandon. He walked around looking. Still, no sign. Cars came and went. Students moved on from the right and left of him. He felt antsy with each passing second. *What the hell is taking 'em so long?*

Maybe they got in some trouble. He walked to the school's front office where he asked one of the clerks if any kids were waiting in the office. Nope. None.

He took out his cell phone and dialed Brandon's cell number. Good thing he had the foresight to give both kids their own cell phone. Both phones were sophisticated GPS tracking devices, but that was something only he and Slick knew about. It took quite a few rings before Brandon's voice answered.

"Brandon, yo', what's up? I'm at the school waiting on you and yo' sister."

Topps' hand clutched the cell tight enough to break it into pieces. He didn't like what he was hearing as Brandon informed him that Hattie had picked them up early.

"But I told y'all asses that I would pick you up. Whose damn idea was that?" He felt stupid getting upset with a seven-year-old. "Fuck it. Don't worry about it. I'm on my way to pick you and yo' sister up. Be ready."

SEVENTEEN

Brandon forgot to tell his grandmother that he had spoken to his father, and that Topps was on his way to get him and Raynita. He had been playing video games in the spare bedroom where he sometimes slept while staying at Hattie's house when his cell phone had burred.

"Thought you had homework?" Hattie queried the minute Brandon strolled into her kitchen looking for a snack. She noticed right away that he had on his shoes, jacket and backpack. Raynita was taking a nap.

"I do." Brandon was standing at her refrigerator staring inside.

"Uh...shouldn't you be doing your homework instead of letting all the cold air out my box?" She was a stickler when it came to studying and homework, believing that a good education was the only way to succeed in the world. "Brandon, you know your mama won't be happy about you not doing your homework."

"She'll get over it."

"What?" Hattie stopped what she was doing. Maybe it was her imagination, but it seemed to her that boy was getting looser at the lips with each passing day. Not accustomed to flippant replies from children, it was consuming all her inner strength to keep from taking a belt to the boy.

"I'll do it at Daddy's house. He's on his way."

"He's on his way? When did he call? I didn't hear my phone ring."

Brandon took out a carton of orange juice and got a plastic cup to pour some. "Yeah. He called my cell phone. He said for me and Nita to be ready. He sounded mad."

"Mad, huh?" Hattie huffed. She thought about how she wouldn't be releasing the kids to him. "Well, he'll be more than mad when he leaves here. I'm just making some lunch. Go wake your sister up, now."

"Do I have to?"

"Brandon, do as I say, please."

The child was gearing up for more protest but stopped when Raynita walked into the kitchen rubbing her sleepy eyes. "Nanny, I'm hungry."

"I'll make some sandwiches."

"We don't have time for no sandwich, Nita. Daddy is coming to pick us up, and he sounded mad 'cause we didn't wait for him after school."

"What kind of mess is going on here?" Hattie said out loud, gathering up lunch meat, bread, mustard and lettuce. "Does your father normally pick y'all up from school?"

"No," Raynita confirmed with a young attitude. "Mama said that no one can pick us up but you and her, and I don't wanna go to Daddy's house. I'm staying with Nanny."

"I'ma tell Daddy what you said."

"So! And I'ma tell Mama you pulled that girl's pants down at school today."

Brandon balled his fist. "And I'ma tell you stole money from your teacher's desk."

"You two stop it now!" She wanted to investigate both allegations but no, they were Neema's kids; let her be the disciplinarian. The two had been at her house for over three hours without one squabble. Hattie knew it was too good to be true. Now she was getting a headache. "I wish your mother would come on. I got my Monday night bingo and no kids are allowed."

The kids ate sandwiches in the kitchen while Hattie tried to call Neema's cell phone. There was no answer, so she tried calling her apartment without luck. Frustrated, she hung up. "She'll be here. She promised."

Raynita whined, "I wanna wait for Mama to come. I don't wanna go to Daddy's house."

Drying her hands on her apron, Hattie mused on the child's words. It was the second time Raynita had made the statement. A statement like that seemed odd to her when most young girls had mad love for their father. "What's wrong, Nita? You don't like going to your daddy's house?"

"Uh-uh. Daddy's too mean. He fuss too much with Mama, and he hits her. I don't like to see my mama crying. Sometimes he spanks me for nothin', and he smokes those weeds, too. I can't breathe too good when he smokes those weeds."

"Daddy don't like us telling his business, Nita. You gon' get in trouble."

"Brandon, hush. What else, Nita?" All ears, Hattie sat down at the table trying not to seem too eager for information. She often could detect that Raynita and Brandon both had been warned not to discuss what went on in the house. But children being children, they too had issues and concerns that needed to be vented. When it came to telling, it was always Raynita.

"Forget you, Brandon. You just mad 'cause Mama fussed at Daddy for giving you some more weeds."

"Is that true, Brandon? Does your father give you drugs?" Hattie waited for an answer she wouldn't get. She couldn't imagine what kind of parent would contribute drugs to an innocent child.

"Nita, I'm telling Daddy on you."

Brandon's eyes were shooting daggers at his sister when Hattie's front doorbell rang. It was the second time she'd heard of Topps giving drugs to her grandson. The more she kept telling herself that it was none of her business, to stay out of it, the angrier she became. She made a mental note to ask Neema about it. "We'll talk about this later." Hattie got up and headed through the living room.

She opened the thick, wooden door to find Topps Jackson standing at the opposite side of her security screen door. "Good evening." Her pleasant face was forced.

"Ms. Hattie. Nice to see you again." Topps had a moist cloth in his hand, wiping his hands like he'd just touched something filthy. "How you doing today?"

Even when he tried to be nice it seemed contrived. There was something too sneaky about Topps Jackson. She had never cared for him since the first time she'd met him. Neema was only sixteen, and he'd brought Neema Jean home drunk at two a.m.

"Topps. What can I do for you?" Hattie made no attempt to open her security door and invite him inside.

"Neema sent me for the kids." He tried the knob on the security door. Locked. "What'up, can I come in?" No sweet smiles or extra pleasantries.

"I'm afraid not." Hattie looked him up and down. The thick, gold and diamond chain around his neck had to be worth more than her car parked outside. Styling in the latest hip-hop wear, he didn't look cheap. Didn't smell cheap. "I don't know what's going on with you and Neema, but she called me earlier and asked me to pick the kids up early from school. She told me to keep them until she comes."

His half-smile changed to a smirk. One eye twitched. "Old woman, I don't have time to play games with you. Those are my kids, and I'm here to take 'em home." Topps made an attempt to call their names through the barred door. "Y'all come on, let's go!"

Hattie stood her ground. "Like I said, Neema wants the children to stay here with me until she comes for them. At least at my house, they won't be traumatized with violence or be given drugs."

"Drugs? Bitch, please. You don't know what the hell you're talking 'bout."

"I'm talking about a man that's trying to corrupt his own children."

A grin. A few chuckles. "Look," said Topps, shaking his head as if he found her amusing. "I'll let all this slide if you send the kids out, so I can be on my way. Okay? You probably been hitting that juice and it's got you talkin' all crazy like a mutha. Brandon! Nita! Y'all come on, let's go!"

Brandon came up behind Hattie, trying to get to the door. "Daddy, I'm coming." Raynita eased into the room and stood looking frightened.

Hattie had no idea where her strength was coming from. "Sit down, Brandon. Your mother will be here shortly."

Topps grabbed the metal door and shook it with all his might. He kicked it twice and spat on it. "Damn you, you fucking hag. You think I have to beg you? Give me those damn kids!" His eyes went blood red. Veins bulged from the side of his neck.

Raynita ran screaming from the room leaving Brandon standing with his fist balled up. "I wanna go with my daddy!"

"Brandon, you get yourself in that bedroom with your sister! You'll leave when your mother comes."

"Old woman." Topps grinned wickedly. "You must have a death wish. You obviously don't know me well."

"I know enough to know that you might be their father, but your name is not on their birth certificates. I know that you're not legally married to my daughter, and you have no legal right to the children. I also know that if you don't get off my property, I'll call the police."

"Oh, so it's like that, huh?" Topps regained his composure, straightened his navy blue jersey. Angry muscles in his face twitched. "I'll leave once I get my kids."

"Someone bring me my cordless phone!" Hattie yelled over her shoulders. "So what's it gonna be, Mr. Big Shot, you leaving or the police coming?"

Raynita ran back into the room with the cordless phone. "Here, Nanny." Crying, she ran back out. Seeing the fear in Raynita's face reinforced her refusal to turn them over to Topps.

Hattie took the receiver and prepared to dial 911. "Like I said, legally, you don't have a right to these kids. Being a sperm donor don't make you a father."

"Is that right?" Topps smirked.

"Last chance. Get the hell off my porch."

His grin turned into a laugh. "Crazy old woman. You crazier than a muthafucker, you know that? I see where Neema gets her stubborn streak from."

"Whatever."

"I'll get off your damn porch alright, but this shit ain't over," he said, removing a packet of Fresh Wipes from his pocket to clean more germs from his hands. "You can count on it."

"That's between you and Neema Jean."

"Crazy bitch." Topps turned to leave, then stopped and looked back in her direction. "You know what they say, old woman. You play with fire, you bound to get burned."

"If that's supposed to scare me, you're wasting your breath. What I fear is the wrath of God. Now, you get off my property and stay off! Your kind is not welcome." She stood and watched

Topps walk back to his chromed-out, black Denali, get in and drive off.

"Nanny, you make me sick! I wanted to go with my daddy. I don't wanna stay here." Brandon walked off to the bedroom and slammed the door.

"You can tell all that to your mother," Hattie yelled behind him. Finally, she could exhale. She felt lightheaded. She had stood up to Topps Jackson saying that she wasn't afraid, but the thin stream of urine running down her leg indicated it had all been a facade. Even her hands were still trembling.

EIGHTEEN

"You should call the police this time, Mama. Maybe something happened to her."

"Myra, how many times I have to tell you, I refuse to traumatize these kids by getting the police involved."

"Yeah, well, Neema promised she would come for 'em last night and she didn't show. That was yesterday and it's almost midnight now. I hardly think that she'll be showing up this time of night."

"I know, I know." Hattie took the phone from one ear and placed it to her other. After cleaning the kitchen and taking her shower, she had been relaxing on her bed and talking to Myra on the phone for the last hour. Despite her eldest daughter being a know-it-all most times, she could also be a source of comfort. At first she'd felt guilty about calling to Victorville so late, but worry over Neema had gotten the best of her. She had to talk to someone. "You know that child, she's full of surprises. Probably off somewhere having fun and not thinking about Nita or Brandon. I used to be young and I know how it is."

"Mama, how many times are you going to keep falling for this little stunt of hers? Calling Protective Services is the best way to teach Neema a lesson."

"Myra, if these were your kids, would you want me calling the police or Children's Services?"

There was pause. "No."

"Don't you think your sister should be treated the same? I called to see if you knew of any of her friends I could try calling. Maybe one of her friends might know where she is."

"Mama, you know Neema and I don't have it like that. We're sisters, but not what you would call best friends."

"Yeah, I know, and it's sad when you stop and think about it. You were always so protective of her."

"Humph. That was years back. Not my fault she chose that lifestyle. I used to try to talk some sense into that girl when we were younger, but she knew what she wanted. Money. Men with money. More money. That fast and wild life. Maybe she got it from Daddy's side of the family."

Hattie reprimanded, "You leave your father out of this."

"I'm merely saying that her wild ways had to come from somebody's side of the family."

"I'm so afraid for her. I keep thinking my phone will ring one night and some officer will be telling me to come down to the morgue and identify her body. I pray for her all the time...I'm so..." She heard a loud crash from somewhere in the house. "What the...what the heck was that?"

"Mama? What is it?"

"I don't know. I heard something loud like glass breaking. Let me go and see what's going on. Maybe one of the kids got up for some water and dropped a glass. I'll call you back."

"Mama, don't hang up..."

Too late. Hattie pressed the off button and tossed the phone on the bed. She got up and slipped into her robe, then her slippers. It was still dark through her long hallway, but at the end she could see a flicker of glowing light. "What in the world... Nita, is that you? Brandon?"

Hattie rounded the corner from her hallway leading into her

living room where the large front window was crashed in by a broken bottle. "Ohmygawd, fire!" First instincts had her stomping at flames on her rug, but her efforts were useless. Spilled liquid from the broken bottle led a flaming path to her living room drapes. The sound of popping and crackling material echoed in the room. "Brandon! Nita!" She ran to her kitchen for a bucket to fill with water. Finding one she ran back into the living room and tossed a useless splash of water that seemed to make the fire worse. Flames on a window joined force with drapery. She screamed for the children, "Brandon! Raynita!"

Running to her back door, she tried pulling her water hose through the house, but once outside Hattie could see that the knob was off the outside faucet. It was her doing to keep the kids from turning on the water and playing in it. She couldn't find where she had placed the knob. She ran back to the living room where to her horror the fire had spread considerably. The thought of trying to extinguish it was futile.

"Ohmygawd, Lord help!" To heck with trying to put the fire out. Getting the kids up and out was her best bet. She ran into the bedroom to see if her shouting had awakened the children, but it hadn't. Their angelic bodies lay in total peace, sleeping in twin beds while the front of the house was filling up with smoke.

Hattie shook them both roughly. "Nita! Brandon! Get up! Get up now. Wake up, I said!"

"Nanny, no. I'm sleepy. I don't wanna get up. We going to school?"

"Nita, do as I say. We don't have a lot of time. Get up, let's go!"

"Did my daddy come back for me?" Brandon wanted to know, trying to rub sleep from his eyes.

If she wasn't so busy trying to get them out of the house and to a safe place, she would have swatted his behind a few times for even asking such a foolish thing. "We don't have time for questions. We have to leave this house."

"I don't wanna go to Daddy's house, Nanny."

"Nita, don't worry about that right now. Hurry up, get your stuff. Get what you can, we have to go."

"Go where?"

"Nita, girl, please stop asking questions and just do what I say! Hurry up now." Just like children are inclined to do, the two grumbled and complained. It didn't stop Hattie from finding some shoes for them to slip on. She snatched blankets from the twin beds and wrapped them around their shoulders. "Let's go, let's go!" They grabbed their backpacks and followed Hattie to the bedroom window where she pushed the screen out and climbed out first to help Raynita and Brandon. It was the same window she hadn't gotten around to having security bars put on. The three migrated through the side gate that led to the front of the house.

"Nanny, how come your house is on fire?"

"I'm not sure myself, Nita. I need a phone. Brandon, you have your cell phone?"

"Yeah."

"Let me have it." Hattie all but snatched it from his hands. She called 911 for a fire truck, realizing that she should have done this first thing. Then she called Myra back to let her know what was going on. To keep the kids from hearing her words, she walked them to her car parked in front of the house. "You guys wait in here." She was able to let the kids inside the car because she rarely locked it. The car needed some engine work and hadn't been driven for weeks. "I'm not going far. I'm right over here." Hattie closed the car door and walked a few feet away. "He tried to kill us," she said when Myra picked up on the opposite end.

"Mama, who? What's going on?"

"The kids' father, Topps. He tried to kill us!"

"What? Why? I mean, how?"

Hattie rattled off the earlier events of the day—how Topps had left her place angry because she wouldn't turn the kids over to him. "He even made a threat about fire before he left. It had to be him. Said somethin' 'bout if you play with fire you get burned. Those were his last words: 'If you play with fire'!"

"Yeah, Mama, but wouldn't him doing something like that endanger his own kids?"

"Hell, yes it would!" Hattie stomped her foot for emphasis. "Obviously, a man like that don't care. Lord, have mercy, this is unbelievable. The front of my house is almost gone. He burned my house!"

"I'm driving down now!"

"Myra, no. Don't make that drive. You're too far away and it's not safe at night. B'sides, it's nothing you can do to help right now. No sense in you driving for over an hour to get here."

"Mama, are you sure? I can wake Glen up and he can drive us."

"No. Don't do that. We're safe right now. No one got hurt. I'll call you again when I know more."

"Are you sure? It's no problem for us to drive down. What will you do? Where will you sleep tonight?"

"I'm positive. You stay put for now. I'll work something out." Myra's drive from the high desert would take an hour and a half, and with the possibility of running into thick fog coming down the Cajon Pass, Hattie felt the trip would be safer in daylight. "A fire truck just pulled up. I'll call you in the morning. Don't worry about us, we'll be fine. I'll see about getting a hotel room for tonight."

Lights went on in surrounding homes. Nosey and concerned

neighbors began gathering in front of her burning house, causing problems for the fire crew members trying to do their job. Soon a flurry of activity was in full swing. Standing there watching, Hattie had never felt so hopeless. What kind of person could do something this awful with young children in the house?

"You poor thing. Are you okay? What happened?"

Hattie followed the sound of the voice. It was Mrs. Sweeney, her next-door neighbor. The elderly widow had a right to inquire, seeing how her house was so close and could be next. "I'm not sure, but I believe it was something electrical." She couldn't bring herself to tell the gray-haired woman that the father of her own grandchildren had thrown a flaming cocktail through her large front window. The thought of her smoke alarms not sounding off popped into her head. For months she had been meaning to replace the batteries in the alarms but hadn't gotten around to doing it.

"Anyone hurt?" Mrs. Sweeney had on her pink housecoat and some fuzzy slippers. Her hair was a mess. Her dark, rheumy eyes flashed true concern.

"No. Praise God for that." Hattie rubbed her goose-bumped arms and looked over at the car where the kids sat to get out of the night cold. She didn't mind Mrs. Sweeney asking questions. The two weren't the best of friends, but after Mr. Sweeney passed away two years back, Hattie found herself doing a few things for the widow. She had picked up her groceries and had driven the forgetful woman to her doctor's appointments. Twice, she'd even taken the woman to church when Mrs. Sweeney's car was down for repairs. Just like herself, Mrs. Sweeney was a God-fearing woman and quite friendly. "I'm grateful I was still awake to get everybody out in time."

"Ain't no telling what all can go wrong with these old houses."

Mrs. Sweeney shook her head. "I doubt if any of 'em are up to code."

"Excuse me. Let me check on the kids." Hattie went over and opened her car door. "You two okay?"

Nita rubbed her eyes. "Nanny, what happened to your house?"

"That's what they're trying to find out, sweetie." Hattie was positive that a Molotov cocktail had crashed through the front window, and she was certain that Topps Jackson was the culprit. Topps' earlier threat of "if you play with fire, you get burnt" kept circulating in her head. Who else would do such a thing?

"We don't have a place to sleep?" Brandon asked. He didn't seem particularly upset over the house burning. "We can call my daddy to come pick us up."

"Brandon, so help me, if you mention one more thing about…"

"Hattie, sweetie," said Mrs. Sweeney, sauntering in her night-clothes over to the car. "I doubt that you and the cheeren' can sleep in that house tonight. Y'all welcome to stay with me until you figure things out."

"Thank you, Mrs. Sweeney. I really appreciate that."

"You welcome. Looks like they got the fire out. I'ma go on home and start some tea. Y'all come on over when y'all ready, or the kids can come with me now if you want."

Brandon looked like he wanted to protest, but Hattie was quick to give him a little pinch as she helped them out the car. "You two go with Mrs. Sweeney here. I'll be over as soon as the firemen get finished. I'll hold on to your cell phone, Brandon. Go on now."

"Don't worry. Everything will be okay. I have some hot choco-late also," Mrs. Sweeney volunteered as she hugged the kids by the shoulders and guided them toward her house. "Y'all like hot chocolate?"

"I like hot chocolate and cookies," Nita chirped happily.

Brandon was tightlipped.

Firemen were all over the place, working around gawking neighbors. Hattie flipped Brandon's phone open and searched the phone listings for Topps' number. She was glad the kids weren't around to hear the tongue-lashing she was going to give him. Then the phone rang. It scared her for a second or two. "Hello?"

"Mama? Is the fire out? What's going on?"

"How'd you get this number?" It was Myra.

"Caller ID."

"Oh yeah. I keep forgetting how that works. They got the fire out. It burned most of the front of the house, but with the water damage and smoke fumes, I doubt if we can sleep in it tonight."

"Can you afford a hotel room for tonight?"

"Without my ATM card, credit card, or driver's license, I doubt it. They won't let me back into the house tonight, but my neighbor offered us beds at her place. You remember ole Mrs. Sweeney to the left of me? That's where we'll be."

"This is awful."

"I know," Hattie agreed, "but it could have been so much worse. Thank the good Lord no one was hurt. I'll try to locate my insurance papers in the morning. I'm so glad I kept those papers in a fireproof safe."

"Still haven't heard from Neema yet?"

"Not a peep, but anyway, we'll talk tomorrow when you get here. Don't worry 'bout us; we'll be fine." Hattie clicked off and continued to peruse the list. A number for Neema's new phone was listed. She tried the number but got no answer. *Where the heck could Neema Jean possibly be?* She tried the number listed as "Daddy." Hattie let the phone ring ten times before she ended the connection.

"Excuse me, ma'am, are you the owner of the home?" a burly, red-faced man walked up and asked. He smelled loud of smoke and burned wood.

"Yes, I am." Hattie shoved the phone in her pocket and pulled her robe belt tighter.

"Do you have any idea of what might have caused the fire?" the fireman asked. His expression and tone was suspicious.

"Someone threw something flammable through my front window; that's what happened. Good thing I wasn't asleep yet."

"Someone?"

"His name is Topps Jackson." She hadn't seen him do the crime, but who else had a motive?

"Maybe you need to speak to one of the officers on site and make a report."

Hattie set her jaw to firm. "Without a doubt, I need to do that." She planned to tell everything. Heck, if she had Topps' address she'd give that to the police as well. The fireman continued to talk, but Hattie wasn't listening. Instead, her attention was drawn away to the midnight-black Denali that had stopped in front of her house. The chromed-out vehicle had tinted windows and twenty-one-inch wheels. It was the same vehicle she'd seen Topps drive up in earlier.

"A damn monster! That's what you are!" She couldn't see the driver through the dark windows, but she didn't have to see to determine his identity. She recognized that a monster was looking back at her.

The vehicle's horn sounded twice before driving off.

NINETEEN

"Mama, be careful."

"I will, but I have to find the insurance papers." Hattie took careful steps, making her way to her bedroom closet where she kept her fireproof safe with other important documents. Once she unlocked the safe, she found a few hundred dollars left from the money that Neema had given her. "Thank goodness. I forgot all about this money." She put the bills in her bosom and found the papers. Now she could call the insurance people and start the process.

"Wonder how long it'll take to rebuild."

"I have no idea." Myra made a face. "What we need to focus on is finding Neema's no-good ass to come pick her brats up. You have enough to deal with."

Hattie shook her head. "What an inconvenience." Since the fire had been contained to the front of the house and part of the kitchen, she was able to get her luggage from her bedroom and pack a few clothes. She gathered up the few clothing belonging to the kids, her Bible, and phone book. Wasn't much she could do about everything smelling like smoke.

"Did you call Neema's cell phone?"

"Myra, of course, and her apartment. I was thinking about going to her place after I'm finished here. She gave me an emergency key some time ago, but I misplaced it. I can look through her phone book and see if any of her friends know anything." Puddles of water, ashes, melted plastic, and things that couldn't be identified were everywhere. Hattie surveyed the mess that was now her living room. Her fairly new color television, boxes of family pictures, and her beautiful new La-Z-Boy chair were destroyed by either fire or water. It brought tears to her eyes. "Twenty-six years of living here, ruined."

"I know, Mama. But you can always get another house." Myra frowned up at every direction she looked. Her nails and hair were too perfect to be touching much in the house, not while wearing her favorite APO jeans and new white lace blouse. She had driven down alone, explaining that her husband, Glen, couldn't take off because he had a heavy surgery schedule. To make sure that she had enough room in her pearl-white Lexus RX 350, she left her three kids with the nanny she used occasionally. The idea of her mother and two more kids coming to live in her house wasn't the best-laid plan, but they were family and she needed to help. Hopefully, the arrangement wouldn't be for too long.

It took most of the day to get some day workers to nail the house's windows. No one could walk in off the street and help themselves to her belongings.

"Don't worry about a thing," Mrs. Sweeney assured Hattie as they all filed into Myra's brand-new SUV. "I'll keep an eye out on your place and I'll call the police if I see so much as a mouse trying to go inside."

Brandon and Raynita whispered and giggled at the old woman who looked comical talking without her dentures. Hattie felt a sense of comfort, knowing that the kids were in good spirits after what they had experienced. "Thanks a lot, Mrs. Sweeney. You have my daughter's number where you can reach me in case Neema shows up here."

"I certainly will." Mrs. Sweeney turned and moseyed back to her house.

"Where to now, Mama?" Myra asked once they were moving.

"You remember where Neema's place is up in the Crenshaw area?"

Myra played it off like she did. "Off Martin Luther King, right?"

"We'll stop there first to see what we can find out." Hattie took a deep breath. "Who knows, she might be at home sleeping."

"We don't live there anymore," said Brandon too matter-of-factly. He had his face to the window, blowing steamy breath onto the glass.

"What do you mean, you don't live there anymore?" Hattie tried to turn fully around in her seat, but sleeping on Mrs. Sweeney's old sofa had her back stiff.

"Daddy said that we're moving in with him. He told Mama to pack up her stuff so we can move."

"And why is it that no one mentioned this before?" Hattie wanted to know. She stared at the side of Brandon's head and wanted to thump it. Every time she turned around, it was something she didn't know about. She wondered what other information they were withholding. "What about your mother; she's still your mother, right?" Perhaps they knew something about that as well.

"Nanny, that's silly." Raynita giggled. "I wanna move with you. I don't wanna live with my daddy 'cause he's a mean man and he fuss all the time. And he likes to hit people too hard."

"Oooo. Wait 'til I tell Daddy what you said," Brandon threatened. "You gon' be in big trouble."

"So, tell 'im! I don't care. I'ma live with Nanny. Just me and Nanny and not you!"

"Poor things. Imagine feeling like that about your own father."

Myra shook her head. "Why would Neema get involved with a person like that?"

"Don't be talking about my daddy!"

Hattie and Myra chorused, "Shut up, Brandon!"

Brandon had told the truth. When then arrived at Neema's old place, Hattie must have knocked and banged at her door for a good five minutes before one of the neighbors told her that the apartment was empty. "What? For how long now?"

The young black woman was dressed in pants that looked like pajamas and she was wearing a dirty white rag on her head. "About two days now. Some big moving truck came for her stuff, and some man was here supervising. Her boyfriend, I suppose."

"Have you seen Neema lately?"

"I sure haven't. Not in a week or so, but normally I'm at work during the day."

"Thanks." Hattie went back to the SUV. She huffed and puffed getting back in. "Guess that takes care of that. The apartment is empty. Her neighbor said she didn't see her when they were moving her things out."

"Neema moved and didn't mention it?"

"I guess so." Hattie buckled her seatbelt. True, Neema had flaky behavior, but this was taking it a bit far. She would have mentioned the move.

"Something is wrong, Mama. This is the third day, and now she's moved from her place without even telling her own family. It's not like her."

"Maybe Mama is at Daddy's house. We should go see."

"Brandon, we are NOT going to your father's house. Get over it and stop asking."

"How come?" Brandon wanted to know.

His inquiry was innocent enough. Hattie didn't have the heart to tell the child his precious daddy was the reason her house was burned. "Because I said so, that's why."

"She's not at Daddy's house 'cause she was mad at Daddy. Remember?" Raynita was playing with her doll. "I bet Mama ran away 'cause Daddy was so mean to her. One time he hit her face and made her cry."

"Nita! Stop telling Mama's business."

"It's my mouth. I can say what I want!"

"Okay, you two, settle down back there." Hattie felt like her head was trying to start hurting. She checked one of her bags to make sure she had her hypertension medication.

Myra headed for the freeway. "It's bad enough that she hasn't called to check in with you, but now we learn that she wasn't even around when her own things were being moved out." She paused to reflect.

"Neema is funny about people touching her personal stuff. I don't know, it just sounds peculiar."

"Yeah, it does. Mama, something is up. We should head to the nearest police precinct and file a missing persons report."

Hattie took a deep breath and let it seep out slowly. "Maybe you're right. There's a police precinct on Seventy-seventh."

TWENTY

*T*he warehouse normally powered down by midnight. Women dusted off cocaine residue before being allowed to dress and go home. It wasn't unusual for Topps and Slick to hang around late talking and going over future plans for the business. Money was counted and stored in a clever floor-installed safe beneath Topps' desk. Most times the safe was too full. Overflow cash had to be delivered to Topps' house to be stored in a safe hidden deep in his closet. Deliveries had to be accounted for, and discussions of who needed to be popped, switched or put down were all part of the operation.

The three people left in Topps' office still had business. Stacks of twenty and hundred-dollar bills were piled high on a table next to the wall. Slick had two counting machines flashing cash while Topps gave instructions to a soldier on his killing crew—pop a female worker leaving the business. If the soldier had a problem with the order, he didn't let on.

Dressed completely in black, the tall, dark-skinned soldier had the piercing eyes and face of a man that could snap a woman's neck and go out for ice cream later.

"Yo, no witnesses. Keep it clean and quick. You know where she lives." Topps handed him an envelope full of cash.

"Piece of cake. When? Tonight? Tomorrow?" The grinning soldier sounded like he couldn't wait to do his job.

"You got three days. And remember, screw this up and you're screwed, too."

"Oh, it's done." The soldier turned and left.

Listening, Slick clicked his teeth. "Man, that's fucked up. You know that skank won't rat out. Give her a break."

Topps sneered over at him. "Screw that. You know the drill. Can't have loose ends running around knowing about the business. I can't do no hard time."

"True that, but damn, man. Sheila been loyal for almost five years. That skank got three mouths to feed. So what if she moving to Atlanta to see about her moms."

"Like I said, you know the mutherfucking drill. It's nothin' personal. And what, she one of yo' pussy givers? Is that it?"

"Nah, man." Slick looked insulted. "I'm just saying that's fucked up. Homegirl got kids to raise."

"Sound like you getting soft on a nigga."

"Nah. I just think loyalty should count for somethin'."

Topps acted like he didn't hear his last words. He got up and left Slick counting money while he went to the front of the building to set the alarm. In no time he was back in his office washing his hands before putting on rubber gloves.

The two never worried about an invasion robbery because the place was locked down like Fort Knox with alarms and cameras all over the place. Of course, it helped to keep a few police officers on his payroll in case a bust tried to jump off, which was highly unlikely. Only a ghost could infiltrate the surroundings without being detected. For added security, it would take an army of men to break down the steel-framed office door where they were. It would leave ample time to escape through the secret door that led to a tunnel out the back of the building.

The secret tunnel had been constructed when his father was

running the business. The only two people that knew about the tunnel were Topps and Slick. To Topps, it was one person too many.

"Man, we might have to open up a few more Swiss accounts to hide all this damn money."

Slick grinned over at him but didn't stop his work. "Got that shit right." Just like Topps, he was dressed entirely in black. The attire wasn't a uniform requirement, but would make it hard to be detected in the event they had to flee into the night.

"Hell, I'm tired. I need a break." Topps was sitting at his desk passing stacks of money over to be counted. The latex gloves felt too tight, but he didn't dare take them off. It was his strong belief that money was one of the nastiest things that people touched and passed around without a second thought. Drugs were snorted with rolled-up money. Men slipped money into women's thongs. He'd seen more than one stripper pass a bill across her pussy. Money was full of germs. Topps got up and went to his sink where he took off his gloves and washed his hands, again.

"Hey, man, where that lady of yours? Neema. Haven't seen her in a few. What's up with that?" Slick gave him a sideways glance. He knew that three days ago Neema set out with a package delivery, and he hadn't heard a peep from her. It wasn't like her not to call and check in with him after a drop. He hadn't planned to, but he'd caught feelings for the girl. Several times even, he'd thought of what it would be like if Topps was out of the picture and he could hook up with Neema and make a decent lady out of her. Make her his main woman.

"Guess she's doing her thing. You know bitches. They always have somethin' to do." From the bottom of his sink, Topps pulled out half a bottle Hennessy Timeless Cognac and two glasses. "Dawg, I gotta tell you that I'm getting tired of this business. It's been long enough. A nigga got enough money not to work another day in his life. Maybe me and Neema and the kids might take off for the islands and build us a house by the ocean. I dig that shit. Know what I'm saying?" Topps poured two drinks and pushed a glass toward Slick. "Hey man, that shit can wait; take a break. Shit. We can always lock that shit in the safe and finish tomorrow."

"Yeah, you right." Slick turned both machines off. He had to wash his hands first because Topps didn't play that shit if he didn't. He walked over and sat, took up his glass and downed the four thousand-dollar-a-bottle brown liquid with ease. "You say you tired of it?" Looked like he needed a refill, so Topps obliged him.

"Man, what you think about us callin' this shit off?" Topps filled his glass halfway. "I'm tired, you look tired. Or even better, you can buy me out."

Slick grinned at that one. "Buy you out? Nigga, please. This a dope business, not a damn Burger King franchise. And how much you think it would take to buy you out?"

Topps looked serious. "Two million and it's all yours. Everything. I walk away."

"Two million?"

"Cash money, and I'm out."

"No shit?" Sounded like a fair price. And it wasn't like he didn't have the cash. The dope business had been good to the both of them, plus Slick owned property he could sell. "Two mil, huh?" The more Slick thought about it, the sleepier he felt. It didn't take long for him to realize that Topps hadn't sipped his drink once, and he must have put something in his. "Damn, man, what's the muthafucking matter with…" He was out like a light.

There was no sense of time lost. When Slick woke up, he was tied—no, duct taped. He was duct taped to a chair. His hands, his feet. It had to taken a good amount of time for a person to utilize so much duct tape. He couldn't move, and Topps was sitting across from him with a wooden baseball bat and a nine-millie in front of him on the table. Beside the bat lay a large manila envelope.

"Welcome back, bro. I'm sure you had a nice nap. It's good to keep the right pharmaceuticals around when you need to put a nigga to sleep. Know what I mean?"

"Man, what the fuck?"

Topps had that crazy look in his eyes. Slick had seen it before, always before he popped or tortured some poor fool.

"All that noise ain't necessary, Slick. I suggest you use your inside voice about now."

"Topps…look, what's up with this, man? Why you trippin'?"

"You my boy, Slick. Always was." Topps leaned into his face. Grill to grill. "We like brothers from the same mother. That's why this here gon' hurt me as much as you, but I'm only going to ask yo' punk ass two times. You can count, right?"

"Ask me what? Man, I'm not playing, take this shit off me! What the hell's wrong with you?!"

"Where is she?"

"Nigga, who you talkin' 'bout? Where is who?!"

"That's number one. We talking bout Neema, fool. You know damn well who we talkin' 'bout. I know you the one hiding her ass from me." Topps fought the urge to bitch-slap him. "Damn shame it has to end like this, dawg. I trusted you."

"Look, man, I don't know what's up with you, but let me go and we can get back to business like nothing happened. We boys like that."

"That's what I thought, too." Topps took the envelope up. "Guess you and Neema thought I was too stupid to find out what was going on, huh?" He pulled the pictures out. The detective he had hired left nothing to the imagination. He watched Slick's eyes buck at photos of Neema and him kissing, hugging, bodies meshed together after coming out from one of their motel spots. "Guess you can't trust no damn body."

Slick hung his head.

"When I was a kid, my mama was an addict. She blamed my father. She hated him." He set the envelope down and went to his sink. From the bottom cabinet he pulled out a water hose, a jug of bleach and a bottle of dishwashing liquid. A clean toilet brush was next.

"Topps, man, I know you upset, but let me explain. It didn't mean shit."

"You know when mothers hate like that it can manifest to a child. She was always taking shit from me. New clothes my dad bought. My new bike. Toys and sometimes even food. She was crazy." He stopped and looked away, reflecting, then stared at his reflection in the mirror over the sink.

"TJ, listen to me...we boys. No woman should come between us like this. We boys!"

"That's why when my mother had that stroke and couldn't walk, her luck had finally changed." Topps smirked. "Couldn't do a damn thing for herself 'cept drool out the side of her twisted mouth."

"TJ, listen to me. Neema loves you. We wasn't trying to hurt you. She just needed someone to talk to 'cause she was scared. That's all it was."

"My mother's caretaker. That's what I became. Luck is a mutherfucker, ain't it? She couldn't take shit away from me again. Not one damn thing." He hooked the water hose up to the faucet. "Crazy bitch. She deserved what she got."

"Man, what the fuck is wrong with you? Take this shit off me! Now, mutherfucker!"

"Yo'," Topps swung around to look at him, "check this out. You ever see what a woman looks like when she don't eat or drink water for weeks?" Topps laughed. "That shit is hilarious, dawg. Look like leather. I know one thing, that shit ain't pretty."

"What the fuck you fin' to do?" Slick was straining, trying to free himself.

"Give yo' azz a bath 'cause you stink, dawg. All people stink to me. Germs and bacteria do that. Know what I'm saying?"

"Man, please...just let me go. You won't have to worry 'bout me again. I swear. You sick and you need help."

Topps wasn't listening. He whistled a tune while he went on with his business, happy as a worker at a car wash on a hot day. First he poured bleach over Slick's head, then squirted dish-washing liquid all over him, took up a toilet brush and got busy scrubbing the man down, head to feet. After three good lathers, he hosed him off.

"Man, stoppit!"

"You should thank me for this shit, dawg. People should be clean coming into this world and clean going out. Tell me another friend that would do this for you."

Slick could barely beg for the bleachy suds in his face. His eyes burned like hell, making him grind his teeth to keep from screaming.

"Now," Topps concluded, cutting the water off. He was in his face again, so close he could smell the bleach fumes coming from his mouth. "Topps is very upset because his boo-bitch is missing, and the drugs she was dropping are missing. And Topps thinks that you know where his bitch and his drugs are. Tell me."

"Man, I swear, I don't know."

"I tried to track her on the fuckin' computer, but it's not working either. You probably had somethin' to do with that shit, too. Now, this the last time I'ma ask you nicely. Where is she?"

Slick kept his eyes shut, trying to squeeze out bleach and soap residue. "Man, I swear, how the fuck should I know?"

"Sorry, dawg, wrong answer." Topps picked up the bat and swung at his head. Blunt force sent the chair backward. Mouth wide open, Slick lay on the concrete floor with blood seeping from his mouth and ears. He was barely conscious.

Topps stood over him looking down. "Topps can't stand mutherfuckers taking what's his. You knew that shit! Not my product, not my bitch, not my kids. Nothing. Got that, you piece of shit!" He dropped the bat and picked up the water hose, placed it in Slick's mouth, and fed the hose deep into his throat. Some duct tape helped to secure it. He turned the water on slow flow.

"Looks like it's gonna be a long night, dawg. But no sweat, we boys. We can hang like that."

Later, his task done, he dragged Slick's water-bloated body out through the secret tunnel before heading back to wash the germs from his hands.

TWENTY-ONE

yra's house was beautiful. The 4,000-square-foot mini-mansion boasted six bedrooms and seven baths with a slew of custom-designed touches. It sat on two acres of desert-landscaped property, complete with an outdoor kitchen, pool and spa. To Hattie it was the kind of home you couldn't feel cozy and comfortable in because it was too luxurious, too clean, and too perfect for everyday living.

The patio where they sat was equipped with a system that sprayed a fine mist of cool water every ten minutes to help fight off the day's typical desert, ninety-six-degree temperature. Myra was glad that it wasn't one of those 110-degree days that she didn't care for or they wouldn't be able to sit outside for more than fifteen minutes.

"Did you talk to that detective today?" Myra asked, fanning her face. She was still a little warm despite only wearing her bathing suit and matching sarong wrapped around her slender hips.

"Yes, I did," Hattie said, smoothing down her beige Bermuda shorts. Even with her white tank top she was warmer than she cared to be. "They said they were doing all they could to find Neema, but just like everybody else with missing loved ones, we have to be patient." She swatted at a pesky fly. It was amazing to her that any flying insect could live in such heat.

"That means they're not really looking." Myra removed a small apple from the bowl of fruit on the patio table. She shielded her eyes to gaze over at the kids to see what they were doing. "That's how they do us; take their time about everything."

"Mama, what about Topps? Did you tell the police about him making threats?"

"I sure did. Until he actually causes me body harm, they can't go after him."

"I bet he knows where Neema is." Myra sipped her icy lemonade.

"I just keep praying she's okay." A missing persons report on Neema had been filed, but it was like Detective Freeman had said; they had to wait for news. Hattie couldn't help feeling that they didn't think Neema was missing or had met with foul play. She simply didn't want to be found.

Myra took a small bite and chewed. "I know, Mama. I know."

"I really appreciate you letting me and the kids stay here. Don't worry, we'll be out of your way as soon as the DMV sends my license and I can get to the bank." Hattie picked up her glass of iced lemonade and kept her eyes on the kids in the shadow part of the lagoon-inspired pool. After ordering a new ATM card, the bank clerk had assured her that it would only take five to ten days to receive it. Without proper identification, an ATM card or her checkbook, it almost took an act of congress to withdraw money.

"I'm only doing what family would do." Myra turned her attention to one of the twins splashing water in Brandon's face. She had to nip it before a fight ensued. "Kalena, stoppit! Leave your cousin alone. I'm not going to tell you again." She turned her attention back to Hattie. "Glen said you guys are welcome to stay as long as it takes. He wanted to tell you himself, but he drives down the hill early in the morning for his rounds at the hospital."

"Bless his heart, and don't let me keep you from going to the shop. I can watch the kids, if you want." Hattie figured that if she was staying for a while, she might as well earn her keep. What's three more kids in her charge?

"Mama, I wouldn't dare dump more kids on you. Actually, I'm thinking about closing the pet shop for a few weeks. I need a vacation, too. But I will have to train my new clerk to do daily feedings and meds while I'm out." She dabbed at her hair in braids, something her husband Glen hated, but Myra couldn't care less. It was the end of August, hot and getting hotter. "If you need any money until you can access your bank account, let me know." A tiny, white dog ran up and jumped into her lap. "How's my baby Princess today? Huh? How's my baby?"

Hattie turned her gaze away to keep from watching Myra let that dog lick her face. She had nothing against dogs, but dogs licked other dogs' privates and ate poop sometimes. Cute was one thing, but it was sickening to watch people all but tongue-kiss dogs. To her, that's what happens when black folks try to act white. Myra probably kissed more on Princess the dog than her own kids.

Brandon and Raynita started arguing about something silly, as usual. To Hattie's horror, Raynita pushed her brother into the pool's deep end. "Nita, no!" Alarmed, she shot up from her seat but relaxed when she saw that Brandon was an excellent swimmer. "Umph. Yeah, now that you mentioned it, I need to get to Target later and buy the kids some clothes so they won't have to smell like smoke."

"Target?" Myra frowned at the name. She was more inclined to shop at Robinsons-May, Nordstrom, and Neiman-Marcus. Target and Walmart did seem more her mother's speed though.

"Yeah. I would go to Walmart, but we've been banned from there. Thanks to Raynita."

Myra only shook her head. "Lordie, I would have died of embarrassment if my kids got caught stealing."

"Imagine how I felt. Anyway, yeah, I could stand some money."

"Here, let me go get it now." Myra shooed Princess from her lap, got up and went to go get some cash. She came back and handed Hattie two thousand dollars before plopping back down. "If you need more, let me know."

"Thanks. Neema will be paying this back. I can take all five kids with me, if you want."

"That's okay, Mama. My kids have some chores to do. They'll be fine."

Hattie didn't fret. There couldn't be too many chores because Myra utilized the services of a cleaning lady three times a week. She had a nagging feeling that Myra feared for her own kids' safety. In a way she couldn't blame her. "I'll need to borrow your car."

"Let's get this clear now," Hattie told Brandon and Raynita two hours later as they stood in front of the Apple Valley Target store entrance. Myra had a problem offering up the keys to her new SUV, but did give up the keys to her old car, a Toyota. "There will be no asking for things we didn't come to get, and absolutely no stealing. Do you hear me, Nita?" She gave a stern look.

"Yes, ma'am."

"We don't want a repeat of what happened at Walmart, right, Brandon?" Hattie asked with a raised brow.

"Yeah, yeah, Nanny. Stop sweating me."

Their shopping time went off without a hitch. Hattie purchased underwear and three outfits and a pair of pajamas for each. She was on her way back to Myra's house, feeling proud of how good the kids had been, when she exited the Target parking lot going right instead of left.

"Nanny, where the hell we going?" Brandon asked after ten minutes of driving east on Bear Valley Road.

"Watch your mouth, young man. And for your information,

we going home." The thought tugged at her heart. She wished she was going home, to her own house, but that wasn't the case. Boarding up her damaged home and having to leave had been the hardest thing she'd ever done. "Back to Aunt Myra's house." She looked to the right and then to the left. Nothing looked familiar. The streets were long between lights and the more she drove, the more rural and undeveloped the surroundings looked. Instead of Apple Valley, they should have named it Death Valley. That's what some parts reminded her of. They drove past large fields of tumbleweeds and Joshua trees.

"Nanny, I think we're going the wrong way."

Like he should know. "Brandon, I know what I'm doing." Truly, she didn't. She'd only visited the city of Victorville twice, and the last time was more than six months ago. "Sit back and let me figure this out." Hattie moved her rearview mirror to look at Brandon. The hard, cold stare of Topps Jackson was looking back at her. She blinked hard and looked again. Darn if he wasn't the splitting image of his father.

"Nanny, can we go to McDonald's?" Raynita wanted to know.

"Sure." Hattie didn't see why not. They had been good at Target. So far, Brandon had used profanity only once, and Raynita hadn't stolen one thing. "As soon as I see one, I'll pull in." She kept looking for something familiar—a landmark of sorts. It was time to turn the vehicle around and head back in the opposite direction. She executed a sharp right onto a side street so she could turn around when she noticed the big, black Denali behind her. The same rims, the same tinted windows. It was the same vehicle she had witnessed parked in front of her house the night of the fire.

"Ohmygawd, no."

"What, Nanny?"

She ignored Raynita's inquiry. Hattie turned the car around and sped back to the main street, putting pedal to the metal as she whipped a left on Bear Valley Road.

"Ah shit, it's Daddy!" Brandon squealed, turned around in his seat.

If she'd had the time, she would've stopped and thumped Brandon's head, but she didn't. Hattie raced up Bear Valley until the traffic slowed. She copped a right into the parking lot of a strip mall and drove to an exit. She had no idea of where she was going or how far she was from Myra's place.

Raynita asked, "Where we going, Nanny?"

"I have no idea. Just hold on tight." Hattie veered to the left before making another quick right onto another side street. The black Denali was still behind her and gaining. Up ahead she spotted a 7-Eleven store. She didn't know if it would do any good or not, but she had to get to it. Topps would be a fool to try something in front of witnesses.

Raynita whined, "Nanny, I'm scared."

"That's cause you a scary-cat baby. I ain't scared of shit."

"Brandon, hush!" With her heart racing, Hattie screeched the car to a stop in front of a gas pump at the 7-Eleven. "Hurry up, get out!" She unbuckled and hopped out, making sure she had the Dooney & Bourke purse Myra had given her, especially with the rest of her cash inside. "Get inside the store," she ordered. "Hurry up!"

"Why we running from my daddy?"

"Brandon, we don't have time for silly questions right now." Hattie escorted the kids inside the cool building. A few customers gave them curious looks before going back to their business.

"Nanny, I'm hungry," Raynita announced for the second time. "Can we get some chips and soda?"

"Yeah. Whatever." Hattie's attention was out the large store window watching the black Denali pull up to the side of the old Corolla. She watched a hooded man dressed in black get out. She couldn't see his face well or his eyes through the dark shades he wore, but she watched in horror as he took out some kind of squirt bottle and sprayed liquid all over her car.

"Oh no, somebody stop that man! Stop him!" Hattie ran to the door but didn't dare step one foot outside. Not with that fool out there. He was crazy! No telling what he would do to her. "Call the police. He's doing something to my car!"

Not one passerby tried to stop him. It had to be Topps Jackson. Hattie almost fainted, watching him light a piece of paper and toss it into her open car window. Screams rang out the second flames burst to life.

"What the hell is he doing?" somebody inside the store screamed. Customers gathered at the window for a look, fearful that the fuel pumps might blow next. Gasps and "ohmygawds" rang out.

"Somebody call nine-one-one. The tanks could explode!" The clerk used speed dial and called for help.

Flames engulfed her car. "Ohmygawd, Lord help us. He's crazy." Hattie watched the hooded man casually climb back into his vehicle and drive away. She felt a sense of relief that he was gone. She shuddered to think of what may have happened if he'd come inside the small convenience store. "You guys okay?"

The children both shook their heads.

A flurry of activity had customers leaving their selections to run for their vehicles and drive away before the fire caused an explosion. A fire truck rolled up on the scene. Two minutes later, Brandon's cell phone rang. Hattie had been holding on to the phone to keep Brandon from having unsupervised contact with his father behind her back. She flipped it up.

"Hello." She was hesitant to put the phone to her ear, like it could be a bomb, then listened to the familiar icy voice.

"Second warning, bitch. Give up the kids or give up your life. What's it gonna be?"

"Never. Over my dead body." Hattie hung up on him.

TWENTY-TWO

"Damn, baby. That was some crazy shit!"

Topps pulled the hood from his head. He was about to burn up from being out of his air conditioned whip handling his business. "For sho. That ol' woman better be glad it was too hot for a nigga to walk up into that store and set it off right."

"For a minute, I thought it was on and cracking." Energized, Gina rubbed her hand along his thigh. "That was fun. Can we go shopping now?"

"Yo', don't give me no grief." Topps licked his lips looking over at her. Now that Neema was missing in action, he and Gina were kicking it pretty heavy. The short, black skirt Gina had on had her luscious brown thighs showing like a mutha. He was digging that red halter top she wore, too. Gina was sexy as hell. "Is that all you can think about? Spending my damn money." For a hot minute, he was glad that she had made the long drive up with him to Victorville. Long drives made him antsy. His appreciation wouldn't last long because Gina was all about Gina. She knew damn well he was going through something heavy dealing with his kids, their missing mother and that damn Hattie, but all she could think about was shopping.

Gina popped her gum, smiling. "No, but you promised that we could check out the outlet stores in Barstow. It's only a half an hour up Highway 15."

"Yeah, I said that shit, but that's after I take care of business."

"Ain't that what you just did?" She popped her gum twice and rolled her eyes.

Topps hated to see women drink too much, smoke nicotine and pop gum. "Do you see my damn kids in this whip?"

"No. I just saw some poor woman scared outta her freaking mind and trying to get away from you."

"What the fuck you say?"

"Nothing."

See. That's what he didn't like about Gina. She was opinionated and mouthy. Mouthy bitches had to be kept in their place at all times. He felt like smacking her good. "What? You have a problem with me trying to be a father to my kids?"

"Baby, no. Forget I said anything. I didn't mean nothing."

"Oh, you meant somethin' all right. Just say what the hell you mean." His fist clutched the steering wheel so hard, his knuckle started swelling.

"I just think that…well, that maybe the kids need to stay put 'til they mama can get them. How you gon' run yo' business with two kids underfoot?"

This ho is mad crazy. Topps pulled the vehicle over and slid the gear into park. "You gotta damn problem with me gettin' my kids?"

"Not really."

"Better not. Shit. You knew the drill before we got involved."

"Baby, I don't have a problem. Damn. Sorry I said anything."

"Damn right, 'cause I know what the hell I'm doing. You in Topps' world right now." He felt like slapping her to get his point across. "They mama is missing and so is my shit she was transporting. She didn't deliver my product and I don't know where the hell she is. She may have left me, but she ain't left them damn kids for good. I know Neema. She'll be back for them kids, and they'll be with me, waiting for her lying, conniving ass."

"Is that right?"

"My word on it, ma. My word." Topps had been thinking about it long and hard. He was closing the business down. Going legit, or something close to it. He'd made up his mind and had already begun moving money from all locations. A shit load of his money was stashed at Gina's condo and she didn't have a clue where. He had so much cash that it was getting harder and harder to hide and keep up with it all. Once everything was all settled, he could relocate to another state. Maybe Florida or Georgia. A couple of times he thought about taking Gina with him. But nah, women like Gina couldn't act right for long. It wasn't in them. "Besides, it's my son, and my daughter. I should be able to have 'em when I feel like it. They my kids!"

"Hell yeah, you should." Gina patted his thigh. "I'm sorry, baby."

"Yeah. You need to be." His lips curled as he rolled his eyes.

"I'm sorry, boo. Don't be mad. Here, let me make it up to you."

"Make it up how?"

"Let me think of something."

Topps blew out hard air. They were on a side street with little traffic. Large, barren fields could be seen in the distance. "Depends on what you have in mind."

"Maybe something like this," Gina said, rubbing the bulge of his crotch. Scooting over, she freed his manhood from his Rocawear sweats, lowered her head to his lap and got busy slurping and sucking.

"Ooh, baby, it's so big. Tastes good, too."

"Damn, girl, you a freak for sho." Topps squeezed her breasts and kept a lookout for anybody walking up on them. For a minute it was hard to concentrate on Gina's lips gliding up and down his shaft when he had so much on his mind: money, shutting down his operations; finding Neema, picking up his kids, and of course, getting revenge. He couldn't let Hattie get away with trying to punk him. "Let me pull around to the back of this building."

The coast looked clear enough for the two of them to climb into the roomy backseat where Topps discovered Gina didn't have on panties beneath her short skirt. In no time he had her skirt hiked up over her hips and one of her breasts hanging out from her black lace bra. With Gina on top, his tongue flicked around her hardened nipple as his hands kept pulling her soft, fleshy rear into his pelvis. Topps had his sweats pulled down enough to get the job done, sliding in and out of her warm wetness with hard, but smooth gliding.

Gina threw her head back. "Oh yeah, baby, do it. Do me harder. Make this pussy work, baby. Squeeze my ass. I'm coming..."

Dirty words to his ears made him pump faster, harder until he couldn't hold back any longer. Spent, the two disengaged breathing hard. They fixed their clothes before some nosey person walked up and caught them with their pants down, literally.

"Can we go shopping now?" Gina didn't give up.

"Hell yeah, girl. We'll get a room first, get cleaned up, then we can go shopping."

TWENTY-THREE

yra was a nervous wreck when she arrived at the 7-Eleven to pick them up. Hattie couldn't blame her. The whole situation with Topps, the kids and not knowing if Neema was kidnapped, hurt, or dead or alive was starting to take its toll with nervous energy and more than her usual share of headaches. She'd even noticed two strands of gray hair growing at her edges and she couldn't have that. The pit of her stomach was starting to get that burning feeling with each passing day—all from worrying.

After the police had taken a report and talked to all cooperating witnesses, there was nothing more to talk about. Myra had felt like crying watching Sutton Towing load up her old vehicle to be carted away to some wrecking yard. She never drove the thing; still, the car held some sentimental value. It was a reminder of where she had come from.

"One of the kids had to tell him where you were, Mama. How else would he know that you're up here in Victorville?" They were loaded in Myra's SUV and on their way back to her house.

"I asked the kids, Myra. They didn't call and tell 'im."

"What if they're lying? It wouldn't be the first time." Myra gripped her steering wheel and looked back at Brandon through her rearview mirror. The boy was crazy about his father, and in his eyes, Topps, could do no wrong. Yeah, he was probably the culprit. It was a shame that his twisted parental love was about to get all three of them killed. "You called your father, didn't you, Brandon? Admit it?"

"What's it to you?" Brandon sneered back.

"Boy, so help me, I will pull this car over and beat the snot…"

"Myra, please. He's no perfect angel, but I believe that he understands we have a serious problem going on here. I don't think the kids would call and tell their father where they are." Hattie blew out a weary breath. "Besides, I've been holding on to his cell phone."

"Mama, think about it, if that lunatic followed you to Target, chances are he knows where I live, too. This is too much. If Glen finds out, he'll have a fit."

"Well, we don't want that." Her words hit hard. Myra didn't have to say it. Hattie could feel it. Staying at her house put her family in jeopardy. Still, it was too late for what she coulda or shoulda done. "Sweetie, I know this is a real inconvenience for you. Maybe me and the kids should go back to the house. We could stay in the garage 'til the house is ready."

"Mama, don't be ridiculous."

"Maybe a hotel or motel." Hattie turned her gaze out the passenger's side, hoping Myra would disagree. The thought of sleeping in a bed once occupied by a host of strangers made her skin crawl. And if she was fighting a war against a monster, she needed all the family support she could get. Obviously, Topps Jackson was a madman that didn't care who got hurt as long as he got his way.

"When will our mama come get us?" Raynita wanted to know. "I miss her."

Hattie swiveled around in the plush leather seat. "Soon, I hope. Real soon." Words easy to say. She wished she knew for sure.

What if Neema ran off and abandoned her kids? The horrible thought kept popping into her head, taunting her. "Baby, don't worry, she's probably taking a little break."

"Yeah, and I'm the Queen of Egypt," Myra mumbled.

"I wanna go home to my own damn house," Brandon announced. "I wanna play with my friends and ride my new bike."

"Soon, Brandon, soon." Hattie sighed. She was too tired to make a fuss over his profanity. What she had noticed about the kids, in a disturbing way, was how immune and nonchalant they were to drama. Seeing the car go up in flames had Raynita upset and teary eyed for a minute, but a bag of chips and ice cream sandwich had taken care of that. And Brandon? Humph. Nothing seemed to really faze the boy. He had gazed at the flaming vehicle like it was bonfire around a camp site. "I hear they have a nice setup at one of those Extended Stay hotels."

Myra shook her head. "Yeah, if you like giving money away. Nah, y'all need to stay put for a while. I only wish Neema would bring her behind home and put an end to this madness."

Hattie couldn't agree more. "I guess I should put my own car in the shop and have the engine repaired. I'm really sorry about your car. The police should be mailing out a report for your insurance company."

"Mama, don't worry about it. Everyone is safe; that's what's important. We'll get through this." Myra smiled over at her. Of all the times she'd tried to persuade Hattie to come up and spend some time at her house, it would have to be under trying circumstances.

"Where's the kids?" Hattie noticed that Princess the dog came with her, but not Trayvon and the twins. Princess was dressed in a rhinestone doggy-jacket.

"At home with the nanny. The twins had homework to finish

up. And you know Tray. If there's no video game involved, he can't be bothered."

Hattie wasn't listening. Her house was unavailable; her car was in need of repair. She couldn't get to her own money. Her life was upside down and she wasn't sure what to do about it. And Neema. She never prayed so hard in her life for Neema to call or show back up. She simply wanted to know if her daughter was alive and well; she would even forget about being mad at her. Well, maybe after she slapped her a couple of times.

Later that evening, after a good supper of pot roast, garlic bread, mashed potatoes, and salad, after the kids were bathed and in bed, Hattie sat on the bed in the guest room where she had been sleeping, trying to make sense of everything that had happened. She'd called the precinct earlier to see if Detective Moon had learned anything new of Neema's whereabouts. Nothing. No activity on her bank account. No phoned-in tips. It didn't seem like they were trying hard enough to find her daughter. Hattie had slammed the kitchen phone down in the detective's ear.

"I'm sorry," she said when Myra had looked at her like she was crazy. "This is so frustrating. It's driving me crazy not knowing."

"They still haven't heard anything?" Myra asked, removing items from her top-of-the-line dishwasher. Princess was at her side, watching her every move. The dog was devoted. "At least we know that she's not in some hospital or the morgue. They do check."

"So they say. According to Detective Moon, there's still no activity on her bank account. They've been interviewing people from her home phone contacts, but no one seems to know anything." Her eyes welled up. "This don't feel like one of her little stunts. Something is wrong this time, Myra. I believe that fool has done something to her. I can feel it."

"I know. I was thinking the same thing." Myra had made some

chamomile tea. She was ready for bed with her cream-hued satin robe, gown, and matching slippers. "Here, Mama," she said, bringing her a cup of steaming tea. "This should help you sleep." The two sat down at the elegant dining room table. It was mainly a room for show, as Myra rarely entertained or ate at the five-thousand-dollar, hand-carved table.

"I need some sleep. I feel so tired."

"Oh, and if you need a car to get around in, I still have my old Honda stored in the garage. Dusty, but it runs good. I've been saving it for Trayvon's first car."

"Thanks, Myra. You have really been a big help."

"No problem. I just wish there was more that I could do. And, well, that's why I wanted to run something by you."

Hattie perked up. "Something like what?"

"I was thinking that…well…" Myra stirred her tea furiously. "I know this guy, and he helps people with problems."

"What kind of problems?" Hattie's tone was calm, curious.

"Whatever problem you have. Actually, he's a friend through Glen. Glen was his doctor when he was diagnosed with colon cancer some years back. His cancer went into remission and he sort of took a liking to Glen, you know, like a good friend."

Hattie raised a brow. "And?" She'd been at Myra's house for several days and seen her son-in-law, Glen, only once. Doctors stayed busy. She knew that, but goodness, what's the point of having a man if you never get to see him? "You bring this up to say what?"

"Uh, well…that he can help you. He's what you could call an 'equalizer.' He can make it all go away. He can make Topps go away."

Surely she wasn't suggesting what she thought. "Go away, like in kill somebody?"

"Mama, if that's what it takes."

"You want me to have the kids' father killed?" Hattie was staring at her incredulously because that was exactly her suggestion. "Myra, you can't be serious."

Myra blinked and looked away, then made eye contact again. "Mama, look, sometimes people are put in situations where they don't have choices. That's how life is." Her eyes glistened and there was an urgency in her tone to help her mother resolve this matter. The sooner, the better before Glen put his foot down. "His name is B. Kelly, but he goes by the name of Bruno."

"Myra, it's a sin to kill. You need to read your Bible."

"And it's a shame to sit back and let yourself be killed. It's not like I'm talking about you killing the man yourself."

"Girl, what is wrong with you? It's like I don't even know who you are." Hattie shot up from her seat. "I'm a Christian, not a killer." She wanted the madness with Topps Jackson to be over with, too, but one thing was certain: She wasn't about to take another person's life.

Myra shot up, too. "Mama, you can't sit back and do nothing!" she fumed. "You either have to solve the problem or give the man his kids. Just give the damn kids to him! Why can't he have 'em?"

Was she out of her damn mind? Hattie glared at her with hot resentment. This wasn't about solving the problem for the kids' sake. It was for Myra's sake. Myra's perfect little world was being disturbed and she couldn't deal with it. It was as clear as glass.

"You can talk until you're blue in the face, but he's not getting his hands on Nita and Brandon. If he does, it'll be over my dead body."

"Mama, he's their father. Give the man what he wants, so he can leave you alone! You can always take him to court and get the kids legally. He's their biological father, for crying out loud!"

Hattie narrowed her eyes at her. "He may be the father, but

that don't make it right. Neema left those kids with me, and I promised her that I would give them back to her. Not the father."

"But what if she don't show back up, then what?"

It was a horrible thought to consider. "Well, I'll have to cross that bridge when I get to it."

"Mama, you're just being stubborn."

"Myra, mothers give up on kids every single day. I know I can't save all the kids in the world, but I plan to do all I can to save just two. Just two!"

"Mama, I know you love those kids; I'm just saying it's not worth getting killed over."

"If that's the Lord's will, so be it. At least I'll leave this earth knowing I did the best that I could, which is more than a lot of mothers and grandmothers can say. As long as I have God's love on my side, we'll be okay."

"Mama, if you think love will get you out of this…" The phone rang, startling the two women.

Being that it was close to midnight, the only person Myra knew that called the house so late was her husband, Glen, to let her know how much longer he would be. Myra sucked air through her teeth before going to answer it. "Hello."

An unfamiliar voice asked to speak to Hattie. Actually it asked for "that bitch Hattie."

"Who is this? How'd you get this number?"

The voice demanded to speak to Hattie.

"Mama, it's for you." Myra reached the receiver out to her, then stood watching.

Hattie put the phone to her ear. "Who is this?"

The voice said, "You know who the fuck it is, ol' lady. Last chance. My kids or yo' life. Make a choice."

"Over my dead body!" Hattie slammed the receiver down so hard that a searing pain resonated in her hand.

TWENTY-FOUR

"That stank-assed witch!" Topps took Gina's cell phone and flung it against the living room wall. The instrument made a small hole in the thin drywall before it shattered. Gina ran out from her bathroom to see what was up. "Neema's mammy think I'm playing with her ass."

"What the hell? Nigga, why you do that? I just got that phone last week."

"Yo', who gives a shit, Gina. I'll get you a better one."

"That's not the point, Topps. It was my phone, not yours."

"I said, who gives a shit!" His malcontent was like a sickness eating away at him. Each passing day was another day of failure. He still didn't know where Neema was. Still didn't have his kids. Couldn't move on without closure. "I'm sick of shit, I know that."

Slick was gone. His ashes scattered here and there. His soldiers had been disbursed. All three warehouses were shut down until further notice. It was a notice that wouldn't be coming. Former workers were lucky. They had been spared their lives. His first inclination had been to pop every last one of them, but such a task seemed tremendous, even for him. What did it matter if they told about his drug business now? He was closed down, all product moved and sold. The bulk of his cash was stashed in Swiss accounts, fat and waiting. Secret safes had been filled to the brim with his money. *Money, money and mo money.* He was a man set for life. He had everything except for his children.

Between moving drugs, buying up old land, loan-sharking and a few scattered franchises, Topps Jackson had accumulated enough money not to have to work another day in his life. Still, he was discontent. Restless syndrome. With no drugs to run, no business to oversee, he now had time on his hands. Too much time was driving him crazy. He glared at Gina, waiting for that skank to say one more thing he didn't like... He didn't have to wait long.

"Baby, maybe you need to get out and get some air. You agonizing too much about those kids. Leave 'em be for now."

"Say what, Gina?" His eyes locked on her like radar. She had just gotten out the shower and was standing there with a large white towel wrapped around her. Gina was jealous of his kids. That's why she kept making little snide remarks about them. Just like a bitch. Always jealous about some shit she can't control.

"Baby, look, I'm only saying that you're getting too upset about those kids. It's not like they're with a complete stranger. Let 'em be with they grandmother 'til their mother shows back up. That's all."

Topps got up. Gina's jealousy reminded him of his mother. Lanette had been a jealous bitch, too. That jealousy had seeped out of her daily, like a stench. It had caused her to treat him like he were somebody's stepchild that didn't deserve much in life. Always taking shit away from him. Taking everything that could cause him some happiness. He grinned, thinking of how the last laugh had been on him when her ass had starved to death.

He had been an only child for Lanette Wrider. The perfect little boy to a young mother who couldn't seem to find the right path in life. Lanette had tried college. It wasn't for her. She had tried opening her own business, a dress shop. That didn't work for long. Then, Mack Jackson had blown into her life some time after that. According to his mother, Mack was handsome and smart. Mack loved her. He would make everything better. Mack had brought hope, security and dreams. Then, Mack brought hard drugs into his mother's life.

Finding a needle sticking out the arm of his passed-out mother became the norm. Days when his mother was good, she was good; but those days became as rare as having food in the house, heat to keep them warm—clean clothes to wear. Topps had been young, but saw depression slipping in like some lowly thief. His father, Mack, came around every now and then—long enough to keep his mother addicted. Then came the hate. Topps' young eyes had watched resentment eat away at his mother day after day. Mothers who hate men sometimes hate the sons they produce. Unnecessary scolding and beatings proved it. Hatred was like jealousy.

Topps couldn't stand an envious woman, and lately, he was spending a hell of a lot of time with one. Gina didn't have any kids, so she couldn't stand his. Gina probably didn't care if Neema showed back up or not. That's how jealousy worked.

Gina was walking away from him.

"Yo', what the hell you trying to say, Gina? Why you keep jaw-jackin' and trippin' about my kids?"

"Fuck, Topps, ain't nobody trippin' but you. You the one keep drivin' back and forth to the damn desert terrorizing folks. They livin' with they grandmother, big deal. Stop trippin' and leave them people alone."

That was all she wrote. For a tall man it was amazing how fast he could move. Blam. In her face. He was at her side like a blown gust of winter wind. He grabbed and started choking on her neck. "Bitch!"

Gina tried to scream, but with no exchange of air, it was a major task.

"This is the last time I'm warning you about yo' damn mouth. Ain't nobody asked you a damn thang!" He had her pinned to the new beige carpet, gagging, trying to scream. Each time it seemed that she would pass out for sure, he let up. Stingy with air, but she could breathe.

Eyes bulging, Gina coughed and gagged.

"Ain't nobody taking shit away from me as long as I live! You hear me, Gina? No damn body!" He released the grip on her neck, grabbed her by her long blondish-brown weave and dragged her to the bathroom kicking and screaming.

"Topps, stop it. I didn't mean nothin'! Let me go!" The carpet burned her skin.

"Not 'til yo' ass understand what I'm saying. That ol' tramp ain't keeping my kids and that's word. Them my fuckin' kids. Mine!"

"All right already! I'm sorry."

Like a man on a mission he ignored her pleading.

In the bathroom he turned on the water in the tub, and saw the terror register in her eyes. That pleased him. "I wish yo' stank ass would try to get up and scat."

Gina tried to claw her way up, but Topps was much stronger. He did a perfect execution of grabbing her frame and grappling her down into the cold water. "Stupid thoughts come from a dirty mind, Gina. That's why yo' thoughts are so fucked up; you need to clean out yo' mind. Wash those dirty thoughts out."

"Get the hell off of me. You crazy mutherfucker! I ain't play-ing with your ass!"

Topps wasn't playing either as his big hand saddled her face and pushed it down into the water. "You a strong bitch, Gina, but dirt is dirt. I'ma help yo' dirty ass get clean."

She fought and splashed with all her might but couldn't stop his assault. The fear of dying flashed in her eyes, and then Topps allowed her up for air only to push her head back into the water. Maybe next time she'd keep that mouth of hers shut. "Are you clean yet? Huh, Gina? I can't hear you."

Finally, when he felt her struggle getting weaker he let her up for air. "That's better, ain't it? Clean as a mutherfucker. See. That's what I'm talkin' 'bout." He stood up straight. Gina was a hot mess to look at with wet snot hanging, face twisted, hair all wild. Pleased, Topps smiled. Keeping bitches in line was a neverending job. Tiresome, too. He could hear his stomach growling.

"Yo', Gina. I'm hungry! Get yo'self together, woman. Fix yo' man some food."

After washing his hands and towel-drying off, Topps went into the kitchen to check on the food supply. It was Gina's idea for him to move in with her while he listed and sold his big house. At his former residence too many of his soldiers knew where he lived. A lot of his enemies knew, too. He couldn't have that. The plan was to start new and fresh once he got the kids back and settled. He could move to another state and buy a new house, maybe even start up a new drug business where he could start training his son. Brandon was nearing the right age to be recruited. He even had big plans for Raynita. Her innocent face could probably move a lot of drugs without suspicion. Keeping it all in the family. That's what it was all about.

"Gina! Don't keep me waitin'!"

Sharing habitats with Gina was okay for a minute, but like a lot of skanks he knew, she talked too damn much. He couldn't have no skank trying to run his business, personal life or otherwise, especially when it came to his kids. That was the downside. Another problem staying at Gina's place was its size. It was a small dwelling with only two bedrooms. Still, he liked that none of his former associates knew its location. Though he still slept with a gun beneath his pillow, he felt somewhat safe. After pulling up the carpet in the spare bedroom closet and pulling up a few floorboards, he'd found the perfect place to store some of his cash.

Pearly, Gina's white Persian cat, padded softly into the room. The animal purred before rubbing up against his leg.

"Hey there, little pussy." He picked the cat up, stroking its soft fur. "You hungry, too?" He had weakness for defenseless animals. He had a puppy once when he was around nine. Found the poor thing shivering under a bus stop bench on his way home from school. Topps still recalled how he took the puppy up, happy to have something to love—and ultimately, something that would love him back. He had taken the puppy home and fed it warm milk and cold cuts, prepared to raise it. But when his mother had awakened from her drug-induced coma, she was livid.

"Little negro boy, you must be crazy! I ain't tryin' to feed another damn mouth!" his mother had screamed at him. His nine-year-old eyes had watched in horror as she took up the puppy, and marched it out the house to the fence. His mother put the frightened puppy outside the gate with a hard swat to its little behind. "You git now! Gon' now. Get on outta here!"

Two days later, he discovered the puppy's maggot-filled, ravaged body. He had cried two days behind that incident.

"Yeah. You look hungry." Topps put the cat down and located some cans of cat food. He opened a can and put it on a paper plate. "There you go, partner. Handle that for now." He washed his hands two times before heading to the living room to click on the fifty-two-inch plasma television. Maybe some tube would help settle his nerves. Smoking a blunt would probably do the trick, but he wanted to keep a clear head when he drove back to Victorville later. "Gina! I'm still waitin'. Damn, boo, what's taking you so long?!"

Dressed in a red sundress with wide straps, Gina appeared. Her eyes were bloodshot red, almost a perfect match to her dress. She had a bruise on her forehead and a few scratches on her face. More battle scars. For some reason her nose looked larger.

"Boo, I'm sorry. You know how I get." Topps pulled a small vial of coke from his pocket, and then used a credit card to section off a few thin lines on the glass coffee table. "Look what I got for you, baby. Come try this shit. It's good stuff."

Gina stood looking skeptical.

"Baby, I said, I'm sorry." Topps looked up, making his face appear as sympathetic as possible for a brutal man who secretly believed that women were beneath him. "You know how I feel about my kids. I'm stressed like a mutha' right now. But it's gon' get better. You'll see. Once I get my business handled, find another house, things will get better."

Gina didn't crack a smile. Didn't say a word.

"I'ma make it up to you, boo. You'll see." He waited for a reply that didn't come. "Can you fix me a sandwich? Throw some of that Cajun turkey and black forest ham on some bread. Don't forget the mustard and some of those little peppers I like."

Gina stared at him. Her still-nervous hand rubbed at the tender redness along her light-complexioned neck before dismissing herself to the kitchen to fix Topps something to eat.

"Thanks, boo. We can go shopping later, if you want. Maybe go look at that silver Range Rover you been wanting so bad." Topps fixed his attention back to the large plasma screen where the sad and pitiful faces of hungry children stared back at him. *Feed The Children*, that's what the show was called. "Look at that shit," he mumbled. A damn shame, if you asked him. *Hell*, he thought indignantly, *Why can't the folks over there with the camera doing the exploiting feed they asses? What's up with that?*

He had a wad of money sitting on the table. Topps picked it up. He waited for the program to show the address so he could freeze it on the screen. It couldn't hurt to send a few bills that way. Help some starving black kids with a meal or two. He got up to go find some stamps and an envelope.

TWENTY-FIVE

"Wake up. C'mon now. Open your eyes."

The voice was clear but unrecognizable. Neema Jean's eyelids fluttered before opening. She remained calm even with the intense green eyes that stared down into hers. She'd never been so close to eyes that green in her life. At least not that she could recall. Green eyes in a pink face she'd never seen before. It was almost spooky. The white jacket he wore hinted toward the medical field. Lips smiled down at her.

"How you feeling?" Green-eyes asked, then sat in a wooden chair next to the small bed.

The room was large and nondescript. A bed, a small dresser, a wooden chair. Nothing on the off-white walls, but the smell of peppermint and strong ammonia was distinct. Her eyes swept around her unfamiliar surroundings. If this was a hospital, it looked cold and cheap. If this was someone's personal residence, they needed a serious decorator. Her trembling hand fumbled to the top of her head where it was bandaged.

"What happened to me?" she queried through dry, cracked lips.

"First things first, let's have a good look at you." Green-eyes aimed a pin light at her eyes, raised one lid, then the other. "Pupils are more reactive. That's a good sign."

"Who you?" Bad English, but that was the least of her problems.

"Relax. I'm a doctor. You've suffered a concussion from a head injury. Do you know what day of the week it is?" He stood and produced a stethoscope to listen to her heart. "Take a deep breath and let it out slowly."

"What day?" Neema tried to think. That information was on the tip of her tongue...somewhere. "It's...uh..." *Dang. What day is it?* Neema's attention flew to the door where another white man entered. Wearing a white knit shirt and dark Dockers, he was dressed as casual as Green-eyes. Average build, not too thin or too fat, his blue-eyed expression showed genuine concern.

Blue-eyes walked over to stand next to the doctor. "How's the patient?"

Dr. Green-eyes stood up. "She'll live."

"I really appreciate you making a house call to check on her."

"No problem. She might have some lingering memory problems for a while. That's normal for this kind of head injury. Aside from a couple of bruised ribs, she's pretty darn lucky for not wearing a seatbelt. Oh, and here's something for pain." Green-eyes passed a bottle of pills to Blue-eyes. "Just follow instructions. Can't stay. I have another house call to make."

"Thanks again, Doc."

"Sure thing." Dr. Green-eyes packed up a new-looking black briefcase and left.

Suddenly the idea of being alone with Blue-eyes hit her. Neema threw off the bedcovers and swung her feet to the floor. "I'm out of here." Her attempt to stand up was greeted with a weakness to her knees. The room was spinning, making her clutch her nauseated stomach. "Oh God..." Her head felt like a container full of cotton balls. Blue-eyes rushed over before she hit the floor.

"Hey. Not so fast. You need to rest until you're feeling better."

"I need to go home." Home. She tried to think of where that place might actually be.

"Let me help you back to bed."

If he meant to harm her, he could have done so by now. Neema felt nothing but good vibes radiating from his persona. He was a stranger with whom she felt an uncanny amount of relaxation. She allowed herself to be made comfortable. He fluffed her pillow.

"There. Are you hungry? I'm not the best cook, but I can make toast and eggs."

"Who are you? How'd I get here, and where am I?" His attentiveness amused her, reminded her of a doting father. If she had to guess, she would put him in his early sixties. Warm eyes. Warm smile, but how did she know him?

Blue-eyes took a wooden chair, flipped it around and straddled it backward, which was pretty good for a man in his sixties. "John West is printed on my birth certificate. Friends call me West. I'm a private investigator. I was hired to follow you and that boyfriend of yours."

"Boyfriend? Hired by who, and follow me for what?" Neema watched him with the sharpness of an eagle. She didn't dare blink lest she miss something.

"Let's just say that this guy named TJ wanted to see if you were creeping on him. Wanted dates and pictures. He hired me and I gave him what he wanted."

"TJ? Creeping?"

"Yeah, you know, sneaking around behind his back. Sleeping with his friend, Slick. Damn adamant about it, too. The best-paying customer I ever had. I tell ya' if all my jobs paid like him, I'd be rich." What he wanted to add was how much she reminded him of his late daughter.

She had no idea what he was talking about. "And was I cheating?" Her stomach was growling on the low, but eating could wait.

"Pretty much so. I kept some of the photos. The way it was looking, your man, your boyfriend, whatever you want to call him, was going to have you terminated. My job was to get him his proof, get paid and be out the picture, but there was something about that guy TJ I didn't like. I could see murder coming. I kept following you, keeping track to see what was up."

"You're lying. I don't know a TJ, and I don't know you."

"Your memory is on the blink right now, but your name is Neema. Neema Jean Sims. You have two kids. A boy, a girl. You were slammed from behind by a truck almost two weeks ago. It was a hit-and-run because the driver took off. You hit your head pretty bad. I loaded you back in your vehicle and brought you here before the police arrived. With that hidden cargo you were carrying, you'd be in jail by now if the cops had gotten to you first."

"What hidden cargo? Wait a minute…I have kids?"

"They're with your mother right now. Her name is Hattie Sims. I'm very good at doing my homework."

"TJ?" Neema forced herself to think as hard as she could, but the name was elusive. If what West was saying was true, she really was experiencing some kind of memory loss. "If my mother has my kids, where is she now?"

"Good question." West ran a liver-spotted hand through his brown hair graying at the temples. "I've been too busy seeing after you."

She wanted to see proof. "ID. Where's my driver's license?"

"That, I should be asking you. When I took you from the scene, I checked the vehicle you were driving. There was no purse. No wallet, just a cell phone that I tossed."

"Why do that? I could have called somebody that knows me."

"TJ would have found you by now. He's pretty cunning. He would have tracked you through your cell phone."

Neema surveyed the room. "I told you, I don't know no damn TJ!"

"Don't worry, it'll come to you." West stood up and looked at her.

"And where are we?" The room's drabness was bringing her mood down.

"A house I own in Palo Verdes. Nothing fancy, but I keep it as a place to crash when I'm in town. I brought you here after the accident."

Her hand reached for her face to confirm a few cuts, scratches and bruises. "How long have I been here?"

"Close to a week, in and out of consciousness. Anyway, little lady, enough questions for now. I'll get you something to eat. You get some rest. I'll be right back."

Neema must have dozed off. The next thing she knew West was back with a tray of food: Lightly scrambled eggs, crispy bacon, toast with jam, orange juice, and creamed coffee.

"Here you go. My friend Doc been taking real good care of you, keeping you hydrated, but you gotta be starving by now."

"Hell yeah." Her voracious appetite had her chowing down like a homeless person that hadn't eaten in weeks. In a sad way, that's exactly what she was. She stopped to reflect for a minute. She had kids somewhere, a mother, and probably a home, too. But where? Tears found their way to her eyes, but she went back to eating. Pleased, West sat watching her.

Much later, Neema had some of her strength back, enough for West to help her get in a tub of water. Soaking in some fragrant liquid was like floating up to heaven to ease her aches and soreness. West was the perfect gentleman that kept a towel draped around her the whole time. Not once did he try to sneak a peek or cop a feel on her bruised, slender body. Not that she had anything to be ashamed of. One thing she did know, her body was tight. A few stretch marks on her stomach, but still it was so flat that it was hard to believe she was somebody's mother. Alone in the bathroom, she lifted her gown and ran her hand over her C-section scar. "Yeah, it looks like some birthing been done."

She sat on the toilet. Taking up the hand-held mirror for a peek below made her smile. Still, it looked good and tight. On impulse she touched the pink pearl of her womanhood, ready to make pleasure, but there was a knock on the bathroom door. "Yeah?"

"Everything okay in there?"

"Yeah. Be out in a minute."

"If you feel dizzy or you need any help, let me know."

"Thanks, West." Neema stood up and put on the T-shirt and thick, white robe West had given her, obviously his. "Wow, I can't believe I'm really somebody's mother."

After her much-needed bath, West sat talking to her in his spacious kitchen, revealing bits of information about her that she should know. It was like he was talking Greek.

"Here's a picture of you and your kids." West passed the photo to her. He always made extras of his work, in case a client lost the ones he turned over.

"These are my kids?" Neema experienced a tug at her heart, but that was all she felt. Try as she might, the two young faces held no recollection. "What's their names?"

"I believe I heard you call the boy Brandon and the girl Raynita." He didn't tell her how he had once sat next to her on a park bench. She talked on a cell phone but took time to stop and yell at her kids on the playground equipment. He had taken pictures with a hidden camera each opportunity she moved away from him or turned her back.

"And my name is Neema?" She made a face. "I don't feel like a Neema."

"That's the name my client referred to you as. I ran the license on your Land Rover and it's registered to a Neema Jean Sims."

"Wow. I have a Land Rover?" She had no idea what a Land Rover was but it sounded like something worth having. "And you say my kids are with my mother?"

"The last time I checked. The problem is, your mother might be in danger as well. I drove by her home the other day and saw some fire damage."

"And?" The more she heard, the more the story sounded like a bad dream.

"Her house was boarded up. I doubt she's staying there." He passed her a picture of a woman standing out in front of a house watching a black car pull off. "That's Hattie, your mother. You have a sister that spends every other Sunday at your mother's house. Her name is Myra. Here's a picture of her and her kids leaving your mother's house. I ran her license plates to find out she lives in Victorville. I'm thinking that your mother might be there. I'm sure they're very worried about you by now. "

"Hattie?" Nothing he was saying sounded familiar. She accepted the next photo from him. "And this is?"

"The father of your children. My client. The man that's probably looking for you as we speak. He introduced himself as TJ, but I checked him out as well. Topps Jackson, one of L.A.'s biggest druglords. Hiring my services was probably his way of keeping a lid on his personal business."

"I...I don't recognize any of these people." Hattie Sims. Raynita. Myra. Brandon. These were the names of her people, yet they were all the names of strangers to her. She kept challenging her brain cells to come up with something but couldn't. Nothing. Nada. It was all so frustrating, not to mention, exhausting. "I must be a bad person." Neema wiped at the tears that welled. "That's why my life is jacked up. I was a bad person, right?"

West stood up from the table. He cast sympathetic eyes down at her. "Not bad, just involved with some bad people. It happens." He sniffed and looked away before running a hand through his hair. "You remind me of my daughter. Her name was Sandy, but she's gone now. Murdered by a cold-hearted drug dealer like TJ. I waited too late to save her."

Neema's eyes met his. "Is that why you're helping me? Because I remind you of your daughter?"

"You need to get some rest." West moved to the kitchen window and peered out. The sun was just slipping behind a purple-pink horizon. He could smell the honeysuckle he'd planted last spring. This was his temporary crib, and he missed his Kent, Washington home. "Look, I have to go out for a few hours. You'll be safe here."

"You're avoiding my question?" Neema persisted, keeping her eyes on him. "You don't know me and I have no money to pay you. Why are you doing this for me?" She tugged the robe close to her. "What's in it for you, West?"

"I don't know." West shook his head before heading out the room. "Another young woman with kids. Lives in danger. It's like I said, it's too late to save my daughter the first go-round. Maybe it's my way of saving her the second time around, through you. Call it restitution." He perked up. "Anyway, I'll bring some dinner back. Stay in bed and get some rest." After throwing that out into the universe, he left.

TWENTY-SIX

"Glen, this is my family we're talking about. Surely you don't expect me to just throw them out to the wolves."

Myra felt close to tears, not that tears would help. They had never been effective on Glen. Maybe it was something that they taught doctors in med school.

"Myra, I'm doing what we should have done to begin with." They were in the massive kitchen where Glen was stirring sugar into his morning cup of black coffee. He took three sips from the cooled brew before sitting the cup down. "I don't want another incident like the one that happened the other day."

"Mama needs more time before the insurance company repairs her house and she can move back home." She thought about what she'd just said. Even that didn't seem like the right solution, not with that…that maniac still out there.

"That's understandable, Myra, but she can't stay here. Not with some lunatic on her trail. If you'd told the truth about this situation to begin with, I would have paid to put them up in a nice hotel. Admit it. You lied about what was going on."

Glen had finally expressed that Hattie and the kids would probably be safer at another location. Normally, to keep peace, Myra went along with whatever program was passed down from Glen. But, for crying out loud, this was her family. "Glen, Mama is scared, and I'm scared for her. She needs to be around family that can help her with this. Not kicked out like some dog that has too many fleas."

"Look, Myra, I understand what you're saying, but you're being overly emotional about this. I care about your mother and your niece and nephew, too, but we have to consider the safety of our own family. I'm scared for you and the kids. You never mentioned some crazed maniac burning her house. And then he burns the car she was driving. Sorry." He shook his head. "It's too dangerous."

"I didn't care about that old car."

"Myra, that's not the point. My mind is made up about this. I called and talked with Mr. Kelly. He assured me that he could keep her and the kids safe until this mess clears up or blows over. He'll be greatly compensated."

"But Glen, honey…."

"Myra, it's end of story." Banging down his mug, Dr. Glen Bradshaw huffed and stalked out of the cheerful, yellow room.

Myra watched his wide shoulders walk away from her. She felt like taking off her shoe and throwing it behind his big, stubborn head. Glen made her sick—sometimes made her question why she'd chosen him for a husband. This was one of those times. He wasn't the most handsome man she'd dated, not with his head seemingly too large for his frame. He possessed the most piercing gray eyes that could stare clean through you one minute and melt you down with his warmth the next. An average girth looked good on his five-foot-ten frame, but it was his confidence that made him appear taller. Once he spoke, anyone with a brain could tell that he was educated, cunning and articulate with his speech. Glen could sell a box of fresh air.

"What if this were your mother? Would you be so quick to put her out?" The master bedroom was on the first level, a vanilla-hued room with a custom-made, round bed dressed in vanilla trimmed in burgundy satin. Potted plants were everywhere. Like a petulant child, Myra stomped behind him.

"To answer your question, my actions would be the same to keep my family safe."

"Family should stick together," Myra persisted.

"True, but if you're not careful, family can get you killed. If it wasn't for family, your mother wouldn't be in this precarious predicament." Glen was standing at the wide sweep of mirror running a charged shaver over his caramel-hued face. His attire consisted of dark Dockers, a light-blue shirt and sensible shoes. His tone softened when he spotted the stress that was blatant on Myra's face. "Sweetheart, I know you're upset right now, but I've already taken the liberty to make arrangements for your mother. You have to trust me on this one. It's the right thing to do, and she'll be fine."

"What kind of damn arrangements?" So what if she sounded ghetto or loud; no one treated her family like crap. Her mother had loved and supported her through four years of college and wouldn't accept a dime for rent and food. If it hadn't been for her going to college, she wouldn't have met Glen in the nearby donut shop.

"Instead of us taking a chance driving Hattie to Mr. Kelly's place, we thought..."

"We?"

"Let me explain now. Mr. Kelly and I both felt that it would be better if he came here for her. He should be here at nine to pick your mother and the kids up. This is a huge favor he's doing for me, so try to be understanding."

Myra kept staring at the side of his head. If her eyes could shoot bullets, he'd be dead.

"I need you to make sure everyone is packed up and ready to

go. On my desk in the study, I left two envelopes with some cash. One is addressed to your mother. It should be enough cash to hold her over until she gets her business straight with her bank. The other is for Mr. Kelly."

"And what if Mama don't wanna go into hiding with some stranger? I tried asking her how she felt about it…"

"Sweetheart." Glen stopped her with a professional glare. "Sometimes we don't have choices in life. I gotta go." He fetched his briefcase, then gave her a quick kiss. "Any news on your sister?"

Myra's heart squeezed at the mention of Neema. "No. Not yet."

"That's too bad."

"Yeah, it is." She and her baby sister had never been the closest. Too much sibling rivalry for their mother's attention was the culprit. Still, she'd give anything to hug Neema about now, to talk to her, to know that she was safe. Tears welled up.

"Just keep checking with the detective that's working the case. Something is bound to turn up."

Myra stood with her hands folded at her chest. "God, I hope so." She wiped her tears away. Every time she tried to think positive, negativity kept slipping in. What if Neema was dead? What if she was being held hostage and being tortured? How long could her mother keep her distance from the kids' father? All thoughts overwhelmed her. She wasn't eating, wasn't sleeping good. And her pet grooming business was being run by her staff. It was no doubt they were doing more goofing off and stealing her blind than work in her absence.

"I have a meeting at six, and late patient rounds at the hospital. I'll grab something to eat while I'm out. Maybe you should keep the kids inside for the rest of the week, and keep the doors and windows locked until Mr. Kelly gets here." Glen stood for a few seconds and looked at her good. "Honey, I know you're worried, but if anybody can help your mother through this, Mr. Kelly can. You know he's an old gangster himself?"

Myra nodded. "Yeah, you told me." Over and over again. Glen had met Bruno Kelly over three years ago when he came to him as a patient in the early stage of colon cancer. It was Glen's aggressive course of treatment that had sent Bruno Kelly's cancer into remission. The man had been grateful ever since, striking up an odd-couple relationship between a polished doctor and a ruff-neck patient. According to Glen, the two still shared lunch once a month. Bruno kept it real that he was forever in Glen's debt. Glen was God, at least to Mr. Kelly he was.

"Gotta run. We'll talk later." Glen kissed her forehead again.

After Glen pulled away from the house, Myra checked all the doors and windows before engaging the house alarm. She went to the kitchen where the aroma of beef stew filled the room. Not having to cook much since Hattie had been staying with them was a blessing. "Something smells good, Mama."

Hattie was at the Viking stove stirring a large pot. "Just heating up the leftover stew from last night for breakfast. We still have some salad left, too, and the cornbread is almost done. Will Glen be eating with us?"

"No." Myra sighed as she ambled over to the table and sat down. "He has a full day planned with patients and meetings."

Hattie cut a side glance at her. "You okay? You look tired."

Myra ran a hand through her shoulder-length, auburn hair. She needed a touch-up, but with everything going on with her sister and mother, her life was on hold. Her business was suffering. Her kids complained about having to share toys and space. And lately, she could feel her heart fluttering as it sped up when she tried to rest. "Mama, remember when I was telling you about this guy Glen knows named Mr. Kelly?"

"The killer? Umph. I certainly do."

"He's like an equalizer, or what you could call a protector of sorts. He steps in when people need help with a problem they're having. It's something he does for a living."

"I understand all that. What about him?"

Myra took a deep breath. "Glen…well, uh, Glen seems to think that you and the kids would be more protected staying with Mr. Kelly until this situation you're in is resolved."

Hattie stopped stirring the stew. "Glen thinks that?"

"Yeah. He's adamant about it. I tried to tell him that you need to be around family, but he's so….so damn stubborn at times."

"He's putting us out?"

"Mama, no. It's not like that. Glen is trying to find protection for you. He's so worried because he's away a lot and the idea of that fool busting up into this house on us, you know, hurting his kids…"

"I see," was all Hattie could say.

"Mama, Glen has total confidence in Mr. Kelly. He's a good friend of his. He says if anyone can help you with this problem, it's Mr. Kelly."

Hattie squared her jaw. She couldn't look at her. "When do we leave?"

"Tonight. Glen said that Mr. Kelly will arrive to pick you guys up. He left money for you to live on until you have access to your bank account. He left money for Mr. Kelly as well."

"All this money being passed out…" Hattie grunted toward her, drying her hands on a towel. "How you two expect me to pay all this money back?"

"Sounds like something for Neema to worry about when she shows back up."

That's when Hattie broke down sobbing.

"I'm sorry, Mama." Myra jumped up and went to her, allowing her mother to get it out of her system. "Please don't cry. I can't stand seeing you like this. I don't know what else to do." She patted Hattie's back hoping that a good cry would purge and renew her mother's good spirit. Hattie was a strong, proud woman who stayed in church. She supposed that even the strong can become disheartened.

"I'm sorry, baby." Hattie wiped her eyes and took control of her emotions. "I'm just so tired of running. Tired of worrying. Tired of waiting, and tired of being tired."

"I know, Mama. This is a strain on all of us."

"I swear…" Hattie sniffed. "If I felt that he was any kind of decent father, I would end this madness and turn the kids over to him. I would, but I promised your sister. I promised."

"Mama, I understand." And in a crazy way, she did. If the script were flipped, she wouldn't want a maniac like Topps getting his hands on her kids either.

"I've been praying so hard for Neema. Praying for all of this to be over with. I need her to come home to her kids, Myra. Don't she love them anymore?" Hattie looked ready for round two of crying.

"Mama, please. Don't even think such a thing. Neema loves her kids more than life. She may not be the best mother, but she does love her kids."

"Lord, I hope so." Hattie wiped her eyes. She managed a weak smile. "I'll go tell the kids to pack up their stuff. Nita's been crying and asking when her momma was coming back, and I keep making up dates. I don't know what else to tell her."

"Just tell her 'soon,' Mama. She'll be home soon."

"Yeah, you're right," Hattie agreed, putting on a brave face. "What time will we be leaving?"

"Between nine and ten tonight." Myra looked at her Cartier Tank Française watch. Lately, the only place she felt comfortable wearing the expensive piece was around her house. "It's after eight now. Maybe we can watch some movies after we eat our breakfast."

Hattie kissed her cheek. "You're a good daughter, Myra."

"I love you, too, Mama. I wish I could do more."

TWENTY-SEVEN

Shit didn't feel right.

It was an eerie feeling that had soaked into Topps all day—a feeling that something was about to jump off. Something big. For one thing, Gina, his boo-bitch, was acting too nice. She had fed him a good supper of fried pork chops, creamed spinach, and buttery mashed potatoes. Homemade, not from a box. One thing he knew certain about Gina, she wasn't the type of woman that enjoyed cooking. This disturbed him.

After dinner, Gina had put the pussy on him good, getting down and dirty with the freaky the way he liked it. Had a nigga feenin' like a junkie and feeling whipped and weak for a hot spell. They'd gotten up and showered without him even asking her to join him. Normally, Gina liked to lie in bed and bask in the afterglow of sex. He couldn't stand the scent of sex lingering on his body.

Secondly, she got up and changed the sheets on the bed without him asking. Hell yeah, he'd noticed it. He hated getting his freak on lying on soiled sheets. After that, Gina had smiled and told him that there was more good loving coming later. Wow. Hard to believe that he had to whip on that ass two days ago for running her mouth again about him trying to get his kids back. *To'e that ass up*, Topps mused with a sneer on his face. He didn't mean to blacken her eye that way, but sometimes shit happened. And her lip had looked a little swollen, but he'd helped her put some ice on it and afterward gave her a chunk of cash to go spend. She always forgave him after spending some of his money. It almost made him feel sorry for her—having to get on her like that, but Gina knew how he felt about women with loose lips. Loose lips sank ships.

"How 'bout some dessert, baby?" Gina was looking over at him with that fake innocence that only a trained woman knew how to put down good. "Want something sweet?"

Damn. His boo was really giving him the royal. "Yeah. I could stand something." Topps lay back on the red satin sheets, his head propped up on a myriad of satiny pillows. His hand was stretching the elastic of the black satin boxers he wore, playing with his thick, black pubic hair. Feeling drowsy from sex, he watched Gina get up and stroll naked across the room to get her robe from a chair. Hips swaying, her luscious breasts bounced like new rubber against her chest. Baby had back for days, but not like Neema's big rounded ass. Hell, he mused, Neema had an ass that could win a contest. High, round and firm. Hell, the girl had enough ass to give some away to women in need.

"Girl, you looking damn sexy." Damn, in a kinky kind of way he missed Neema. Not a night went by when he didn't wonder what had happened to the mother of his kids. Her last drop had been a set-up, but she never arrived. Not knowing what had happened to Neema or the large package she was supposed to drop was a constant reminder that she was the loose end. He needed to find her and bring closure. And getting his kids away from that pesky Hattie was a sure way to lure Neema back into the picture. When he did find her, maybe he could forget about the "termination," forgive her, and they could start all over again. So what if she fucked and sucked on Slick behind his back. Pussy was like wash-and-wear fabric. Germs could be washed off. That's what he liked about it.

"Be right back, baby."

"Take yo' time, Gina. No rush." Once Gina was out of the room, Topps reached under the bed for his piece. Gina was under the impression he'd left the weapon locked in his trunk, but fuck that. His piece was part of him. He checked the silencer. Tight and ready for whatever came his way. He was probably just being paranoid from the blunt they'd smoked earlier. Too bad. Paranoid came with the territory. Being cautious could keep him alive.

She treating a nigga all good and stuff. Hell, that's all my boo needed was a good ass-whipping to bring out her good side. He chuckled to himself. It proved his theory that women liked to be slapped around every now and then. It was confirmation of endearment—made them feel that a man really cared enough. Topps placed the weapon under the pillow next to him.

"Here you go," said Gina, smiling as she sashayed back into the room with a tray containing two bowls of sherbet and two glasses of sparkling wine. "Your favorite sherbet, coconut pineapple. I brought a few grapes, too." She plucked one off and fed it to him.

"Damn, boo, you in a good mood this evening. What's up?"

"Hell yeah, I am. My man just bought me a brand-new Land Rover HSE. Who wouldn't be in a good mood?"

"You damn right." Topps grinned. Once Gina had found out that he had Neema rolling in a Range Rover, she wouldn't stop going on about it until he took her behind down to the dealership. He didn't care much for the color Gina picked, dark silver, but the whip was nice. Chromed out with all the extras. The thing about Neema though, her black Rover was locked up in one of his warehouses. Waiting.

"I'ma be nice for a long time, too." Gina smiled, showing perfect white teeth that had survived a few punches to the mouth. "Now that I got me some new wheels."

"Ain't nothin'. Not really. You deserve it, boo. You been hangin' tight with me. I know it ain't easy with me trippin' and all, but things gonna fall back on track. Keep being my ride-or-die chick, you'll see." Hell yeah, she should be grateful. How many niggas she knew handed over seventy-thousand dollars cash for a new vehicle? "You can show some more appreciation tho."

"Love you." Gina kissed his lips before climbing onto the bed. She allowed her white silk robe to gap, giving ample view of her taut breasts. Dark nipples peeped out at him.

"Damn some sherbet. I'd rather slurp on you." Topps emptied his wineglass.

"Sounds like a plan." Gina eased back on the bed with her head against the headboard.

Topps wasted no time removing some sherbet with his hand, smoothing the cold sweetness between her thighs. "Open wider."

Gina threw her head back and did what she was told. At first the cold on her clit was shocking, but not entirely unpleasant. "Ooh, yeah," she moaned as Topps got busy, licking the sweetness much like licking an ice cream cone. "Feels so good I wanna talk Spanish."

"Talk it then." From this vantage he liked to sneak glances up at her. Women made the oddest facial expressions while in the throes of orgasmic pleasure. That shit was funny, but still turned him on.

Still, something was different.

Gina was watching him like a hawk. Actually, she almost seemed nervous. Her eyes should have been closed, her face a scrunched-up mask of ugliness with each lick to her pink, swollen pearl.

"Better yet," Topps said, flipping the script on her. "You do me."

"What?"

"Yo', you heard me, boo." Topps came up and sat with his back against the headboard. "Show some appreciation and do me."

"Why you being so selfish? It was just getting good to me. Why you stop?" Griping, Gina moved into place. "Thought you liked making me feel good."

"I do, but I'm not the one got a new vehicle yesterday. Do yo' thang, boo."

Gina mumbled something and got busy stroking his love stick. "My sweet, selfish one," she swooned.

Topps had situated himself to the left of the pillow where his weapon lay underneath. While Gina did her thing he reached for it, just in case.

Gina was running her long, hot tongue up and down his engorged member, almost taking him to the level he sought. His eyes were about to roll back into his head until he heard something that put him on alert.

Sucking faster, Gina's head was like a piston in a high-performance engine, up and down. The next moment was like a blur. In the blink of an eye, a rough-looking intruder he'd never seen before rushed into the bedroom shooting. *Pop. Pop. Pop.* Topps zipped to the right. He had his gun ready, too. A flash of instinct had him grabbing Gina up as a shield. One bullet whizzed past his head, but two caught Gina in the upper back as she screamed.

"What the fuck! You want some of this, mutherfucker!?" Topps reciprocated with two shots, one to the neck, one to the chest. The intruder went down. "You crazy bitch, I shoulda known!"

Gina had set him up. No doubt she had discovered the large cache of cash he kept at her place. He let her limp body fall to the floor. "You stupid, stupid bitch!" She looked dead, but as mad as he was he wanted to kill her again. Topps pumped two more bullets to her head, then kicked her body so hard it felt like he'd broken his toe. "Damn you!"

That skank Gina had ruined everything. He couldn't stay there at her condo now. He couldn't go back to his house that was already empty and in escrow. Maybe it was time to pull up and leave California for good.

Topps heaved a big breath looking around at the damage and mayhem. He walked over and turned the intruder over for a better look. "Damn. A fucking kid." The boy couldn't have been more than seventeen or eighteen. He wondered how Gina had swung that deal? Did she promise him some 'monussy?'

Time to get the hell on. Where could he go to start over again? Someplace nice. A lot of greenery and not a lot of summer heat that plagued Los Angeles or Phoenix. Seattle, Washington. Yeah. Up north sounded pretty good.

First though, the matter of getting his kids had to be solved for once and for all. Obviously the scare tactics he'd been employing hadn't worked. It was time to get serious. The sooner he had his kids back, the sooner he could get the hell out of dodge.

He pulled out his cell phone and called for an accomplice. A bona fide killer that went by the name of Zoot. Not that he had a problem popping a nigga himself, but maybe some back-up could help him get the job done faster.

"What up, my nigga? Got a job for you. Easy money, but it could be an overnighter. You game? Good. I'll slide by your crib in about two hours."

Later, after showering twice before opening the safe that he kept at Gina's condo, Topps had all his money packed up in two large duffle bags, He used a smaller bag for clean underwear and clothes. His money stored in Swiss accounts could sit for a while, but it was his habit to keep large amounts of cash on hand in case he needed it to score drugs or for a payout. After he loaded the money bags in the new Land Rover he'd bought for Gina, he cleaned out all his personal effects from his Denali and wiped it down good for fingerprints. He did the same for Gina's condo. The Denali was two years old and had served its purpose. After the job was done, he'd give the vehicle to Zoot along with some cash. Perfect planning. Gina wouldn't be needing that new Rover anyway, and him sporting a new whip might do him good.

Tonight he and Zoot both would make the hour-and-a-half drive to that hot-ass hell-hole they call Victorville. Once his business with Hattie was done, Zoot could go his way, and Topps could hit the highway going north. He didn't care who had to lie, cry or die, this was the final showdown. He wasn't leaving California until he got what he wanted.

TWENTY-EIGHT

Great. Another thug.

Hattie couldn't take her eyes off the big hulk of a man that arrived at the house on time. Not five minutes before, not five minutes after, but at nine o'clock sharp. Dark and muscular, Bruno Kelly was an inch shy of six feet. Judging from his confident persona, that inch was the only thing shy about him.

"Bruno. Good to see you again." Myra held the door open.

"Likewise. You're looking well." Bruno Kelly stepped inside and gave her a quick peck on the cheek. "How's the family?"

"The kids are fine. How about yourself?"

"I can't complain. Wouldn't do any good." His deep, Barry White voice was calm and steady. "I know those twins have to be keeping you pretty busy."

"You know it, too." The two shared a brief chuckle.

Hattie stood to the side taking it all in. So this was the Bruno Kelly that was supposed to keep them safe? This was the great black hope. She scanned him up and down. "Umph." His wide chest looked like it would burst the seams of the dark-blue tank he wore, and the thickness of his thighs was evident through his jeans. Already she hated the tattoos on his thick arms. Only crazy people marked up their bodies. Hattie immediately thought of the actor, Ving Rhames. That's exactly who Mr. Bruno Kelly looked like, but in a sexy-thug-kind-of-way. She guessed Bruno Kelly to be somewhere in his early fifties. Seasoned, but obviously in good shape. *Maybe he's some kind of fitness nut.*

"Uh, Bruno, this is my mother, Hattie Sims."

"Pleased to meet you, Hattie."

"Umph. You don't look so tough to me." Hattie half snorted. Not that she was trying to come off as rude, she wasn't so sure about this Bruno Kelly thing. How could Myra ship her off with a complete stranger?

"Mama, please."

"What? I'm just speaking my mind."

Bruno chuckled. "I don't? Maybe I need to put on my serious face." Frowning up, he narrowed his eyes and growled.

"Oh yeah, now I see it." Hattie grinned, admiring Bruno's puffed-up chest. "I feel better already." Hattie felt a little tingly but dismissed it as nervous energy.

"That's all I need to hear," Bruno retorted, going back to his business manner.

Myra suggested, "Why don't we go into Glen's study and talk." She led them into a spacious room with a large mahogany desk, potted plants, and shelves of medical books. "I'm sure that Glen has told you of my mother's situation." She took a seat at Glen's desk as if she was president of the company.

An hour later, after filling Bruno in on what mayhem had transpired, Bruno took the floor.

"I have two residences we can use, but the one I have in mind is just down the hill. It's gated and patrolled by guard dogs. Miss Hattie, you and the children are to bring clothing only. No toys. No electronics. No cell phones."

Hattie huffed. "What? No cell phones?"

"Cell phones are notorious for GPS tracking, which might explain how this Topps guy knows where you are."

Hattie didn't like him, nor the thought of staying with him. The idea of not having a cell phone wasn't sitting right either. "But how will my daughter Neema get in touch with me? I need my cell phone." Actually it was Brandon's cell phone she was keeping. Hattie usually bought the cheap pre-paid phones but always disposed of them after a short use.

"Mama, it's okay," Myra said soothingly. "Nee knows where I live. If she calls me, I can call Mr. Kelly."

"That'll work," Bruno confirmed, watching for Hattie's reaction. "However, I do want to stress that the less family contact, the better. It's the best way to maintain strict security."

Hattie resented Bruno acting like such a know-it-all. "How long will all this take? I wanna be able to go back to my own house in this lifetime."

"Mama, how would Mr. Kelly know such a thing?"

"Well, somebody need to find out, Myra. This is stressful for all of us. We need things to get back to normal."

"Mama, hopefully, Neema will be back…" Myra halted her words. The subject of Neema was too touchy for the moment.

"So," said Bruno Kelly, looking around with the utmost confidence. "Where are the children?"

"Upstairs playing." Myra got up. "Forgive my manners. Would anyone care for something to drink? Coffee, tea, lemonade, or perhaps some water?"

"Cold water," chirped Bruno.

"How about you, Mama?"

"Lemonade is fine."

When Myra returned to the study, Brandon and Raynita were present with their suitcases. Myra had searched and found some old luggage stored in her garage. That way her mother, niece and nephew wouldn't be toting their belongings away in trash bags.

"Here we go," she said, placing a tray of tall glasses down on the desk. "What's going on?"

"Mr. Kelly here is going through all the kids' belongings to see what goes and what stays." Hattie gave a half-hearted smile.

Two large rolling suitcase were open, the contents piled along the carpeted floor. Mr. Kelly was going through each piece of clothing, searching pockets and hems for tracking devices.

"Like this here." Bruno held up one of Brandon's sneakers. He took out a pocket knife and cut the sole. "Tracking devices can be put in the soles of shoes."

Hattie wanted to run over and sock the wind from his gut. "I just bought those shoes last week."

"Don't worry, we can get him some new ones."

"As long as you're paying." Bruno Kelly was getting on her nerves already. "Humph."

An hour later, they arrived at Bruno's place. Raynita and Brandon had fallen asleep during the half-hour drive down the Cajon Pass. It was a good thing because Bruno's white panel van had no windows for the children to gaze out. Their soft, even breathing was a blessing to Hattie. It gave her some time for her own thoughts. "Where exactly are we?" she inquired. Her back felt achy from sitting too long and rumblings from her stomach threatened. The drone of a large metal gate opening woke her in time to glimpse the cobblestone driveway Bruno was pulling into. The full view of the house was hidden behind a curtain of tall hedges.

"The city of Rancho Cucamonga."

"This is high desert?" It was dark out but strategically placed lighting provided a view of green, lush surroundings.

"We're in low desert." Bruno replied as he carefully steered his van into a spaciously neat garage. Two large and serious-looking

Rottweilers wagged their bobbed tails eager for Bruno to get out and show them some attention.

"Those dogs look vicious."

"They are," Bruno assured her, putting the van in park and cutting off the engine. "But well trained. Don't worry, you're safe unless I tell them to attack."

"Nanny, are we there yet?" Raynita stirred in the back of the van where the two had been sleeping on the reclined seat. "I'm hungry."

"Me too," Brandon chorused.

Hattie confirmed that she had the envelope of cash that Glen had left for her. She had peeked at the cash earlier before they left Myra's house. It had to be over five thousand dollars to help with the children's expenses until she could get to the bank. Her stomach rumbled again. Maybe she should have suggested stopping at a McDonald's to feed the kids. Obviously the supper of beef stew for dinner wasn't enough. "I'm sorry, but you think we can find a McDonald's or a Carl's Jr. before we turn in?"

"That won't be necessary," Bruno assured her.

"I beg your pardon?"

"The less places we stop, the better." Bruno opened his door and got out to pat both dogs. "How my boys doing? Huh? Miss me? Yeah, you did."

"The kids are hungry. We should have stopped for food."

Bruno stuck his head through the driver's window. "I went grocery shopping earlier today. There's plenty of food. Let me put the dogs up."

Hattie waited for him to put the dogs outside the garage and unlock the door leading into the house before getting out. "Come on, you guys. This is home for now."

"I wanna go home," Raynita whined. Crying soon followed. "I want my mommy."

"Why can't we go to my daddy's house?" Brandon asked. "Our momma can't find us at this house. She don't know this house."

It took all Hattie's strength not to get upset. Were they that blind to what was going on? If it wasn't for them, she wouldn't be in this situation. Heck, she wanted to go home, too. Cry about that. "Don't cry, sweetie. All in due time. Just be patient."

"This is not our damn house and I'm not going in!" Back to stubbornness, Brandon pouted with his arms crossed. "I wanna go to my daddy's damn house now!"

"Little boy, what did I tell you about your mouth?" Hattie couldn't blame him. Moving here, moving there. It had to be taking its toll. "C'mon, Nita. Let's go find something to eat." The two got out the van and headed into the house.

Bruno stuck his head into the van's window. "Ice cream and cake. I got it. Pizza and hot dogs. Got that, too. We can pop some popcorn and watch a movie. I got some of the best PlayStation 3 videos, man. Come check it out."

"You got Conan the Barbarian?"

"Sure do."

"That's phat." The mention of videos seemed to do the trick.

After Hattie baked a frozen pizza, heated up some canned soup and made a salad, the four sat at the table while Bruno went over the "house rules"—mostly suggestions for keeping everyone safe. "Just so you'll know, I set the house alarm each night at eleven. No opening the windows or doors after that. And I have to warn you about my dogs. Two dogs patrol outside and there's one that's trained to stay in this house. His name is Bull and he won't come out unless I give him a signal to do so. Do not, and I repeat, do not open the bedroom door that says 'Bull' on it. My dogs are highly trained, but they don't know you yet, so don't try to befriend them. They need time to get used to your scent."

"Will your dogs bite us?" Brandon asked, chewing on pizza.

"Only if you behave in a threatening manner toward me. Bull can let himself out the room where he stays, but only after hearing my signal. Follow the rules and you'll be safe. Each day I'll have you to feed the dogs something to help them to get used to you."

"Nanny, I don't like big dogs," Raynita whined. "I like puppies."

"I know, sweetie. I won't let nothing happen to you."

"Nita tried to steal a puppy from this girl where we live, but Momma made her take the puppy back."

Hattie looked at Bruno and shook her head. "Thanks for that information, Brandon."

Bruno grinned. "We'll get along just fine."

The house was large and nicely furnished. Brandon and Raynita would share a bedroom with twin beds. Hattie was shown to her own bedroom after getting the kids dressed for bed and tucked in. She felt tired, drained. Before turning in for the night, she pulled out her Bible and said a quick prayer before reading a few chapters hoping to feel better—for her ordeal to end and for Neema to show back up. That's all she wanted. "Lord, please. Please send my child home."

Unbeknownst to them, two hundred feet away, a brand-new silver Land Rover was parked across from the house. Tinted windows obscured its occupants who had followed the white van from Victorville. Topps had watched Hattie and the kids through a pair of high-powered binoculars climb into a white van. He couldn't believe his luck. The right time. The right place. It looked to him like he had caught them in the act of trying to relocate. In a way it was a good thing because he hadn't wanted to storm the doctor's house and have to pop unnecessary people to get what belonged to him, especially young children. "Now ain't that a bitch. Looks like mama skank brought in some help," Topps told his accomplice, Zoot, who sat in the passenger seat smoking a blunt. "I hope you in for doing some time out this way."

"Man, hell, I don't have shit else to do. My woman left me. My job played out, and my mama wants me out of her crib. I need to make that paper, my man."

"Good 'cause it might take more time than I thought." Two large, prowling dogs on the property presented a slight problem. But he knew exactly what to do. Not too many dogs could resist some ground-up sirloin. The best seasoning was anti-freeze and rat poison. Oh yeah. No problem at all.

"Yo', be careful with that blunt. Leather seats aren't cheap."

"No problem." Zoot put the blunt out. "When can we get busy?"

"Like I said before, we gotta do it right. I don't want my kids to get hurt."

"Hey," said Zoot, smiling to reveal a bottom row of brown, crooked teeth. "As long as a nigga gets paid, I don't care how long it takes."

TWENTY-NINE

wo days later, after leaving her three kids in the capable hands of a nanny, Myra drove from Victorville to Hesperia to check on her pet care business. The sun was up early this morning, preparing to wreak havoc on the desert landscape. Expecting another heat wave, she dressed light in a yellow T-shirt, cut-off jeans, and yellow sneakers. Her auburn hair was off her neck in a ponytail. It was far from the designer look she loved sporting, but casual dressing was a must for dog grooming, something she enjoyed.

It had been almost two weeks since she'd showed up to check on the three employees that had been running the place while she was off on her family emergency "hiatus." She dreaded the disaster that awaited her. She supposed that profits had no doubt dwindled since her absence, which happens when owners attempt to run a business via a phone line instead of in person. Stealing and goofing off came with the territory.

It was a little after seven when she let herself into the shop, and canceled the alarm on the modest-sized dwelling that was sandwiched between a deli and 24 Hour Fitness. The venture had started out as a pet grooming facility, but had morphed into the sale of pets and pet products. My Pampered Pooch had been in business all of three years, thanks to a generous investment from Glen who had agreed that his wife needed something more than kids to occupy her easily bored mind. A few low-maintenance pets could be found like fish, turtles, lizards, birds and hamsters. Small dogs were her preference. In fact, if it wasn't for Glen, she would no doubt have a house full of small dogs, mostly tea-cup poodles and pugs. Two local breeders occasionally supplied her with pure-bred puppies on consignment. But thank goodness, there were no hungry, whining puppies crying for her attention before her morning coffee.

"First thing first, some coffee." Myra turned on her coffee-maker and pulled out her Gevalia blend. For the first time in a while, she felt happy and relaxed knowing that her mother and the kids were safe and secure. She could get back to her own life. In no time the aroma of fresh-brewed coffee filled the air. Pouring a cup she headed to her office to check the day's grooming appointments.

"Umph. Miss Shone's prissy little poodle, Whitey, at eight." Not exactly her favorite, but Miss Shone was a good tipper. Twin Spaniels at nine. *That should be interesting.* A new customer at ten, and another new client at eleven. There were a few others on the list, but they were regulars. Looked like a busy day was planned. Sipping coffee and perusing through a stack of receipts and invoices, her heart almost leaped out of her chest when she looked up and found a stranger standing at her office door.

"What the hell!" Myra shot up from her padded chair prepared for a good fight. "What do you want?" Her eye-to-eye contact with the pink-faced stranger conveyed both suspicion and anger. "Why are you here?" Her immediate assumption was that the stranger was affiliated with Topps Jackson, working for him and looking for her mother.

The stranger stepped into her office, smiling. "Didn't mean to scare you."

"Who are you?"

"The name is West. John West. I'm trying to locate a Miss Hattie Sims."

"Why? I mean, may I ask what is the nature of your inquiry?" Myra stole glances around for a suitable weapon. Her large crystal paperweight? Her sharp letter opener?

"Relax. I come in peace. Your front door was unlocked."

"You're lying!" Or was he? She couldn't recall if she had locked that darn door or not.

"Mrs. Bradshaw…I…"

"How do you know my name? Look, I don't know where Hattie Sims is, and even if I did, I wouldn't tell you." It was the truth. She really didn't know the location that Bruno Kelly had taken Hattie and the kids. Even if she did, she had no reason to trust this man. "If Topps Jackson hired you to find her, you're wasting your time. She left two days ago."

"I'm a private investigator, but you're way off track. I know that Hattie is your mother."

"Who hired you?" The sound of the store's front door opening and a female calling out her name calmed her. Marva Moon, her trusty assistant, had arrived early. "Marva, I'm in my office!" Thank God. She could relax a little knowing she had backup in case this John West tried anything. "Well, who hired you?" she prompted impatiently.

Marva, who was Hispanic and black, was at her office door as perky as ever. "Hey, boss lady. Good to see you."

Myra returned a salutation but kept her eyes glued to John West, who looked more like a school principal in his navy-blue dress shirt and matching slacks.

"I work for no one right now. You could say that I'm a friend of Neema Sims, trying to help her out. Perhaps I came at a bad time."

Marva asked, "Is everything okay here, boss?"

"I'll just see myself out," West announced casually before turning and walking away.

"Boss, you need me to do anything?"

"Uh…yeah, Marva. Put all invoices in order by date for me. Thanks." Myra walked after West. "Mr. West? Hold up…I'm sorry. Please forgive my behavior. I've been under a lot of stress lately. Tell me what's going on."

"That's understandable. So has your sister."

"May I ask how you know Neema?"

After West ran down the situation about Neema's accident, her memory loss and how she was being taken care of until she was herself again, Myra looked flabbergasted.

"Are you serious? She doesn't remember her own kids?" That would explain why she hadn't called to check up on them. She'd seen TV episodes of people having their memory lost after head trauma, but had always surmised that it was a Hollywood gimmick. It was hard to believe that such a thing could actually happen. "Does she remember anybody?"

"You can talk to her, if you like. I can't guarantee you anything." West took out a cell phone and called his house where Neema was still recuperating. Once Neema answered, he passed his cell phone to Myra.

Skeptic, Myra took the phone to her ear with her heart racing like crazy. "Nee?" The voice she heard on the opposite end brought joyful tears to her eyes.

While Myra fired one question after another, Neema kept repeating questions. "Who is this? What's your name again? How did you know where to call me?"

It was Neema's voice for sure. "Oh, my God…Nee? It's you! It's really you."

THIRTY

"Nanny, is our momma ever coming back?"

"I don't care if she never comes back," Brandon deadpanned. "When I go live with my daddy, I'll have my own room and I can do whatever I want. I can even smoke weed if I want to. That's what Daddy told me."

"Brandon, you shut up. Momma's coming back, huh, Nanny?"

Hattie was at the stove cooking scrambled eggs for breakfast. "Nita, I think so. Sometimes mothers need time to themselves. She's just taking a long vacation by herself. Think of it like that." *What a liar,* she thought. The truth was, she didn't know if Neema was still alive or not. The more she called the detective working on the case, the story was pretty much the same. Not one clue to Neema's whereabouts. Hattie could only imagine that having to deal with a monster like Topps Jackson, something terrible had happened to her child. She prayed morning, noon, and night, but she couldn't let herself cry about it now. A brave front. That's what she had to put on for the children's sake.

"Mama don't give a shit about us," said Brandon, like cursing was so natural for a seven-year-old boy. The two sat at the table waiting for Hattie to feed them. It was almost noon and Bruno was outside dealing with his guard dogs.

"Brandon, you watch your mouth now."

"It's true," Brandon confirmed, his face twisted. "Mama is a selfish whore who only cares about herself. That's what Daddy said."

"Brandon!" Hattie removed the skillet of eggs from the flame and walked over to where Brandon sat at the table. "Don't let me tell you again about your mouth."

"All women are bitches," he smarted.

"You just won't listen, will you?!" Hattie yelled, snatching Brandon up from his seat. She dragged him to the nearest bathroom and turned on the faucet. Brandon squirmed and tugged but couldn't get away from her. "I am so sick of your dirty mouth! You hear me? I'm sick of it!'"

"Get offa' me, bitch!"

"I warned you. Didn't I?!"

While Brandon was yelling, "Bitch! Leave me alone," Hattie took up a bar of soap and shoved it into his gapping mouth. She had warned him continuously about his dirty language, but he obviously didn't heed the warnings. Now, she had to show him that she meant business. Her own kids never talked to her that way, and she had no intention on allowing some little snot-nosed, know-every-damn-thing, mannish-acting grandson to do it. "You will not use that kind of language with me, young man. You will not!"

Raynita was watching with the excitement of a back alley fight. "Want me to get the belt, Nanny?" The anticipation of watching her brother get a whipping glowed in her eyes.

"Go find me a belt, Nita!" Tackling that child was more than Hattie expected. She couldn't believe how incredibly strong his little behind was. The more she struggled to restrain his hands, the more Brandon kept breaking free and pounding his small fist against her thighs. Sweat dotted her forehead, and Hattie had the brief sensation that she was wrestling with a wild bear. "I have told you over and over again about your mouth! You just won't listen, will you?"

Brandon tried to clench his mouth shut, but it was hard to do and call his grandmother names at the same time. The bitter taste of soap on his tongue made him gag and cough. Soap bubbles came out of his nose while he frowned and spit the offensive taste out.

Raynita ran back into the room. "Here, Nanny. Here's a belt. Whip his little butt good!"

Brandon was yelling and crying, but Hattie could see that he still hadn't had enough by the fierce look he gave her with his balled-up fist. It occurred to her that if the boy was a little taller and older, she'd be the one getting a beat down. "Oh, I see. You need some more convincing that I mean business!" She took the belt and began wailing away on Brandon's legs, ignoring his fake tears, careful not to strike his face. "This is because I love you. You remember that. You hear me, Brandon? I'm whipping your tail outta love!"

Yelling and crying brought Bruno running in to see what the deal was. "What's going on?" Of course, it was obvious. Seeing Hattie dance Brandon around with a thin, leather belt brought a smile to his face. For the three days they'd been at his place, he had witnessed the boy talking to his grandmother and sister with so much disrespect that he had wanted to intervene. "It's about time." He closed the bathroom door to give Hattie some privacy, then turned to Raynita. "Hey, how 'bout some ice cream?"

"For breakfast?"

"Why the heck not? How does strawberry sound?"

"Sounds good," Raynita squealed. "I like strawberry."

Bruno took Raynita's little hand and led her to the kitchen. They hadn't been sitting down with their cold delight a good five minutes when Hattie slow-dragged into the spacious kitchen.

She looked like she'd done battle with the devil himself. Breathing hard, she plopped down into a chair.

"Shoots, I forgot how much work it is to spank a child. I need a nap and a Red Bull." Her hair was wild, her blouse stretched out of shape. She was tired and her arms and back ached. "Sorry I had to do that in your house," she panted, out of breath, "...but... but it couldn't be helped."

"No problem. The Bible says, 'Spare the rod, spoil the child.'" Bruno regarded her, looking perplexed. "I'd rather see a parent knock some discipline into a child instead of the police."

"Absolutely, and that's why I did it. What?" Hattie asked, noticing the odd way Bruno was looking at her.

"Nothing. I didn't think you had it in you."

"Well, I did, but it's been wrestled out of me now. Dang, that boy is strong."

Hattie went over and put some now-cold eggs on a plate. She poured herself a cup of coffee and moved to the table to sit again. "Nita, you eating ice cream for breakfast?" Whatever. She was too tired to fuss about it. "You still eating some eggs, young lady?" She set the plate down in front of Raynita.

"Yes, ma'am."

"And what do we say when someone gives you something?"

"Thank you, Nanny."

"You're welcome." She was going to mold the kids into shape even if she had to go to an early grave doing so.

"Hey, what say we spend the day out and about? A nice outing would do us all some good. How would you like to have a makeover?" Bruno waited for her reaction.

Hattie raised a brow. "What kind of makeover?"

"I don't know. I was thinking that if you changed how you look a little, you wouldn't be such an easy target. Some new clothes, a new hairdo, maybe even a change in hair color."

"I look that bad?" A hand flew up to pat her hair into place. "I'm telling you that child put up quite a fight." Hattie thought about it. The last time she'd had her hair done was after the breakup with her last boyfriend, Harold. The relationship had lasted over a year with some hints toward marriage, but Harold had a slight drinking problem that had him acting like a lunatic. That put the brakes on marriage. After the split, Hattie simply gave up on dating and men. There was no need to keep her hair and nails up after that. "I don't have a beautician. I wouldn't know where to go."

"No problem," Bruno assured her. "I have a play sister that owns her own shop in Fontana, not too far from here. I can give Queenie a call to see if she can work you in. How 'bout it?"

"Well…I suppose it couldn't hurt." Shoots. Who was she fooling? She'd been needing some personal pampering for months now.

"Be right back." Bruno excused himself to go make a call. Back in ten minutes, he announced, "Get the kids ready and let's roll. She says she can squeeze you in."

THIRTY-ONE

"Man, this shit is the bomb," said Zoot, using his rubber-gloved hand to mix up a bowl of poison to be fed to the guard dogs at the place where Hattie was staying. "Rat poison, anti-freeze, and ground-up glass mixed into a savory ground beef with a hint of spices. Now that's what I'm talkin' 'bout."

"Yo', as long as it does the trick. I'll shoot a mutherfucker in a minute, but I ain't into shooting innocent animals. That's not my thing."

Zoot was grinning like a mad scientist. "Man, we could probably kill up a bunch of niggas with this shit. Throw a big barbecue and cook up some nice big, juicy burgers. I heard that anti-freeze has a sweet taste to it. That's why stupid dogs lap it right up."

Topps ignored his accomplice's remark as if he hadn't heard a word the man said. He was checking out his gun and actually thinking about shooting Zoot to put him out of his no-bathing-ass misery. The man stank and Topps didn't know how much more torture he could take.

"Ain't a dog around can resist this shit when I get through pumping flavor into it. Smells so good I feel like eating some myself."

I wish you would. Topps remained quiet. He had rented a large room with two beds twelve blocks away from the gated house he'd followed Hattie and his kids to. He needed time to hash out a plan. Plus, having to take care of more personal business caused a delay.

Three days now. That's how long he'd been holed up in the room with human funk that made him want to retch every time he took a deep breath. It tempted him to plug his nose with cotton, and then blow a hole clean through Zoot's ass so some fresh air could get to it. If it wasn't for the fact that he needed Zoot's help with the task at hand, he would have skied up. But he had to make sure they knew what the hell they were doing when invading the house. A tall gate around the house's circumference, security bars on the side windows of the house, guard dogs patrolling. Hell, he even saw a couple of surveillance cameras. Yeah, they had to take their time and do it right. Errors could get them both killed.

Zoot was excited like a chef finishing his first culinary master-piece. "Man, this shit actually smells delicious. Come take a whiff of it."

Shit. The hell with it. He had to tell the truth. "Yo', my nigga, all I smell right now is ass. What you need to do is hop yo' ass in the shower."

"Say what?" Zoot looked up, his expression a mix of curiosity, anger and disbelief.

"You heard the fuck what I said. You need to hop yo' ass in the shower and get acquainted with some soap. Know what I'm sayin'?"

"Nigga, what the hell you talkin' 'bout? I washed up." Zoot looked slightly offended, even though he could smell for himself that he was ripe.

"Man, we been on this fucking mission for three mutherfucking days now and I haven't seen you wash or brush shit. Not once. That ain't right, bro."

"Are you for real?" Zoot raised a brow. "I didn't know you hired me to see me wash my ass. Hell, you wanna swing that way, it's gonna cost you more money."

It was meant as a joke, but Topps wasn't laughing. In fact, he took the implication as an insult to his manhood. He was twisting the silencer on his gun. Mostly admiring it. "Damn all this waiting around. We need to seal this deal tonight so it can be over with. You go yo' way, I go mine. But for real, how you gonna be there when you can't even ride in my whip?"

"Dang, nigga. You for real or what?"

"Yo, you can't ride in my whip smelling like that, man. Take a shower. That's all I'm sayin'. In fact, take two and a wash-up. I can't take yo' stank another day. You killing me."

"Man, fuck you," Zoot hissed loud. "I smell like a man should smell. It's not like I brought my overnight bag with me."

"I'll give you a pair of clean drawers, my nigga. I got deodorant and a clean shirt you can have, too. I always travel prepared."

"Man, I'ma grown-ass man. Nobody tells me when to bathe."

Topps was glaring at him. Maybe he didn't mean to point the gun in Zoot's direction, but it was aimed that way. "For sho, but I'm a grown-ass man, too, partna', and I say get yo' punk ass in the shower or get popped. The choice is yours."

Zoot stood and peeled off his rubber gloves. "What? You gon' shoot me if I don't? Man, this is fucked up. You one crazy-ass nigga, you know that?"

"Yeah. That's what I've heard." Topps kept the gun aimed at him. His look couldn't be more serious. "But I smell clean."

"Ain't this a bitch." Mumbling, Zoot swiped the bowl of poison meat onto the floor. "You wrong for this, man. Wrong." Despite his complaining, he went in to take a shower.

Topps went outside to fetch some fresh clothing from the Rover.

It was close to noon and hot already. It was an oppressive heat that reminded him of being in Vegas. How people enjoyed desert living was a mystery beyond his comprehension. He couldn't wait to be done and get the hell away from this town. Before going back inside, he fired up a blunt and took his time smoking inside the vehicle while listening to some rap music. He counted out some cash from his duffle bag to put in his wallet.

"We can wrap those gourmet doggie burgers up and take that shit over now," Topps suggested, walking back into the room with a clean T-shirt and underwear rolled up. He tossed the roll over to a sour-faced Zoot who was walking around with a blunt dangling between his lips and a towel wrapped around him. "No telling how long that shit might take to drop 'em."

"Hey, man, what's this beef you got with this lady we going to pop anyway?"

Topps sat on the bed, his mind thinking about all the bodies that had slept there. Years of other people's dirt, sweat, body fluids, and fallen dead skin cells. It made his skin crawl. "Who the hell said anything 'bout poppin' her old ass? I'm just taking my kids, that's all."

"Seem like a lot of trouble. Can't you just call her up and ask for 'em?"

"Nigga, what you think? What, you think this shit is a pleasure trip we on?"

Zoot headed back to the tiny bathroom to get dressed. "Damn, man. I just asked. Don't bite my head off."

"Don't be asking stupid shit about my damn business. I didn't hire yo' ass for that."

Zoot was back in the room staring at him a few seconds before grinning. "Hired? Man, you one funny dude. We've been in town three days and I ain't seen a dime."

"Yo, once the job is done, then you get paid."

"Damn, Topps, how I know I can trust you? You be trippin'."

"Money ain't a problem, so don't worry about it. You'll get paid."

"Yeah, okay." Zoot sniffed. "But on the for real, TJ, I don't appreciate having heat pulled on me like that." His expression went from jovial to serious. "Don't do it again."

Topps got up and walked over to him. His favorite mode of intimidation was getting straight in a person's grill. Like now. "Is that right?" Topps sneered. Zoot was close enough for Topps to smell the mint scent of his breath. "And what'chu gon' do about it?"

Two bull-headed men squared off, both too stubborn to bow down.

Zoot made it obvious that he wasn't afraid of him. "Like I said, don't let it happen again."

"Yeah. That's what I thought you said."

The icy silence warmed when Topps said, "Pack that shit up so we can roll. We got business to take care of."

The ride back to the gated house was ten minutes of thick silence. Topps didn't give a damn. In fact, the more he thought about that nigga Zoot giving him grief, he might be paying his ass with a bullet instead of the promised cash. Obviously that fool didn't know who he was dealing with. "I was just playing with you earlier, man." A lie to ease the tension between them.

"No sweat." Zoot sniffed. "I was playing, too."

"We straight then?"

"Yeah, partna'. We straight."

Topps cruised the Rover to the side of the tall hedges that surrounded the front of the house. The gate was ornamental black iron connected to sides of tall brick. He surveyed their surroundings to see if they were being observed. Not one soul was out walking the neighborhood. Looked like the intense heat was a plus—made people stay inside their air-conditioned homes. "You know what to do, bro. Get busy."

"I'm on it." Zoot hopped out and moved to the front of the vehicle where he lifted the vehicle's hood. After a few seconds of giving the illusion of having engine problems, he eased over to the tall hedges and slipped between the thick curtain of green.

One of the two massive Rotties caught his scent and charged in his direction, running, growling and snarling. It banged its thick, muscular body against the iron gate trying to get at him. All Zoot could see were sharp teeth and drool.

"Easy, boy," Zoot cooed as he removed the small patties of poisoned meat from a plastic bag he had tucked inside his shirt. "Here you go. That's it, smell it. Smells good. Yeah. Taste it. There you go. That's some good shit, ain't it? Good boy."

Rottie Number One took the bait with no problem. Rottie Number Two ran up on the scene growling and almost foaming at the mouth. Sharp teeth promised a gruesome outcome, but that didn't stop Zoot from trying to soothe the beast. "Easy, boy. Easy now. Calm down. You want some of this, too? Yeah? Sure you do." Rottie Two was different, untrusting. The snarling beast took his time sniffing at the pattie, growling in protest, then sniffing some more. "Taste it. It's good stuff, boy. There you go, just a little bit. Now try some more." Once all the meat was exhausted, Zoot walked back to the car and put the hood down before climbing back in.

"They eat that shit up?" Topps asked, flying some white powder up a nostril with a rolled-up hundred-dollar bill.

"Like candy to a kid."

"Good. Want some of this?"

"Hell yeah." Zoot held his fist out for Topps to tap out a small pile of powder from the tiny brown vial he held. He took up the rolled bill and flew the pile in one strong sniff, then licked the residue from his hand. "Damn, that's straight pure."

"Only the best. So how long before them bitches are down?"

Zoot sniffed hard. His nostril burned and felt numb as heck, confirming good stuff. "Uh...we should be good to go by nightfall. If they ain't dead, they should be too sick to care who comes over the fence. And that's for real."

"I'm sure there's an alarm on the house. The element of surprise might be our best chance." Topps started the engine and drove a few blocks down, turned the vehicle around and parked. "We'll squat here for a while to see who comes and goes out that muther. That way we'll know what the hell we dealing with." He left the engine on so he could run the air conditioner. Too much heat might start Zoot to smelling again. He'd pop him for sure then.

"This area is the bomb. Shit, I could live up in this muther," Zoot observed, looking around at his surroundings. Fairly new, large homes with manicured lawns painted a pleasing picture. "Probably mostly white folks, I bet. Maybe even a few Klan members waiting to burn a cross on a nigga's lawn."

"Screw this place." Topps snorted. "I couldn't stand being no desert rat. Once I get my son, I'ma get ghost outta here quick. Maybe head up north. Nothing but green and more green."

"Your son?" Zoot raise-browed him. "Thought it was two kids."

"It is, but...you know how it is with girls. They like they mama. Walking trouble and hard-headed. The more I think about it, I might have to leave her ass behind. Once I get my business back and runnin' up north, the plan is to get my boy trained for it. Know what I'm sayin'? Gotta keep my shit poppin'."

"Ain't never havin' no damn kids."

"Good for you." Topps snorted. "I love my son. He'll be rich like his father."

"Need some new soldiers, let me know. I'm game."

"Yeah, I'll keep that in mind."

Luck was on their side. The wait wasn't long before the massive black gate opened and the white panel van pulled out. The cautious driver paused to look both ways before pulling onto the street.

"Well, looka' here." Topps grinned, pleased. "Looks like the little family is going on a little excursion." He took up the binoculars for a better look at the driver. Male. A face that looked hard, but unfamiliar.

"Whad'up?" Zoot sat up looking excited. "Shit, man, let's run up on 'em now and blast they asses!"

"Man, my kids might be in the back of that mutherfucker. You hard trippin'."

Zoot looked insulted but held his tongue.

"Nah, let's do it right. Give them dogs some time to die while we go get somethin' to eat. Don't know about you, but I'm starvin'."

"Yeah, I could stand some grub."

"They'll be back," Topps sneered. "That's when we have the element of surprise and no witnesses. It's perfect."

THIRTY-TWO

"Afterwards, we can take the kids shopping for a few things, then head over to the Cheesecake Factory at the Gardens." Bruno sounded excited.

"The Gardens? What's that?" Hattie asked. This thing about her having a makeover was making her a little nervous. What if she looked too young or like some floozy? What would her church members say when she returned?

"Victoria Gardens. It's an outdoor mall off Foothill. A few major stores, a few places to eat. My favorite is the Cheesecake Factory. Hopefully, it will be a little cooler by the time we head that way." After being in the house for three days, Bruno was almost like a child on his way to the toy store. In a strange kind of way, it felt like he was part of a family—his own family, something that he had wanted for a long time, but had to put on the back burner when the cancer had reared its ugly head. "Having dinner out might do us all some good."

"I want ice cream after dinner," Brandon announced. For most of the ride he'd been quiet, his way of letting Hattie know that he was still upset about getting spanked.

"Is that how we ask?" Hattie corrected. She hated to ride him so much, but if that's what it took, so be it.

"Sorry, Nanny. Can I please have some ice cream after dinner?"

"That's much better, Brandon." Hattie smiled with a sense of pride. "You sound like a little gentleman, and yes, you may have some ice cream after dinner." If she had known that a good spanking would do the trick, she wouldn't have waited so long to give therapy. She was almost looking forward to Brandon's next "treatment."

"Nanny, may I have some ice cream, too?" Of course, Raynita wouldn't be outdone.

"Of course you can, sweetie." Hattie winked over at Bruno, who obviously was impressed at her disciplinarian skills. "Oh, don't let me forget to call Myra later to see if she went by to check on my house and pick up my mail."

"I won't."

Hattie sighed. Actually, it wasn't so bad being at Bruno's house. In an odd kind of way, she felt more comfortable being at Bruno's than at Myra's place. How odd. Still, there were spells when she missed her own place. "My bank finally mailed me another ATM card, so that helps. I wish they could speed up working on my house."

"Stop worrying, it's all coming." Bruno exited Interstate 15 at Baseline and headed east into the city of Fontana.

"Easy for you to say." Hattie snuck a quick glance over at him. A nice-looking man with no wife. No kids. How strange. She hadn't been made privy to the full history of his life, but it wasn't difficult to put some of the pieces of the puzzle together. The man had been in a serious relationship before he became sick with colon cancer. His ex-fiancée couldn't deal with his illness, packed up and split. He bred and trained dogs at another residence he owned. He had run with a gang in his younger days, but after witnessing his brother being shot down like a dog, he had enough of death and destruction. Bruno, being shot two times and surviving, sealed his removal from the lifestyle. That was twenty years ago, in a place called Tacoma, Washington. According to Bruno, he never looked back.

"This play sister of mine is good at what she does. You'll like her."

"I hope so." Hattie sighed, folding her hands. For this excursion she had worn some form-fitting denim and a black top with a wide belt around her waist. Soft leather flats on her feet. It was a youthful look she had to get used to.

The Dashing Diva salon was small but clean. Hattie and the kids followed Bruno into the shop and took a seat while he went looking for his play sister Queenie. Seeing the two walking toward her made Hattie more nervous.

Queenie looked to be in her early thirties. She was a tall woman with gentle brown eyes. Small on the top, and wide on the bottom, her fleshy face suggested a woman that had once been larger. The black apron she wore was faded some, but her hair was tight.

Brandon pointed and grinned. "Ooh, she got a big booty."

Hattie shot him a look. "Did you say something, Brandon?" For good measure, she'd brought the leather belt with her and Brandon knew it.

"No, ma'am." The child put his head down.

"I didn't think so."

"Hattie, this is my play sister Queenie," Bruno said proudly. "She'll be hooking you up today. Queenie, this is Hattie Sims."

The two females exchanged pleasantries with Queenie touching and examining Hattie's hair like she'd discovered a patch of peat moss on her head. "Give me a good two hours."

Bruno frowned. "You need that long?"

"For intense conditioning, yes I do," Queenie sassed back.

"Okay then. Guess I'll take the kids to the Mills to play some games. Is that okay, Hattie?"

"Ah…yeah, that's fine." Hattie gave Brandon a stern look. "I'm sure that Brandon will be on his best behavior. Right, Brandon?"

"Yes, ma'am."

"Good."

Two hours later, Hattie was ready to go. The kids ran into the salon excited about the video games they had played at the Ontario Mills' game center. Bruno was right behind them. The three stopped dead in their tracks at the sight of Hattie. Mouths sagged open.

"Nanny?"

"Hattie?"

"Nanny is a babe!" Brandon yelled.

The woman that had come in harried and dowdy-looking had been transformed into a younger-looking diva mama with shoulder-length, dark-auburn hair. Hair that swayed. Add to that, a facial, pedicure, and a manicure with French tips. The little makeup she wore was perfect.

Hattie was a little nervous about her new look. "Well? Is it too much with the hoop earrings?"

"No way." Bruno kept checking her out. "Wow." He liked what he saw. In fact, he liked it a lot. "You…you look great."

Brandon got in the mix. "Yeah, Nanny. You look young and sexy."

What in the world would a seven-year-old know about sexy? Hattie didn't even want to ask. "Thank, you. What about you, Nita? You like Nanny's new look?"

"You look pretty."

"Thank you. Here, let me pay the lady." Hattie opened her purse.

"Hey, it's my treat. I got this." Bruno walked over and paid Queenie, which wasn't much because the woman owed him a big favor. Good-byes flowed back and forth as they headed out for Victoria Gardens.

After shopping at the mall, they dined at the Cheesecake Factory before heading back to the house. Bruno made a point of checking out every vehicle coming and going around him. Earlier he had spotted a new Land Rover with tinted windows parked not too far away from his gate. The windows were so dark he couldn't see if it was occupied or not, but it was gone now. Probably belonged to one of his neighbors that paraded a slew of Mercedes-Benzes, Land Rovers, BMWs and Lexuses up and down his street. He used a remote to open the iron gate before pulling the van in.

"That's odd," Bruno observed.

"What's that?" Hattie asked, feeling sluggish from the wonderful meal she had eaten earlier. Her plan was to sleep for hours. The kids had fallen asleep already in the back of the van.

"My dogs didn't come greet."

"Oh Lord." Hattie perked up quickly. She felt her heart speed up.

"Calm down. They've been known to dig out at the rear of the house. Dogs will be dogs. They might be roaming the neighborhood. I'll let you and the kids in the house and go check to see what's up."

Hattie looked alarmed. "But…what about Bull inside?" The only time she'd been around the large dog that lived inside the house was when Bruno was present.

"You and the kids go straight to the kitchen and stay 'til I come inside. Wake the kids. Bull is trained not to enter the kitchen unless he's summoned."

"Are you serious?"

"Hattie, it's okay. Get the kids inside."

Bruno got out and unlocked the door leading into the house from the garage, turned the alarm off before going in search of his prized Rotties. At the rear of the house, he found one dog laying in vomit, barely breathing.

He knelt down to the animal, a sick feeling in the pit of his stomach. Poisoned. "Son of a bitch!" He was about to rise to go search for the second yard dog when a baseball bat came crashing down on his back. The hard blow knocked instant fear into him as he shot up and swirled around to deal with his assailant, Topps Jackson. The two men struggled hard, breaths coming quickly. Bruno managed to knock Topps into the pool, giving him time to reach for the gun strapped to his left leg. Bruno fired off one shot at Topps coming up for air, but missed. So busy aiming for another shot at Topps that he didn't hear the bullet that struck his leg, Bruno felt a sudden burning and knew he was hit. He grabbed his leg, at the same time seeing another assailant rounding the side of his house coming at him with a gun.

Bruno fired back at the second attacker, barely grazing his shoulder. Zoot aimed and fired again. The second bullet whizzed past Bruno's head, prompting him upright to hop toward the garage leading into the house. More bullets whizzed by as he made it to the door and attempted to get inside, but his two assailants were right behind him. He dragged his wounded leg across the tiled floor leading into his living room, bleeding. It was him against the two of them. His small twenty-two was no match. In a situation like this, his thought was that cooperation might save Hattie and the kids. "Don't shoot, please."

Zoot aimed the silenced metal at him. "Drop that damn gun, partna."

Bruno did what he was told. The earlier blow to his back had him dizzy with pain. His vision was blurry, almost like he was seeing double. The bullet in his leg was screaming for medical attention. "Look, you guys…this can all be worked out. Whatever it is that you want, let's talk about it."

Topps kicked his gun to the far end of the room. "Man, don't shoot his ass yet. We need him to open up the safe. I'm sure he got one up in this muther. I can smell money."

Having heard gunfire, Hattie told the kids to stay in the kitchen. She ran back toward the front of the house to find Bruno on the living room floor bleeding from his leg, obviously in pain.

Water dripping from his clothes, Topps stepped from behind Zoot. "Oh my God! Bruno. Oh no. I'm so sorry." She turned hateful eyes toward Topps. "Why won't you leave us alone! Just leave us alone!"

Bruno laid his dizzy head on the floor. "Hattie, don't even sweat it. If he's a real man, he'll sit down and talk like a man."

Topps lowered his gun, grinning. "Ain't shit to talk about. Know what I'm sayin'? I'm here to take what's mine. I didn't have no beef with you, but you in it now. End of story."

THIRTY-THREE

*B*runo had one last ace up the hole, but the timing wasn't right. He listened to Topps yelling for the kids to come out. Brandon was quick to show up. He ran to his father, and hugged him like he hadn't seen him in years.

"Daddy, I knew you would come for me."

Hattie couldn't believe that boy. *Little traitor.*

"That's my little nigga." Topps rubbed his head playfully. "Where's yo' sister? Go get her ass now. We'll be leavin' soon."

"Yeah." Zoot grinned. "Tell her to get herself on in here, so we can get this party goin'."

Topps snapped at him, "Man, shut the hell up!"

Zoot turned the gun on him. "Nah, nigga. You shut the hell up! Now toss that piece on the floor."

"Man, what the fuck you think you doin'?" Topps sneered over at him.

"Looks like I'm 'bout to clean house, that's what." Zoot waited for him to toss the gun to the floor. "Don't make me have to pop yo' ass first. What? You think I forgot about that little episode you pulled at the motel? Hell nah, nigga. You punked the wrong nigga this time. For real."

Topps dropped the gun to the floor. "You might as well shoot my ass now 'cause you one dead man once you leave here. I got too many soldiers I can call."

"Oh, don't worry," Zoot assured Topps with a nasty sneer. "You can be the first. You crazy-ass mutherfucker! Thought I didn't know about all the cash in the back of your car, huh? I figured, why just have some of it when I can have it all. It's gotta be some cash up in this muther, too. It's all about timing, my nigga, and this is perfect timing."

Brandon came up behind Zoot holding a gun on his father and sprang into action. "Don't shoot my daddy. Don't you shoot him!" With all his might, he pushed Zoot, and the gun went off but missed. Topps was on Zoot in a flash, kicking the gun from his hand. It slid across the nylon carpet.

The kids screamed. Hattie screamed. Bruno tried to get up but the shattered bone in his leg made it impossible. He yelled for someone to get the dropped gun, then put fingers to his mouth and whistled loud through the house. In no time a large black Rottweiler was at his side. "Sic him, boy! Get him!"

Growling and snarling the dog went straight to Zoot, attacking him. Topps scrambled up and out of the way, barking orders to Brandon. "Get the damn gun!"

Fearful of being disobedient, Brandon ran for the weapon. It was heavy in his trembling hand. His father had taught him how to use it. He could shoot it, but shoot at what?

Zoot's scream of agony pierced the interior. He couldn't get away from the strong animal, but finally managed to get to his feet, running from it. The beast was right behind him.

Hattie screamed for Brandon to give her the gun. "Bring it here, Brandon. Give Nanny the gun!"

"Boy, you listen to me," Topps warned. "You give that gun to her and I'll tear you a new behind. You shoot her! Shoot her now!"

Tears came to Brandon's eyes. "Daddy, I'm scared." He aimed the gun at Hattie.

"Brandon, you listen to me." Hattie knew she had to make him see the truth, that his father had bad intentions. "You don't want to shoot your Nanny. I love you, Brandon. I love you very much, and you know it's true." Hattie was on her feet ready to walk over to him, but Topps charged in Brandon's direction with hell in his eyes.

"Little nigga, when I tell you to do something, you do it. I said, shoot her ass!" Topps reached out to grab Brandon's shaking hand. Hattie ran up and tried to stop him. To her surprise, Raynita ran up and bit Topps' leg hard. Pain took Topps' mind off the struggle, giving Hattie the strength to take possession of the gun.

"You little bitch!" Topps screamed at Raynita. "Just like your damn mama! I'll slap the black off yo' ass!"

"Don't you dare touch her!" Hattie aimed the gun at him. "Brandon, you and your sister go to the room and close the door."

Traumatized, both kids acted like they were in a trance.

"I said, go to the bedroom and close the door. Now!" She waited for them to leave the room.

Topps stood up smirking. He didn't look like a man that was afraid to die. "What now, bitch? What? You think I'm scared of you 'cause you have the gun?"

"I want you to leave. Leave now while you have a chance." She couldn't stop shaking.

"You must be crazy. Shoot me 'cause I'm not leaving without my son." Topps stepped closer.

"Please...don't make me do this."

"What? Kill a nigga?" Topps stepped closer. "Christians can't kill. Remember? Ain't that what you supposed to be, a so-called Christian?" He stepped closer. The second Hattie turned her attention to look over at Bruno, who seemed half unconscious, Topps charged her.

"Bitch, I'll kill you!"

Hattie squeezed the trigger and Topps went down.

"Oh my God!" She dropped the gun and ran to Bruno's side. Kneeling down, she held his head up. "I'll call an ambulance."

Bruno's eyes opened. "Wipe your prints from the gun first and give it to me."

Hattie did like she was instructed.

Bull walked back into the room with blood covering his face.

"Come here, boy. Over here," Bruno called to him. The highly obedient dog went to his master. "Sit."

To Hattie, the dog's bloody face was a gruesome sight, but she felt like she could let her guard down. It was over.

"Thank you, sweet Jesus." Tears streamed down her face.

Feeling a little better, Bruno was able to get on his feet despite the searing pain in his leg and back. After cleaning off Hattie's and Brandon's prints from the gun, he placed a call to the police department. "You take my van and go to a motel room for a few days. Call me after that. And don't worry about a thing."

"But I can't just leave you…"

"Hattie, please do as I say. I can handle the rest."

Reluctantly, she collected her things, took the kids and left.

THIRTY-FOUR

"Okay, Mr. Kelly, where the heck are we going?" Hattie was smiling over at Bruno, but the man kept his attention on the highway.

"You'll see."

"You know I don't like surprises, so tell me."

"Woman, relax. It's a beautiful day and I thought it would be nice to take a long ride. You know, get out of the desert for a while."

"Yeah, it is beautiful." Hattie gazed from her window up into the sky. The air was warm and there was not one cloud to be seen. It was three weeks after the showdown with Topps and she thanked the good Lord every day that it was over. The man that had been terrorizing her was dead. "You guys okay back there?" Angling around, she regarded the two busybodies.

"Yes, ma'am," Brandon replied as he played quietly with a hand-held video game. "I'm on level four now, Nanny."

"Nanny's big boy. That's good." She studied his face for a moment. Hattie had thought that Brandon would be traumatized after the shooting incident that claimed his father's life. He wasn't, at least not that she could tell. After explaining to Brandon that his father was in a deep sleep until the doctors could fix him, the child seemed receptive of the explanation. Resilient. That's what kids are today, Hattie mused. Maybe it was because of all the violence kids watch on television. Should I feel guilty? It was a question she sometimes asked herself. Her answer was no. She felt justified, not to mention blessed. She was blessed that it was over.

"Nanny, may I please have some water?"

"Yes, Miss Nita, you certainly may." Hattie removed one of several bottles of water in the cooler on the front seat and passed it to her.

"Thank you, Nanny."

"You're welcome, sweetie." Turning back around, she looked over at a sly-looking Bruno. Something about the man tugged at her heart. He had been hired to protect her, but in actuality he'd done much more by wiping her and Brandon's fingerprints from the gun that shot Topps Jackson. Bruno's fingerprints were the only ones found on the weapon, along with Topps'. After a short investigation, the law deemed the incident justifiable. Two men broke into Bruno's house to rob him and were killed. One was shot by Bruno, one was attacked by his guard dog, Bull. "And what's with you and Myra and the secret phone calls?"

Bruno chuckled. "You are so suspicious, you know that?"

"Shouldn't I be? Tell me what's going on," Hattie persisted.

"Woman, I told you, Myra was keeping me posted about your house. She says the repairs are coming along nicely and they're almost finished."

"And she couldn't call and tell me that news?"

"Hattie, I'm telling you what she said. You were the one that told her to call me with any news. Remember?" Grinning, he shook his head. "Jeepers, so suspicious."

"Humph. That was before," Hattie confirmed. "Things are different now. Things can go back to normal. No more hiding out. The kids can get back in school. The only thing missing is Nee…" A lump in her throat cut her words off. Thinking of Neema brought tears to her eyes. It had been weeks now and her child's body still hadn't been found, but she knew that Topps Jackson had done something to her daughter. *Lord, help me.*

"It's gonna be okay," Bruno said, seeing her mood change.

"It makes me so mad," Hattie balled her fist. "I've called that silly detective so much that he's avoiding my calls now. I guess a young, missing black woman is no big deal."

"Don't talk like that," Bruno soft-chided. "I'm sure they did what they could to try'n locate your daughter. Maybe with so many people going missing every year and not enough resources, it's hard."

"I know one thing, when I'm settled back in my house, I'm hiring a private detective. I don't care how much it costs, I'm hiring one."

"I hear you. I know just the right one that can help you, too."

"Humph. Might even hire the services of a psychic. A good one. Maybe that blonde woman that be on Montel's show all the time. What's her name? Brown something."

"Sylvia Browne." Bruno could tell that she was serious with her spoken plans.

"Yeah. Her. I'ma find out what happened to my child if it's the last thing I do on God's good earth."

Hattie reached up and pulled down the passenger-side mirror to check her hair. She'd paid the same salon a visit two days ago and she was still looking good. Maybe it was her imagination, but a couple of times she thought she saw Bruno looking at her like he was…well, like he was lustfully checking her out. Goodness, when was the last time she had a man do that?

"I would do the same thing if I were you." Bruno put his signal on and merged into the freeway's diamond lane. "I heard that Miss Browne's services are not cheap."

"I don't care. I need closure. I don't wanna go to my grave wondering what really happened to my child."

"I understand."

After two hours of driving, they exited the freeway on Pacific Coast and took the scenic drive headed west before finally turning right onto Jasmine Court. Two more right turns and Bruno pulled his van into a driveway behind a brand-new black Toyota Camry.

Bruno checked the address. "This looks like the place."

"Who lives here?" Hattie asked, admiring the modern, two-story house with neatly trimmed boxwood and red roses in the front. The house was beige with dark-brown windows. Judging by the surrounding homes, she could tell it was a well-maintained neighborhood.

"Some good friends of mine. Haven't seen them in a while." Bruno climbed out, hurried around to open the door for Hattie, then helped the kids out. "Don't worry. They're good people. You'll love them."

Raynita wanted to know, "Nanny, who lives here?"

"Sweetie, didn't you hear what Bruno said? Some friends of his."

"I like this house," Brandon announced. "It's the bomb."

They walked to the massive wooden door where Bruno rang the doorbell. In no time a blue-eyed man was swinging the door open. He was attired in short khaki pants, a Hawaiian-print shirt of yellow and red and wore brown sandals. He looked to Hattie like a tourist on vacation.

"You're early." John West smiled, opening the door wider for everyone to enter. "Come on in. Make yourself at home. She'll be down in a minute."

She? Hattie gave both Bruno and John West a curious look. The two didn't seem all that friendly to her, but inside the house was gorgeous with a marble entrance, beautiful furniture and a magnificent wrought-iron stair railing. She caught the scent of something good cooking, like a pot roast with plenty of garlic. It smelled similar to the way she cooked pot roast with lots of garlic and some cilantro. "Ummm. Smells like somebody knows their way around a kitchen."

John West yelled up the stairs for someone to hurry up and come down. "She's such a diva. Loves to stay in the mirror."

I know this negro man didn't drive me two hours to meet some hoochie girlfriend of his. Hattie's happy mood was threatening to leave as her blood pressure was slowly rising. She folded her arms, feeling a mad attitude coming on. Or was it possibly some jealousy?

Finally, someone was coming slowly down the stairs. From her vantage point, Hattie saw the feet descend, then two thin legs in black leggings. The body was next, and then she was looking at a vision that almost took her breath away. She screamed as she ran over and hugged her. "Ohmygawd! Neema! My baby!"

"Mama!" Both Raynita and Brando rushed over to hug her. "Mama, where you been? We missed you."

The joy of reunion was noisy, but to Bruno and John West, a wonderful sight as they stood back, watching. For a second Bruno got a little teary eyed. It hadn't been the easiest thing keeping the big secret from Hattie. Several times he had to talk Myra out of jeopardizing the big surprise.

She was so caught up with joy, Hattie barely noticed Myra coming out the kitchen wearing a cute apron and casually announcing, "Welcome, family. Dinner is ready to be served. Let's eat."

"Myra? Oh my goodness." Hattie couldn't control the tears flowing. It was all too much. "How in the world did you keep this from me?"

"Trust me, Mama, it wasn't easy, but I wanted it to be a surprise. Are you surprised?"

More tears confirmed it. "Thank you."

"Actually, Mama, the one who made all this possible is Mr. West here. He was the one that found Neema after her car accident. He nursed her back to health and kept her safe."

Hattie went to John West and gave him a kiss to each cheek. "I really can't thank you enough," she said, giving him the best hug she could muster.

"I would do it all over again if I had to." John West smiled. "She's like a daughter to me."

After an hour more of sharing Joy, Neema excused herself to go back upstairs claiming that she need to take something for pain. Since the accident she suffered from bouts of neck and shoulder pain.

"Sweetie, take your time," Hattie assured her. "We'll be right here."

THIRTY-FIVE

Dear Mrs. Tidmore:

It saddens me to inform you that your daughter, Kaytrina Tidmore, is no longer living. I know this because I was one of the last people to see her alive. I just wanted you to know that her death was an accident at the hands of an ex-boyfriend of mine. They got into a fight and Kaykay lost her balance and hit her head. Trust me when I say that it was an accident. I doubt if she suffered because she died instantly.

I wasn't sure if I should write this letter to you or not, but it was hard for me to accept her death, and even harder for me to accept that you would be spending years wondering if she would ever come home and wondering what had happened to her. Kaykay was a dear friend to me, and just like you I will miss her so much.

Also, you'll be glad to know that the man responsible for her death, Topps Jackson, has also passed away. Not only was he the monster responsible for Kaykay's death, but he also provided a way for her body to be disposed of at Harmond's Funeral Home located in the Crenshaw area. I don't have the address, but I'm sure that it can be found in the Yellow Pages. I'm not saying that they kept her ashes, but you never know.

I should have called or written to tell you this information sooner, but issues with my own health kept me from doing so. I'm deeply sorry about this. I was very fond of your daughter, and not a day goes by that I don't think about her. If I had never invited her over to my place, this tragedy would not have happened. I wish a thousand times that I could turn back the hands of time to see her beautiful smile again.

Regretfully yours
A dear friend of Kaykay

Neema took a deep sigh after reading the typed letter for the tenth time. She had written it two weeks ago after Myra had called to tell her what had happened to Topps Jackson and his accomplice who tried to do harm to their mother. Once her memory had started to return, thanks to Myra driving down each weekend with family pictures, love and patience, she experienced a great sense of closure. Writing the letter to Kaykay's mother would seal the deal.

There was a knock at the bedroom door. "Mama, are you coming back down?"

"Nita, I'll be right there." Neema took up the address-labeled envelope, stuffed the letter inside and pulled off the sealing tape. Maybe she could get the next person going out to drop it in the mailbox. With a sense of accomplishment, she got up and headed down the stairs.

"Mama, I have a couple of more surprises for you," Neema announced as she walked back into the cheery yellow kitchen to join her family. Everyone seemed happy and animated as they waited for Myra to serve her famous pineapple upside-down cake. She took a seat at the table. "You asked a couple of times whose house this is."

Hattie looked at the loving faces surrounding the table. The only person missing was Myra's husband, Glen, who couldn't get out of two scheduled surgeries that day. "Well, here we all are, cooking and eating like we own this place."

"I like this house," Brandon confirmed again. "It's got a big backyard with huge trees."

"Mama, you own it," Neema said, smiling.

"Girl, please. I can't afford a house like this." Hattie patted at her chest, thinking Neema might have some residual brain damage from her hit-and-run accident.

"It's paid for, Mama."

"What?" Hattie couldn't believe what she was hearing. "By who, I mean, by whom?"

Neema patted her hand. "Don't worry about that part. You deserve it for all that I've put you through. Being hardheaded and not listening to what you were trying to show me. I'm so sorry, Mama." Tears welled. "Trust me, things are gonna be so different from now on. I swear to God it will. Oh, and I'm going back to college for my degree."

Hattie was momentarily speechless.

"That new Toyota Camry parked outside, that's yours as well."

"Wait a minute. You saying this house and the car, both are mine?" Hattie looked from one face to another. Her gaze stopped on Bruno's face. "Is this your doing?"

"What? Why you looking at me? I'm just going with the flow," he told her, smiling. Bruno saw no reason to spill the whole story, how after Hattie had taken the kids and fled from his house the night of the shooting, he found the keys to the Rover in Topps' pocket. He then searched for the vehicle, which he located a block over from his house. He'd found the duffle bags of money along with a safe deposit key he traced to a bank in San Pedro. There, he found expensive jewelry and more money. Topps Jackson had amassed quite a fortune from years of doing wrong. Enough to get Neema set up in a new apartment and buy a house and car for Hattie. As far as he was concerned, Hattie deserved everything that money could buy.

"Well, I'll be going now," John West announced as he stood up from the table. "It was nice meeting all of you."

Neema stood up, too. "You're an amazing man, Mr. West. Strangers don't do the things that you have done. Thanks for everything." She was at his side for their good-bye hug at the front door. "I'll never forget you."

"Better not. You're like my playdaughter now. I'll be heading out of town in three days. I'm sure we'll keep in touch."

"I'd like that."

"That's my girl." West gently thumped the top of her head, and kissed her cheek. "The pleasure was all mine." With that he left.

"May I please have some more cake?" Brandon asked.

Myra cut him another piece as Neema walked back into the eating area.

"Thank you, Auntie Myra."

"You're welcome, Brandon."

"Ohmygawd, my kids saying 'please' and 'thank you.' I can't believe how polite they are now."

"Uh-huh," Myra teased. "I bet you can't, so try to keep it moving that way."

Neema picked up a dishtowel and tossed it at her. "Girl, forget you. What about those bay-bay kids of yours?"

"Girl, you know my kids aren't as bad as yours," Myra teased her back.

"In your dreams.'

Bruno and Hattie had their heads huddled together, whispering something that only the two of them found amusing. Hattie's face was glowing as she got up to get her purse.

"Mama? Where you going?" Neema asked, standing at the counter with a glass of fruit punch.

"Uh...on a date."

"A date?" Myra and Neema both stared in disbelief as Bruno escorted a giddy-acting Hattie to the front door.

"The kids are safe and back with their mother. It's time for me now."

Two mouths sagged open as they watched their mother switch her sassy hips to the door and stop. Bruno kissed her cheek and opened the door.

"Oh, before you go, can you drop this letter in the mailbox for me?" Neema walked over and handed the letter to her.

"Whose Mrs. Tidmore?" Hattie queried, studying the address.

"The mother of a good friend. Please don't forget to mail it. It's very important."

"Nee, I think you forgot to put a return address on it."

"I didn't forget. It's my final closure."

"Oh. No problem." Hattie winked back at them. "Brandon and Nita, Nanny will see you two later." Then she turned to Neema and Myra. "Oh yeah, I'll be in good hands, so don't worry. And one more thing. We'll talk more when I get back, but don't wait up for me."

ABOUT THE AUTHOR

An author that refuses to be put into a "genre," D.Y. Phillips enjoys and dabs her pen into various writing projects. She has written romance, poetry, magazine articles, mainstream fiction, a screenplay and several children's picture books (still collecting dust) to quell her love for writing. She lives in the high desert of California, and is currently working on her next book project. You can visit D.Y. Phillips in her humble cyber crib at www.debraphillips.homestead.com

READING GUIDE QUESTIONS

1. In a perfect world, grandmothers naturally love to spend time with their grandchildren, but can they become overwhelmed from too much "dropping the kids off"?

2. Should Hattie have taken her oldest daughter's suggestion to call Child Services for Neema's abandonment of her children?

3. The relationship between Neema and Topps Jackson is clearly a love-and-hate one where she has accepted being abused and degraded. Does this sort of behavior seem more acceptable to young women?

4. Six-year old Raynita was notorious for stealing things. To prevent the stealing incident at Walmart, should Hattie have paid better attention to the child while in the store?

5. Topps Jackson presents himself as a man that is cold-hearted and perhaps even insane. Did it seem right that he would expect loyalty from his accomplice, Zoot, after threatening the man with a gun?

6. Even though Hattie had warned seven-year-old Brandon about his potty mouth, was she being too harsh in washing his mouth out with soap and taking a belt to him?

7. Was Glen, Myra's husband, being reasonable for asking Hattie and the kids to leave his house?

8. Discovering Topps Jackson's drug money left in the vehicle, was it right or wrong for Bruno Kelly to keep the money and share it with Hattie?

9. It's rare for a stranger to help a person in need, but if you were in the shoes of the detective, John West, would you have helped a young woman like Neema?

10. Did you see John West's help as his way of making up for the daughter that he lost?

11. After learning that her sister Neema was alive, but suffering from amnesia, was Myra wrong for not telling her mother sooner?

12. After endangering the lives of her entire family, do you think that Neema learned a valuable lesson from the ordeal she suffered while trying to live the fast life?

13. *Love Trumps Game* is a story of good versus evil; Hattie's love for her grandchildren and their love in return for her. As a good-hearted person, did Hattie deserve what she ended up with, or should she have received more?